Also by L M Hedrick

THE RIGEL AFFAIR **by L M Hedrick** - He's fighting to win the most horrific war in history. She's fighting to bring him home. Fall in love with this epic! **Based on a TRUE STORY!** Get your copy or **View Now** on KindleUnlimited!

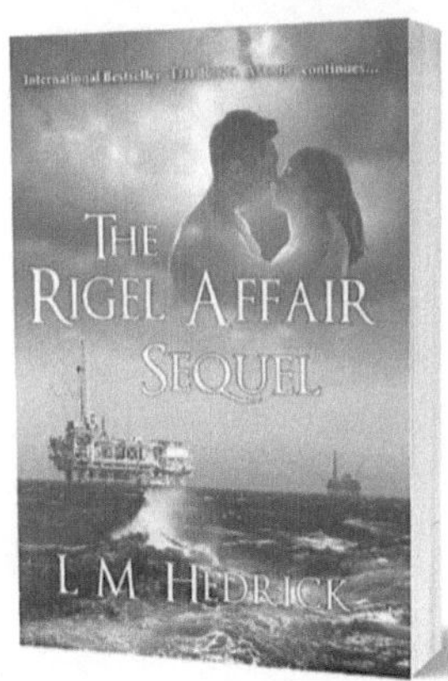

This book needs to be a movie. Highly recommended! Grab a copy of "THE RIGEL AFFAIR SEQUEL" now or **View Now** on KindleUnlimited!

BROKEN WINGS

L M HEDRICK

Chez Blanc Publishing

ISBN: 978-0-473-65373-6 (Paperback)

PUBLISHED BY CHEZ BLANC PUBLISHING 2022
www.lmhedrick.com

Cover Design and Layout by NZ Graphics

Library of Congress Cataloging-In-Publication Data is available upon request

Broken Wings is printed in Chaparral Pro

Printed in the United States of America

Dedicated to the love, strength, guidance, and support of my

Mother,

whisked away too soon by accident...

Broken Wings

CHAPTER 1

It was Christchurch, New Zealand, in 1984 as Allison Brownley leaned over the warm timber railings of the old bridge and tears cascaded - flushed by the River Avon, ebbing downstream, rippling away and disappearing around the bend, like her marriage of fourteen years.

"Jack's a bastard. I'm thirty-five and trapped. He's up to his neck in something," Allison screamed her fears into the River Avon.

The brisk, Southerly wind rudely tossed golden oak leaves into the sky, allowing their sad tumble into recent rain pools. Across the park she caught a glimpse of Jack's car racing around the corner to their house. The children were at school. *Why is he home now?* She gripped the folds of her jacket, and ran towards the road. It was hard dodging the traffic, but once across, she'd be hidden behind the bushes that surrounded their property. She made it to the corner and up to the gate, fumbling with its rusty clasp.

She crept up the path, past the hapless roses that hung their heads in shame, up the porch stairs, and pushed back the old wooden door to the hallway. Sunlight burst in, highlighting doors on both sides of the hallway. She breathed a sigh of relief. Jack hadn't seen her.

Jack's voice boomed out, "Listen, I'll get there as fast as I can, Damn it! I had to come home and get it... Fuckin', back-stabbin' jerk. I'll get that son of a bitch. I've had enough."

She moved past their bedroom, when suddenly a floor board creaked. Her heart missed a beat. She stepped into the huge lounge and hid behind the heavy door dividing the passageway from the dining room, her ear up against the crack of the door. She could hear a tapping sound and Jack's sarcastic laugh.

"When I fix things, they don't come back. Never. Nobody fucks with me and gets away with it. Nobody, do you hear me!" Jack's voice stopped.

Allison ducked down, hoping desperately he wouldn't see her, her legs trembling... she tried to hear...

"Gas cylinders and rock salt... get about three dozen from four or five suppliers. We don't need any more snooping around." Another laugh, his tone louder now, "No, don't worry about that. We'll coat the copper reactors inside with Teflon paint - get five liters of Xylene one oh oh six. I've bought the oven." The tapping sound stopped. His voice raised, "Oh her... she's nothing. I can handle her. She's so naïve. She thinks I don't know. She's stupid... always has been. You know that... her and that stupid, nosey mother."

Allison went over in her mind - how many times in this very room? She remembered Jack's subtle jokes directed at her and her mother. Now she was spying in her own home - her husband a stranger.

Jack continued ranting, "Fuck no, I know you can do it. Listen, I haven't much time."

Allison stood up. She decided to come out, but the swish of Jack's white lab coat startled her. She could hear him in their bedroom. She sneaked towards the bedroom door and peered through the crack. She could see him bending over their bed with something in his hand. He turned. Allison sprang back, her hands gripping the passageway walls, and slid back into the lounge, her heart in her throat. The front porch door slammed. She rushed over to the bay windows, but Jack was gone.

A bitter throb of realization rose up to choke her. Throwing herself down on the carpet, she clenched her fists and lay there. The warmth of the streaming sun marched across her from the stained glass windows high above, and seemed to reach down to her and comfort her. She lifted her head up from folded arms, and slowly sat up. In a misty vision she looked around the room, lost to yesteryears, times when things were different. She fixated on her painting above the mantelpiece in a huge antique frame. It was a Galleon, pitching against a relentless sea at sunset, rich in oils, bold in texture. Allison thought about her artistic skills, her pride bringing strength. Her eyes began to clear. She took in another breath and pulled her knees closer to her chest, rocking backwards and forwards, gently smiling through watery eyes. It was not going to be easy - defying Jack.

Chapter 2

Mattie walked down the long driveway, her small frame not unlike Allison's, with her favorite slippers crunching over the sharp gravel. She leaned over to open the box, but something was stuck in the lid. Mattie's long beads swung out from her floral cotton top, blocking her view.

It can't be. A stab of nostalgia loomed over Mattie as she thought of her husband, Charlie, caressing their newborn Allison in France. She pulled at the letter stuck in the lid. It had an American postage stamp – but with Allison's name on the envelope. What has Allison been up to? Maybe she's like me? Now husband Bob's kind face was smiling at her, as he stood by the large white pottery urn on the front step. Watering the rose bushes with one hand and pruning with the other, Bob queried, "Did you get any exciting mail?"

"Oh, just the usual… some mail from up North. A letter for Allison actually… an old pen friend from America I think… I don't know. What do you think she's up to?"

"Allison? You know my opinion. That girl has always been a bit of a rebel. I think Jack keeps her in line."

Mattie knew it was no good in her heart, trying to fit into life back in New Zealand. She had met Bob again, an old friend from Timaru. He was a pilot, just like Redge, home from the war. Bob put his watering can down, and followed Mattie up the steps.

Mattie sighed. It was useless - poor Bob, he never saw much harm in anyone. Mattie went inside. *I'll have to forget, but I wish I hadn't seen the stamp. I don't want to be reminded*, she told herself, and placed the letter on the ledge by the kettle. The kitchen was dark, but friendly. None of the house felt anything but inviting. The old home had only good vibrations, and the smell of coffee with the hot steam brought a warmth of anticipation.

Bob washed his large, generous hands and carelessly wiped them on the new dishcloth. "Nothing like the smell of fresh coffee," Bob said, sitting down in the little space by the backdoor. "And what have you got to say for yourself this morning, Kimmy, my boy?" his hands gently stroking the old ginger cat.

Mattie came out to the porch, carrying two cups of coffee.

A sudden screech of brakes. They looked up. Allison hopped off her bicycle, looking hotter than usual.

"This is a nice surprise. You've got a letter," Bob said.

Mattie nudged him. "Oh, just a change of address. What brings you here so early? You look upset." said Mattie.

"I am," burst out Allison. "I have to make a phone call."

"A call to who?" asked Bob, still trying to understand the two women.

"I'll explain later," and Allison brushed by him. She was never close to Bob, and knew he was not her father. Mattie had told her only a little piece about Charlie and what happened to him. Why did Mother have so many secrets? Bob seemed to get on the wrong side of her, or never understood her, especially once she reached adolescence. She grabbed the phone book and walked back into the lounge. "I won't be put down!" she raged at her mother, with tears welling in her eyes.

"What's happened, dear?"

Allison began to cry. She sank into the old leather swivel chair by the long windows that opened out to the beautiful back garden.

"Jack must know about Ed Marshall," she said, looking up at Mattie.

"Who's Ed Marshall?" asked Bob standing in the hallway.

"Bob, will you leave Allison alone? I'll talk to you later. I'll go make some more coffee," said Mattie, walking out to the kitchen.

Allison sat there, fumbling the pages of the phone book, and wiping her nose on her handkerchief. She stood up, and walked over to the telephone. Bob was back in his beloved garden, so there was just the quiet rumble of the kettle boiling through the little alcove to the kitchen. Allison dialed Ed's number at his office. There was a busy signal.

"Was he there?" asked Mattie, as she came around the corner, carrying two cups of the steaming brew, and handing one to Allison.

"No, it's busy," Allison said as she sighed, and took a mouthful of coffee. They sat for a while, gazing out to the garden. The lawn was picture perfect with rhododendron bushes marching in tune with the breeze. Allison looked over at her mother, feeling the warmth of the coffee mug in her hand, and viewing the beautiful garden, soothing her soul. *Poor mother, I wish she'd tell me more about herself*, Allison thought sipping her drink. She was old enough to know that some memories never left. She'd find out one day what happened to her father, Charlie, but Bob was a good, kind man and he made her mother happy.

Allison broke the silence. Jack was on the phone this morning. I caught him, but he didn't see me. I bet it was Josh. Who else would it be? That's the whole trouble," Allison lamented.

"Well, you have to face up to it sooner or later. You have no choice," Mattie advised.

"I know... that I know. You don't have to go on. It's my life that's at stake." Allison slammed down her empty coffee and got up to dial Ed's number again. This time a voice answered. It was Ed. "Ed... its Allison Brownley. There's been a new development in my case against Jack. I was wondering if I could speak to you."

"I can come now if you like. Where are you? I have something for you."

"I'm over at my parent's house."

"I'll be there."

Allison put down the phone and turned to Mattie who was anxiously standing by her, "He's coming over. He says he has something new for me."

"Well there you are."

They sat back in the sunlit lounge and waited for the car to come up the driveway. Mattie got up and went out to Bob, "I'm so worried about all this with Jack. Maybe I should just give her that letter?"

"I'd leave it. Too much going on. Next thing you know, she will take off to America. Who knows with her?"

They stood, both concerned, listening to Ed's car crumple over the stones and come to a stop. The car door banged and a man of medium height got out, wearing casual brown trousers and a tee shirt, a bit wrinkled, as if he'd dressed in a hurry. He had a notepad in his hand. He smiled at Mattie and Bob as he walked up the front steps.

"Thank you for coming so quickly," said Allison, standing at the front door. She could smell cigarette smoke as he passed by.

"Oh it's fine. I was going to be in the area anyway," replied Ed.

"Come into the lounge and I'll tell you what's happened," said Allison.

They walked across the sunlit room, and sat in silence opposite each other. Ed wrote something down in his notepad. Allison stared anxiously at the top of Ed's balding head, as he continued writing, unperturbed at her presence.

"Sorry, I had to take some notes down while it was fresh in my mind. It's been one of those mornings," he said, shifting his weight in the swivel leather chair. "Let's get down to business. Tell me... what has happened?"

Allison wadded her handkerchief into the palm of her hand. Her voice began to quiver as she recalled the incident.

Ed took in a breath, coughed and shifted forward in his chair; not wanting to put pressure on her. He coaxed her, "You take your time with this... remember the details," and sat back, looking away from her as if to put himself out of the room.

Allison could feel the emotion creeping up inside her. It was no use, how could she explain all this to a strange man sitting in her parents' house. Ed sat listening, reassured her, and nodded for her to go on. She shuddered, gulped, and somehow found the strength to go on, "I hid from him. He was looking for something... something in the bedroom... and worst of all he was going to get someone. Yes, get someone he knew. Oh my God!" She put her head in her hands, "What have I done?"

"Allison, slow down. You're not making sense. Who is he going to get?"

"You. It might be you!" Allison looked up, her small, oval-shaped face covered in tears. The twisted wet handkerchief dropped as she hung her head.

Ed continued to write calmly. His notepad balanced on his knee, he looked up, not wanting to break her flow of words. "I hear what you are saying, but that is not a threat. It's only your assumption. You see, there are all sorts of harassments out there and this is not one of them."

"No but..."

"Now listen... hear me out."

By this time Mattie had moved into the room. Ed looked over at her, "Mrs Smith, I'm trying to get Allison to see the behavior patterns."

"Yes, it is what I have been telling her, but she has to listen to you," replied Mattie.

Ed closed his eyes for a second and reopened them again as if to push away Allison's curtain of denial. He tapped his pen nervously on his knee. "You have to assume there is nothing wrong to be able to solve this. I know it doesn't make sense, but it does work. Now I have some fresh developments that will bring these events to light."

Allison raised her eyebrows about to speak, when Ed raised his voice, as if to stop her interrupting. "I don't want you to jump to conclusions or get too excited. Investigations don't work that way. I have someone undercover at Jack's work-place. This man you speak of – Josh... I take it he lives alone?"

Allison interrupted, "Oh my God... *Josh*, he's the trouble." She bit her lip and thought she had better shut up and listen.

Ed continued, "He also works with Jack, and there's going to be a private function. Something where the two of them may get more exposure than they bargained for. That way we can nail them. But, you have to play your part. Tell me everything... *and I mean everything*. From your children and when they come home from school, up to when you go to bed at night time. I know that's the hard part, but you have to be strong."

Mattie shifted from one leg to the other as she leaned against the wooden mantelpiece, and made a small, silent acceptance with her head.

Ed went on to talk about Josh. Yes Allison had already told him she thought he was gay, but Ed surprised her by saying the Police were involved. By Allison's expression, he knew he'd said too much. Jack is a very clever research chemist. He and Josh purchased a very unusual assortment of supplies and equipment. It's not being shipped to his work. He even bought a commercial oven.

Ed decided to tell Allison in a quiet, nonchalant manner, so she didn't get too upset, "Is Jack doing food research?"

"Food? Jack only cares if his dinner is late or the peas are cold. No, food is not his interest here. I have no idea what research he does, but I heard him say he'd bought an oven."

Ed glanced at Mattie, but looked hard at Allison, and reminded her of how good her parents were.

Allison knew without having to say how lucky she was.

He stood up and moved towards the door with a positive stride. He gave her a pat on the shoulder. "You see to those kids of yours… you'll be fine. I'll stay in touch." He winked at Mattie. "I'll see myself out," and pulled the front door quietly shut.

It was a moment of relief for both women. Allison went back to sit in the sun. She leaned forward, her mind racing. How could she keep this a secret?

Chapter 3

Allison cycled back to her house, and gave a shove to the old gate. It slammed with a clunk, bringing a sense of satisfaction.

She put her bicycle away in the garage and walked out the driveway down the road to meet the girls. It was a pleasant walk to the back entrance of the school. She strode with her head in the air and her homemade, three-tiered floral skirt blowing in the breeze. She looked longingly at the homes as she passed by, with their well-established gardens, winding pathways and beautifully manicured hedges, thinking to herself all the time about what Ed had said. She could hear the school bell ringing and the shuffle of activity coming from the nearby school buildings.

The children began to appear - the boys dressed in grey shorts and shirts; the girls, in navy-blue cotton pinafores over white blouses, old-fashioned, but very practical. Their vibrant red ties were half-the-time knotted around their waists, much to Allison's disgust. She caught sight of Isabel who was first out, wearing her tie slung around her waist. She was easy to spot in a crowd, with her thick auburn plait hanging down her back.

"Mummy, Mummy, I did well in my project. I got good marks. My teacher said I'm smart." Tendrils of loose hair framed her pretty, round face, as she called out to Allison, pushing her way towards her, balancing her bicycle with one hand and the other hand awkwardly holding a large cardboard poster with all kinds of leaves and particles stuck with glue.

"Yes dear, you have an excellent brain. Let me push your bicycle so we don't lose half the poster on the road," said Allison, smiling at another mother passing by.

Isabel slowed down only a second for Allison to catch the bicycle and look around for her friend, who was coming to play. The children were all out *now*, and there was a mass of boys and girls, all trying to squeeze out of the bike bars at the end of the lane.

"Where's Lucy?" Allison asked, stooping a little as she took the bicycle.

"Here I am," said Lucy in her tiny voice, pulling at Allison's skirt from behind.

"See my poster," said Isabel, jiggling her poster in front of Lucy.

"Mummy, I don't have a poster like Isabel," Lucy's big green eyes filled with tears.

"Oh come on now, you do lots of wonderful paintings. You and I paint together all the time. Hey, why don't we get some paints out… when we get home?"

"But I want to play with Isabel." Lucy pouted, pushing out her bottom lip.

"No she doesn't, I'm playing with Hannah… not with Lucy," Isabel said, skipping past them, her face gleaming with beads of perspiration. She ran on down the road ahead of her friend. Hannah smiled politely at Allison as she passed her, riding her bicycle to catch up to Isabel.

Lucy walked beside Allison, swinging her school bag into Allison's legs.

"Don't do that, dear. Come on… we'll have some nice things for afternoon tea." Allison took Lucy's hot little hand and they walked back down the road.

Isabel had left the gate and front door wide open. Allison placed Isabel's bicycle against the side of the house and let Lucy in first, who rushed to join Isabel in their shared bedroom. Allison went into the kitchen and poured out three plastic glasses of orange juice. She took a handful of snack packets out of the pantry, grabbed an apple off the bench and cut it into pieces.

"I'm thirsty," said Isabel

"Well, sit up at the table."' Allison set the drinks down on the table. "You can share these packets."

"I'll do it," said Isabel snatching at the packets.

"Stop being so bossy, and let Hannah and Lucy have some - and don't forget Chris."

A few moments passed and the front door banged.

"Gidday Mouse," boomed Chris, as he stumbled over Lucy to get to whatever food was left on the table.

"I'm not Mouse, and nobody likes me."

"Stop that Lucy. Come on, you know your big brother teases you," said Allison. Chris laughed, curling his lips to one side in one of his favourite mannerisms. He loved the antagonism he created. All of seventeen years old, he was Allison's first, not Jack's, who had relented to take him. Allison had married in her late teens and divorced almost all at once. Chris, a protégé of his grandfather, was driven by a powerful urge to perform at his best in sport. A tall, slender youth, he had a thatch of wild, auburn hair, and a small face like Allison's. His wiry frame pushed past Allison to make a rush for the fridge. Chris knew he had to be quick, if he was going to sneak any extra food. From the bottom of the open door, Allison could see his dirty knees, sprouting out from oversized dark grey shorts.

Allison stared down at the muddy shoes, crinkled socks and tangled shoelaces, and called out, "I thought I told you to take off your shoes, when you come home."

"Oh, whatever," he said banging the fridge door, shoving a fist-full of leftover meat into his mouth and fingering Lucy's hair as he passed her. She let out a squeal and the three girls sprang back in their chairs.

"Hey! That's tonight's dinner," Allison yelled at him. He grinned, and made another run at the girls and they ran, squealing to their room. Allison's feeble attempts at discipline washed off Chris, and he waltzed past her into his room at the front of the house. He reappeared, in a pair of shorts almost hidden by an oversized white tee shirt branding "Improve your Image... Be seen with Me."

"I'm off to cricket practice," he said, still chewing, holding a cricket bat under his arm, pummeling a well-worn cricket ball in his free hand.

"Don't forget to be home in time for tea," Allison reminded him.

He liked to inform her of his whereabouts, even though she found him hard to understand. He was her best friend in his own quiet way, like his grandfather. Chris had adapted well to his life at home with Jack - he kept aloof and apart.

Allison watched him at the kitchen window as he crossed the road, his hair golden in the sunlight, his long legs racing to catch up to his friend. For a moment she wished she could be free like him. She would have to be patient. She had instructions now from Ed and keeping busy was going to be the only way; she knew how to survive. Taking out the chopping board, she sliced into an onion, wiping at her eyes, from the stinging aroma. Damn the onions, damn the grass clippings. If it's not dirty knees, its grass stains. She cursed as she turned the handle of the old metal meat grinder. Clumps of last night's lamb, and the onion and carrot pieces, tumbled out into the casserole dish; one of her mother's well known cottage pie recipes. It was always a tasty mixture of meat, vegetable juices, layered with a thick topping of mashed potatoes, and sprinkled with grated cheese. She opened the oven and placed the heavy contents into the waiting heat.

Hannah thanked Allison for having her, and the girls settled down to watch TV.

The front door banged and Jack appeared, still in his white lab coat - with something odd on the pocket. It looked like a blood stain.

"Hello... how was your day?" asked Allison.

"Fair. When's dinner?' Jack pushed past her to look in the fridge.

"Usual time."

He closed the fridge door and turned to face her.

Allison felt a shiver run through her. She looked for emotion in his steel blue eyes, but Jack concealed everything.

He leaned against one of the old dining room chairs, with a half-smile, "So what have you been up to?"

Allison shifted a placemat and wondered if the question was cynical, or was it his usual sarcasm. She was about to answer when Isabel burst in.

"Look, Daddy... look what I've done," swinging the poster in front of him.

He turned around and bent down to pick her up, "How's my Isy?" and he smiled at her, their faces locking as he lifted her up.

"But you got to see my poster."

"I can see it. It's good." He put her down.

"Am I late for dinner?" said Chris, appearing from nowhere.

Allison set the pie dish out to cool, and looked at Chris. She said nothing, and soon after everyone was in their seats for dinner.

Allison was packing the dishes away in the dishwasher, when Jack said from the dining room, "Would your mother baby-sit tonight, or what is Chris doing?"

"I have to go out again to a sports meeting, but I won't be long," Chris called out.

"Why?" asked Allison, looking at Jack.

"Oh, I thought we'd go to the movies."

"I suppose I could call my mother. Chris said he won't be long." She picked up the phone and dialed Mattie's number, "Jack wants us to go to the movies. You'd only have to come for a while. Chris will be back soon from a meeting."

"Is everything alright?" asked Mattie.

"Yes," Allison put the phone down and went to tell the girls that their Nana was coming to look after them. They were excited - they loved their Nana - and bounced up and down on their beds. Chris left in a hurry and Jack went into the bathroom to clean his teeth. Isabel came up behind him, nudging in to join him, cleaning her teeth.

"Did you have a wash?" asked Jack.

"Yes," she beamed up at him, wiping her face with the towel and running back around the corner into her room.

Allison went into her bedroom and looked at herself in the mirror. She put her hands up to her cheeks, blazing hot against the cool touch of her fingers, and gave a sigh. Picking up her hairbrush, she tried to untangle the masses of permed, disheveled hair hanging around her face.

Jack's sudden laughter reminded her of today's events, and she stopped. Isabel was half-crying and saying, "Don't, Daddy, don't," giggling and giggling.

Footsteps came up to the front door, distracting Allison's thoughts about Isabel and she called out to Jack, "I'll get it. That'll be Mother."

Jack went on laughing - he sounded so happy.

Allison rushed to the door and took a step back, "Oh, it's you."

"You don't look too pleased to see me, or have you had a bad hair day?' said Josh. He smirked looking down at her hairbrush.

"Well you better come in. Jack... Josh is here," she turned towards the passageway. She hated him for being so quick to put her down, quick with his smart remarks. Her face was even more inflamed now.

"Hello Josh," Jack appeared from the bedroom, looking a bit flustered and pulling at his clothes to straighten them.

"What you been up to? Had a fight with the garbage man?" Josh laughed, leaning up against the passage wall, laughing even more at Jack's serious face.

"Well, where's your mother?" Jack looked over at Allison, ignoring Josh's remark.

"She'll be here," Allison turned and went back into the bedroom. She didn't look at herself much anymore, and fumbled through her drawers to find something to wear.

"Hurry up, it's not a fashion parade... it's only the movies." Jack called out.

Allison could still hear Josh's childish giggle. She pulled out a silk scarf from the top drawer, tied it around her neck, grabbed her plain beige jacket, and joined the two men in the main lounge.

"Well... see that didn't take long. You look like you're copying me." Josh buffed out his chest displaying his impeccably tailored jacket adorned with a lonesome handkerchief.

"Except, your shoes won't do."

He looked down at his shiny shoes and looked at Allison's. "Look... quit the teasing. Mine are sneakers; you can't shine these... so fob off."

Josh laughed again, a mimic of Jack - standing there wearing the same swept-across, thick hair-do. They both had thick, dark hair. Josh was a fraction shorter than Jack. His teeth were perfect - you could see them, as he so often laughed. Jack's teeth, which you never saw much as he kept them hidden - except with the occasional smile when they protruded onto his bottom lip. Jack was a different person when Josh appeared.

Mattie looked around the corner of the lounge, and gently said, "Hello."

"Well, good evening Mrs Smith," Josh said in a very loud, semi-polite manner.

"We better get going," replied Jack and with a quick nod to Mattie, they left the house.

Josh seemed nervous as they made their way into town, still giggling and making unnecessary comments about anything and everything. He was not good at the quiet, controlled deceit that Jack could portray, and it became considerably apparent to Allison that something was up. The lights dimmed in the busy theatre, and the atmosphere between them soon became disguised by the loud bursts of melodrama booming out of the screen. Jack was seated between them and, for an instant, Allison felt almost like an intruder. She twisted at her scarf. She could have been sitting there all alone. Allison, captured by the movie, didn't notice Josh's empty seat. She spoke softly to Jack, "Josh is missing a great movie", when she leaned forward to comment on its excitement.

"I'll go check on him."

·   ·   ·   ·   ·

Jack slipped out the door and walked towards the bathroom. He caught sight of Josh posing by the movie billboard and watching him approach.

"How long does it take to get the message?"

"I'm not dumb. I had to wait for the right moment," said Jack.

"Well she's your baggage. Listen... I got the cylinders. Shit! My apartment's a bloody gas house. It's the neighbors we'll have to watch."

"I know. But something else has come up... that we need to deal with. I've been over to that building in town. I broke in. There's two of them in there."

"Oh really? Who is it then?"

"It was easy. Lazy bastard... files all over his desk with her name on it." Jack pulled his hand out of his pocket and Josh winced at the nasty gash half-bandaged.

"Did your Missus see that?"

"Knowing her, she would." Jack's face was serious. "She's been seeing this cop, Ed Marshall. I followed him. Got the bastard's papers. He's been snooping around alright. Bloody knows the fuckin' lot. I'll kill her. I tell ya... we have to move!"

"Did you get a look at him?"

"No. I just followed him. Stayed undercover." Josh giggled.

"I like your nerve Buddy." Jack walked on back into the movies and turned to Josh. "We have a meeting to go to."

They drove back in silence. Josh didn't say a word as they entered the house. Mattie left and Allison got ready for bed.

"Where the fuck are we going?" said Josh as they left the house.

"Shut up and get in the car."

Jack drove down the back of Fitzgerald Avenue, along towards Ferry Road into the industrial area until he came to a gated building. They stopped on the other side of the road.

"Whoa. Are you going in there?"

"What choice do we have?"

"Listen... drive 'round the block. I've got an idea."

"It better be good. Tonight's the night... before this bloody idiot does something."

"I know someone. Someone you won't believe will get us out of this shit."

"Well this can't wait."

Jack stopped the car and they got out. Jack knocked on the gate and a dog barked. Someone came out holding the dog and dragging the chain. He wasn't pleased to see Jack.

"Listen fuckhead... I thought I said no contact." He was dressed in leather and it was easy to see he was a gang member. The tattoo on his neck blazed iridescent in the streetlight.

"We've got an intruder needs dealing with."

"Wait here."

He went inside and came out, "Move your ass. Motley will deal with ya."

Jack and Josh went inside.

It was dark and only one person was seated at a table, smoking in his cloud. Two punks were standing against the wall. The man at the table had a face nobody could forget. A huge scar ran across his cheek - like the work of a broken bottle in a bar fight. When he looked up and began to speak, his front teeth were gone.

"You gringos... Don't ever fuckin' come back here." Motley was pissed.

"Ed Marshall." Jack leaned forward. "Our deal can't go through. The prick's a bloody pig and knows the lot." Jack sat down. Josh looked shocked.

Two punks stepped forward and seized Jack and Josh. "Wait," Jack called out, "I have a plan."

They let Jack go. "Tomorrow night." Jack pointed to Josh and they released him. "All you have to do is drive him off the road... he won't be feeling well," Jack said, sitting down.

"We don't deal with ignorant, incapable pricks like you."

"By then he'll be spitting blood with buggered vision. You want the work done? We're almost ready for full tests on the new process... but we're only consultants. Get rid of the pig. Here's the name and where he works. Then we can meet and train your cook," Jack winked at Motley and handed him a slip of paper.

"You're lookin at him."

"Good... then we're on. I'll tell you when to make your move. You can keep our next ten grand... just do it."

Jack and Josh left the premises, passed the guard and walked back to the car.

"Fuckin' hell. Why did you need me with you?" said Josh

"What do you think? Would I go alone? These punks are crazy."

"Then why deal with them?"

"They know how to get rid of people. They're the producers... the distributors, you dumb shit. We're not making any drugs. We're only consultants. Listen, if we're to make a stash of money, how the fuck are we to do it? Eh? *Think Boy!*" Jack made a jab into Josh's head.

"Fuck you, you old cunt. I'm not you're wife. Give us those papers I'll do it my way."

"No! You'll fuck it up. We've work to do."

"Bloody hell, what now for Christ's sake?"

"Listen, shit-head, shut up and listen." Jack drove with vengeance. "Now... let's get back to the cop. DMS, buddy... transforms into methanol, kinda ironic, don't you think? Dip your finger in this shit and you're out of here." Jack pulled into the driveway and Josh went home.

The next morning, when Allison got everyone out the door, she picked up the phone to call Mattie, "What happened last night?"

"I should have known Josh would turn up. It's all too much. Everything... Jack's behavior with Isabel. Not Lucy but Isabel," she paused. Mattie listened. "He was in bed with her last night, tickling her. I know... we've been over this before with Chris that time in the bath... but the report came back with nothing. He's a pervert, he's a...," she stopped. She froze... an eye was peering at her through the crack in the doorway. She dropped the phone.

"What did you just say?" Jack sprung out from behind the door, rage in his eyes. "Come on, answer me! I'll have you up for slander. I know what you're up to. You stupid little cunt-face." He lunged at her, spitting saliva. Allison's knees went weak, her mouth went dry, she tried to speak, but nothing came out. He started to shake her.

"I said, I don't like how you treat Isabel. Poking at her. She's your daughter. She doesn't like you in her bed. And I'm sick of Josh coming around. Who are you married to - him, or me?'

"How dare you accuse me? I'll get my lawyer onto you and have you locked up, you wait and see. You think you're Miss Prim and Proper? You, and that meddling mother of yours?'

"You leave my mother out of this."

"You ignorant fool. You have no idea what you're in for," he pushed her back on to the bed, stared down at her, and laughed. He leaned over and with one arm, he swiped all her cosmetics off the dressing table. Her hairbrush flew across the bed and hit her in the face. "Lot of good all this shit's going to do, when I'm finished with you... rat face." He walked out and slammed the door so hard the house rumbled. The car engine roared and he was gone in the dust.

Allison lay trembling; her knees couldn't stop shaking. She hid herself under her pillow, sobbing until she remembered she'd left the phone off the hook. She pushed back the pillow to see her mother standing there, over her bed.

"I heard everything on the phone. I drove up and waited until he was gone." Mattie sat down next to her and Allison fell into her arms and wept.

"I don't know what I'd do without you. I'm so frightened."

"Don't be, it's all got to come out. You just have to be strong for the children. We can get some advice on the way he is with Isabel. But it's his behavior with Josh you can't tolerate. Ed will help. Here, I brought you something," she handed her the letter. "I'm sorry it's open by mistake."

Allison looked up at her, half crying, "It's from Randy, my old pen friend. How did he get my address? Oh, I see, it's re-addressed," wiping her tears on her sleeve and anxiously opening the envelope.

"Put it away safely, or do you want me to keep it?"

"No, I'll read it," she said and opened the pages to read with her mother. Randy had addressed it to her, just like they were at the age of fourteen. She had chosen him out of a column from the Seventeen magazine. He looked like the boy at the hot dog stand with his swish, bodgie hairdo, and strong, dimpled jaw. He went on to say he had become a writer, so his words flowed out of the page and seemed to bounce up at her just at the right time. He went on to describe how he was looking through some old files, and found all her letters.

"He wants to know all about me," Allison looked at her mother sitting next to her explaining his written words. "He wonders if I'd ever come to America? Oh my God, Mother... imagine that."

"Well dear, it's a nice diversion for you. I knew it was good timing, even though your father doesn't think so." Allison looked at her mother with a frown. "Put it away... you can't go on dreaming like this," Mattie said, patting her. "Here... take my handkerchief... blow your nose." They comforted each other, and after a while, Mattie left.

When Jack arrived home, he was strangely quiet. He sat reading the paper; the girls had gone to bed. Allison sat watching television on the couch next to him. Jack liked his favourite chair by the window.

"You'll be glad to know. I'm going away. It's all arranged. I'm going to America."

"But how did this happen?"

"My work", he paused, "They want me to do some research. All this shit you have put on me... I decided this morning to accept the offer for several months' assignment. You can see what it's like to be alone with all your crap and your fucked up mind. You can get a big dose of whatever it is that makes you happy." He threw the paper down and left the room.

What had happened to cause him to simply arrange to leave? She had to call Ed. *The business function must be it.* She sat there, stone cold amongst the dark alcoves and the small empty fireplace with no flames. The dark walls crowded around her. She lay down on the chilling leather couch, gripping her knees into her chest. A sick thought came instantly into her mind. The letter she had shoved underneath the paper cover in her top drawer. *Why didn't I take Mother's advice? Damn!* She stood up and circled the room. What if Jack saw it? The trip to America? He must be bluffing. She'd have to move fast.

CHAPTER 4

On the following night, there was a function at Bellamy Labs to celebrate the launching of their new cancer drug. Jack and Josh left the function and headed to the laboratory. No one would sense their absence, as it was the beginning of the evening.

Bellamy maintained a ready supply of Dimethyl Sulfate as their best methylation chemical to develop new products, but it was a beautiful killer with fatal respiratory tract reactions. The rat experimentation had proved fatal. It was time.

Jack quickly pulled on the organic vapor respirator and special thick butyl rubber gloves to handle the concealed chemical, which he now had in an airtight, vacuum packed cylinder. He grabbed a pipette and they walked down to the basement where Ed's car was parked. Josh stood at the top of the staircase. There were no cameras in the basement. He could spot anyone coming. Jack dropped the Slim Jim down the car window and quickly opened the car door. He opened the cylinder, took out his pipette, dipped it in the solution and carefully allowed the DMS to drop into the dashboard ventilation ducts. Within seconds he locked the car door, and returned to the lab to dispose of his gear in the special chemical disposable unit.

"That should make Ed's emphysema feel better, for a little while anyway," Jack laughed.

"You diabolical old cunt. You know that DMS numbs the tissue before it starts the burning, so it's a quite pleasant way to go."

Josh went back up the stairs, slipping in amongst the crowd. Jack entered by a side door, about ten minutes later, and mingled with the crowd. He heard something about his new grant and couldn't resist butting in.

"Yes... I'm off. They picked me." He started to laugh out loud. The men congratulated him, shaking his hand, nodding and smiling. A clinking sound of glasses rang across the room stopping the chatter and everyone hushed. A waiter, dressed in Canterbury colors, with a black shirt and a red tie, offered Jack a glass of wine. He grabbed it. Took a gulp, and looking around, managed to catch Josh's eye from across the room.

"Gentlemen, friends, and colleagues... may I have your attention?" the man at the head of the main table raised his glass. "Welcome to 'Oysters and Chardonnay'. Allow me to introduce myself... I am the chairman of Bellamy Labs, Ian Crosley, and our sponsors for the evening are "Oyster Bay Winery' from Marlborough Sounds. We have our traditional Kiwi oysters, all the way from Bluff in the Deep South. We have come a long way here in the province of Canterbury with the launch of our new cancer treatments at the Christchurch Public Hospital, and now we have pleasure in announcing... we're going offshore. We have a very special guest tonight, Mr Harold Anderson, from Chicago's Stockholm Laboratories." He turned and tilted his glass at the dapper gentleman standing next to him.

"Thank you. I must say... I can't believe the size of your oysters, they're *Huge*! What do you feed these critters?" There was a snigger in the crowd. "It's a pleasure to be here folks." He took a sip of his wine. "Oh... and thank Oyster Bay! Tell them I'll take a case home with me," he said in his loud American accent. He stood out in the crowd with his bright striped blue and white shirt, white collar, red tie, and braces clipped onto a well-cut pair of black trousers with shining black shoes.

Mr Crosley went on, "Some of us have contributed long hours of research and I know tonight you'll raise your glasses in praise to those who worked hard on our projects. To Bellamy Labs, Gentlemen. May we always show our Kiwi ingenuity? Three cheers, hip-hip-hooray," said Mr Crosley, taking a sip and smiling at Mr Anderson, who seemed to be enjoying the fuss as he sucked hard on a huge cigar.

Glasses clinked and mutters of enthusiasm hushed again as Mr Crosley went on, "I didn't expect such a turn-out," he paused, looking into the audience. "We have several visitors, I see."

Everyone began to look around the smoke-filled room. Jack searched the faces, wondering who his enemies were. He'd never seen Ed before.

"As you know, Bellamy Labs was formed back in the sixties and has stood the test of time, along with all the history of our wonderful city of Christchurch that we are so proud of. Merging with our brothers in Chicago will further our opportunities to invite fellow researchers to share our talents. Mr Brownley, are you here tonight?" asked Mr Crosley.

There was a further hush and Mr Crosley strained his neck, around the room. Jack was not a good speaker and looked awkward as he raised his glass in response.

"Here, thank you, Mr Chairman."

"Mr Brownley, gentlemen, is the first of our research chemists to join Stockholm Labs in Chicago. He leaves this Saturday."

Everyone clapped and Jack raised his glass again. He stood there waiting for the applause to fade.

"It's been a long time for all of us, and I'll do my best... Thank you." He took another gulp of wine. Mr Crosley's voice seemed to migrate into a monotone, as Jack wished he could vanish into the crowd. He stood by the huge windows, the lights of the city sparkling outside. He felt hemmed in by the surrounding tables, draped with white starched cloths, donned with silver bowls of oysters, trays of Marlborough sea foods, pastry, and a vast display of fruit. Jack put his glass down and stabbed an oyster with a tooth pick. It dribbled down his chin, as he leaned back to let it slip down his gullet. He thought about the chemical and how an oyster was not going to cure the raging infection now underway.

One of the waiters, balancing a silver tray, interrupted Jack's dream, "Sir, a serviette."

Jack grabbed it without a thank you and dodged around the waiter, keeping his eye on Josh, who was talking with an older man smoking a pipe. The man seemed to shrug him off and move away. Josh followed him.

Jack took another oyster and swirled its soft contents around in his mouth, feeling the juices flow before biting into its rush. Josh now looked nervous. Jack took another glass of wine and moved over towards Josh, "So which one's Ed?"

"I don't know."

"Well, who's the weed with the pipe?"

"How would I know? Lay off, will ya. Look around yourself." Josh walked off.

Jack knew he was lying. He knew Josh well - better than he knew himself. He could read him. He hung around determined to find Ed. Frustrated, Jack left and went down to the basement and sat in his own car. It wasn't long, before he watched a man of medium height, stopping as he came down the stairs to the basement to light up a cigarette, and write notes on a pad. Jack smiled, as he watched him open his car and drive off. *So much for finding Ed*, he thought.

Jack headed in the direction of Fitzgerald Ave and pulled alongside the curb; he knocked on the gated building. A figure appeared.

"It's time."

Jack drove off.

Ed had driven home to his apartment in the city - his lungs feeling strangely better than they had in a long time. The odorless DMS was feasting on newfound flesh.

The next day Ed awoke. Now his lungs were on fire. He looked at the time and gulped down a handful of pain relief. He must have passed out for hours. It was late in the night when he made his way out. He had work to do. He got into his car and began driving along Madras Street towards Fitzgerald Avenue, when the oncoming red light wasn't there. It shifted. It came towards him. His vision danced everywhere. Suddenly another car. No... he couldn't see. *What the hell*! The horn stuck. His head exploded onto the dashboard and into the windscreen. Blood gushed out covering the whole interior of the car. Another car swerved towards him. In an instant Ed's car was wrapped around a pole. There was no one in sight.

Chapter 5

Allison felt uneasy the morning after the function. Jack had come home so late, slept in and only just left for work. She grabbed the phone and dialed Ed's number.

"Hello, is Ed Marshall there?"

"No sorry he is not," said a rough voice.

"When will he be there?"

"I can't tell you." There was a click with the phone.

Allison went into her bedroom. She wasn't satisfied. Picking up her jacket and car keys, she left the house.

Allison drove into town, passing the long stretch of gardens in Hagley Park bordering the City, her mind set on finding Ed. She didn't like the response from whoever it was that had answered the phone. It worried her.

Ed's office was one of those unkempt rooms in an old historical building turned into an office block. Christchurch was full of history amidst an old English settlement, nestled in the heart of the South Island - more English than England.

Rounding the corner of the building, Allison parked in one of the customer car parks. She pushed open the heavy wooden door with its glistening stained glass window and stepped into a dark foyer. The receptionist continued to type behind the counter. Allison stood erect and still, trying to attract her attention. Allison stared at the brass bell, and then she picked it up. It made one clunk of chime with a hard jiggle.

The receptionist, uninterested, stopped typing briefly, and looked over her glasses at Allison. "Yes... who do you want?"

"Which way to Ed Marshall's office please?"

"Down the hallway and turn left." She went back to her officious typing.

Allison moved quickly down the hallway, around the corner to a door with a glass window in a dimly lit part of the building. She knocked on the glass. No one answered. She turned the handle and the door opened with difficulty. It seemed to be damaged.

"Is anyone there?" she called. She walked in, repeating, "Is anyone there? Hello..."

The office had a stale smell of cigarette butts. Dirty coffee mugs sat on a couple of cluttered desks. She went over and, without thinking, lifted an envelope to see who it was for. *Mark Fenton*. She quickly put it down. Maybe she was in the wrong office?

She moved back towards the door, inadvertently brushing something off the other desk. Picking it up, she saw her name on the front of a manila folder. She opened the folder but nothing was inside. What is my name doing here? Where are the papers for this file? Just then, she heard footsteps. Placing the folder back on the desk, she returned hastily to the door.

A small, wizened man with a pipe in his mouth, still chewing at it, appeared and looked startled at seeing Allison inside, "Who are you?"

"I'm Allison... Allison Brownley."

He took his pipe out of his mouth. "You rang – earlier? Inspector Mark Fenton."

"It's urgent that I see Ed Marshall. I'll wait for him... I have to see him."

"Look... he's not here." He went over to his desk and began shuffling papers around. "It's illegal to enter private property... you know that don't you?"

"I'm sorry."

"Well, sorry's not good enough. Now get out of here."

Allison sat in the car park for a moment, her car keys resting in her lap, and leaned her head against the steering wheel. It's no use, I'm stuck. She banged her fists on the steering wheel of the car. Turning on the ignition, she pulled out onto the busy road. It wasn't far to the laboratories, and a surprise visit might just help her. She parked outside Bellamy Labs, and got out into the cold Christchurch wind tugging her jacket open. She ran up the staircase, and down the corridor.

"Come to check up on me?" said a voice from behind. "I saw your car. You're not a hard lass to spot. What are you doing here?" Jack asked.

"Oh... I was just out. Is there any more on your taking that job in America?"

"Of course. I told you, didn't I?"

Allison sat down in one of his office chairs, fumbling with her car keys as she looked across at him. He sat, twitching his knee.

"They mentioned it last night actually." He kept looking out the window and then at his watch. "Look, I have a meeting. Did you come in for lunch?"

"No, I was just passing. I... oh, it doesn't matter. It can wait," Allison stood up and went to the door, then turned around to face Jack. "I'll see you tonight."

He winked at her, "I'll be home tonight."

Distracted, Allison continued past her home, across town, towards the airport, to Josh's apartment.

Ed's question about Josh living alone prompted her to find a link. Parking the car several houses down from the apartment block, she walked towards Josh's front door. She knocked. She stood there, waiting for an answer, staring through the glass panel. She had been inside several times before, but had never seen so many boxes all around the lounge floor. She peered at a calendar in the living area. It was a picture of Boy George bending over in true butt-cake fashion.

She knew the apartment was usually as immaculate and tasteful as Josh himself. The calendar seemed out of character, but was it? No answer to her knocks. She stepped back and looked across at the next-door neighbor's door. She boldly walked over to it and knocked. A smartly-dressed woman opened the door.

"Good afternoon, I wondered if you know the man next door," Allison blurted out. It was the first thing she thought of.

"Whom am I speaking to?" the elite lady said as she looked straight at Allison through heavy rimmed glasses that darkened in the light of the open door.

"Oh, sorry... I'm Allison... Allison Brownley. I was wondering if you knew Josh next door. I have a problem. My husband...."

"You'd better come in," she said, interrupting her, and closing the door. She showed Allison into her living room, adorned with antiques. "Please sit down," and they glided into the beautiful over-stuffed cushions.

"Allow me to introduce myself," she said with a smile. "My name is Mrs Wilson. Let me see, now. You ask if I know the man next door." She hesitated for a moment, "I don't know him personally, but I do see him come and go. What is it you need to know?"

"My husband comes over here. A thick-set man... he has dark hair, sort of like Josh, only bigger build. They work together." She was reaching out for words to identify Jack, and looking into Mrs Wilson's eyes, trying to glean a hint of information from underneath those thick-rimmed glasses. She went onto tell her he drives a large black car and he might wear a white lab coat sometimes. She watched Mrs Wilson's expression change, and Mrs Wilson agreed, *yes she'd seen a man wearing a white lab coat....* Allison sat there with her, hoping she would remember something else. Finally, Allison got up and thanked her, but suddenly the old lady stopped, and said she had heard a truck right outside her window only a couple of nights ago.

Allison thanked her, and walked back to her car. She quickly called her mother before fetching the children.

Mattie cautioned, "You be careful. It's not your job. It's too dangerous."

"Okay mother, calm down. Listen I have to get the girls. I'll call you later." Allison put the phone down and made her way down the path towards the school, with Ed's words ringing in her ears, *"stay calm."*

When Jack came home for the evening, everything was normal.

Next morning, Allison heard Jack on the phone in the bedroom. She opened the door.

"Get out," Jack slammed the door. Allison pushed it open again. "I thought I told you, *don't interrupt,*" Jack hissed. He stood by the window talking on the phone, the cord stretched across his briefcase, papers sprawled everywhere. Jack's suitcase was balancing to one side.

"I was packing for you." Jack put the phone down and went to shove her. Papers and cases flew off the bed. "Now look what you've done. Just get out."

Allison was frightened. Jack's skin turned fuming red with his dripping sweat. The door slammed in Allison's face.

Jack called out a few moments later, as he slammed the front door behind him.

Allison went back into the bedroom to look out the window. His car disappeared around the corner. She turned around. The bed was empty. The briefcase was gone; only crumbled clothes, lying on the floor over the suitcase remained. She bent down, picked up the suitcase and clothes, and went on packing.

The phone startled her; she grabbed it.

"Have you heard the news?" said Mattie

"No, what?"

"On the radio... someone was killed last night. Head-on crash. You don't think...?"

"It's him. It has to be. Good thing Jack was home." Allison put a hand up to her mouth.

"You be careful. Stay away from that office. I told you it's dangerous," cautioned Mattie.

Allison put the phone down and went on with the packing. She looked around the room and went over to the drawer where she kept Randy's letter. It was on top, not under the paper.

•   •   •   •   •

Jack loaded up the steel parts for the conveyer belt and drove off in the direction of the airport, heading north, over Styx Mill Bridge, towards Belfast. He backed his car into a long driveway towards the only building, and got out, opening the shed door. Josh's car was around the back and Jack gave a shout to him, as he slammed the car door.

"Got the welding and soldering done," said Jack, poking his head into the shed.

"Shit, you did the copper in," replied Jack.

"Who told you that?"

"Well... *look!*"

Jack walked over and glared at him. "Listen, you keep your mouth shut and get on with the job. What happened was my mistake. It won't happen again." He threw Josh up against the wall. "Not unless I'm being double crossed. Eh?"

"Wait... *wait...* just calm down, buddy." Josh straightened up, "You're almost ready to liquefy the gas. Look at your tanks. Who's going to coat the bastards?"

"You did get the right stuff?"

"Of course I did. You just don't get it... do you?"

Jack pushed him away, "Not really. Just dump in the Xylene, swish it around and stack them upside down in the corner." Jack pointed the dark corner which had an alcove. "Listen, I fucked up. It won't happen again."

"What about the thug?"

"They want this new process and are paying a ton of money. Things don't always run smooth. Let's get back to business. We have to build a conveyor belt for the sugar beets."

"Hmmm, seems like a lot of hard work for nothing," Josh's voice was more relaxed.

"The conveyor is a decoy, now wise up, dipshit."

"What about the oven? How does that mix with ethanol?"

"Trouble with you, you've got no imagination. What does it matter? We'll be making bloody pan cakes out of cow dung, for crap sake."

"Well, I'm the stupid bastard that's stuck here while you're gone."

"Well if you don't stick around, who do you think's going to come after you? Why do you think I took you to see Mongrel boy the other night, eh?"

"You fuckin' wouldn't, would you?"

"I fuckin' would."

"Okay calm down. All this's got out of hand."

"Not really. You're in it, whether you like it, or not. You're the one who's going to be teaching the bastard."

Jack walked off and began assembling the plant for the ethanol. The crane had placed the hammermill perfectly on its stand next to the shed. He bolted the conveyor together, ready to be placed tomorrow by the crane next to its feed bin. Lots of people were talking about alternative fuel, and this concept would fit nicely into their plan.

Jack had to praise Josh, liquor him up. They lay in the long grass, by the stony driveway, swilling their beers, sheltered from the end of summer's hot sun. They always found plenty to laugh about, and the heat of the day soon passed.

Chapter 6

Jack, Allison and the children walked into the airport terminal late Monday afternoon. He bent down to hug the girls. Chris was absent, as he had some normal excuse with events at school. Jack hugged Allison briefly. He looked sadly into her eyes and paused. She caught a glimpse of past, happier days when they had vowed their commitment to one another. He had let her see that expression, only to leave her. He turned and waved good-bye.

Back at the house, Allison stood in the bedroom. It felt strange. Mark had called. He confirmed Ed's accident and time of death. That was all he could tell her. His voice sounded pleased that she would be questioned. *Sadistic bastard*, she said to herself as she opened the drawer. She picked up Randy's letter and laid back on her bed, sniffing at the musky pages...

> *Dear Allison,*
>
> *I know it's been a long time but I couldn't help wanting to see your beautiful face one more time... hey... so cute. Yes it's me, Randy. Hey, what's happened to you, are you married? Would you ever come to America? We could meet. Here's my address and phone number, if you ever get to Pittsburgh.*

She threw the letter down, grabbed the vacuum cleaner with a vengeance, and began to clean. *Out of all this shit, someone likes me*, as she banged the long hose against the wooden walls. "If that bloody Jack has stuffed this up, I'll kill him," she said out loud, pulling the hose against her torso, and rounding the corner into their bedroom. The phone rang and it was Jack... with voices in the background.

"Hello, thought I'd call and see how things are. I got here alright."

"Oh, that's nice." Her tone was almost sarcastic.

"How are the kids?"

"They're fine. You sound like you are having a good time."

"Yes, it's different," Jack laughed. Allison could hear women's laughter in the background. "Listen I must go... I just wanted to check in."

She put the phone down, and bent down to pick up Randy's letter. *I just called to say I love you.*" Some favorite lyrics rang in her head, and her eyes watered, until she could hardly see the floor. She heard a loud sucking and motor noise from the vacuum cleaner, and an edge of paper came flying towards her. Bending down, she lifted up the pleats of the valance and more papers tried to make their way up the cleaner. Handwriting was scribbled over typewritten words. She tried to read - pages of scribbled comments, including Ed Marshall's name, covered two pages.

She lowered her head and squinted under the bed, pulling out more pages, staring at them. Formulas with official stamps on them like Government documents. *What does 'molestation,' ...Dimethyl Sulfate mean*? Swiping a hair out of her face, what the hell... *toxic dose edema of the glottis*? "Shit!" flinging the pages down, she grabbed a handkerchief and blew her nose. Maybe he's going to kill someone? She scrambled over the hose and grabbed the phone book. Allison made an appointment to see the Child Welfare Department in the City.

It was a pleasant afternoon's bike ride through the park.

"Where are we going, Mummy?" called out Lucy from Chris's bike, her tiny feet swinging in the spring breeze.

"Quiet, Mouse," said Chris as he raced on ahead, winding his bike through the daffodils that had found their way through the long grass, beneath drooping willow trees.

"Not too far, it's just up here on the corner," shouted Allison. They rode along the dirt track beside the River Avon, sprinkled with a kaleidoscope of spring flowers. They neared the City fringe, all managing to keep together as they crossed the bridge, rounded the corner and dismounted. Chris caught up to Allison as they crossed the road to an old, weatherboard building, on the corner, facing the park.

"Well, come on then," Chris said to Lucy, taking her hand and talking back to Allison. "I don't have time for this. What the hell is this all about, anyway, Mum?"

"Oh, you know, when Jack upset you in the bath? I just wanted to get this all out in the open."

"Listen Mum, it's in the past. Who cares? I don't anymore, and I'm sure as hell these people are not bloody stupid."

They parked their bikes, and climbed the rickety staircase to the top floor. It was another historical building, so old that its paint cried 'demolition', and the staircase felt as if it would collapse. The view at the top was breathtaking. The river could easily be traced as it meandered into the Botanical gardens and past the Museum. Allison stopped for a moment to take in the view, but Lucy was tugging at her skirt.

"Mummy, what's that on your skirt?" Allison brushed at her skirt and felt underneath. Her hand felt sticky, her fingers stuck together.

"Go on inside and over to the counter with the girls Chris. I have to go to the restroom." Allison hadn't noticed what was happening, the ride on the bike had disguised the sensation of the flow and she rushed to open the bathroom door.

Clumps of thick red blood oozed onto her fingers.

She ran cold water to splash the stain off her skirt. Her flow lately had become distressing, with gushes of blood dripping everywhere. She pulled at the toilet roll and stuffed volumes of toilet paper into her panties, and rushed back to join the children at the desk. The three of them stood at the desk looked towards Allison as she approached.

The lady behind the counter looked oddly at Allison, and greeted her, "Good afternoon, Mrs Brownley... is it? Are you alright... did you have an accident?"

"Mummy's got blood all over her."

"Quiet Lucy," Allison's face flushed, as she tried to explain, "Yes, I mean, no. I'm sorry. I'm in a bit of a fluster." Lucy stared up at her, not able to see the top of the desk, nor the person whom Allison was addressing.

Chris poked at Isabel when the lady went on to say, "My name is Helen. Please all come with me." She moved away from the desk and led everyone down the passageway, into the waiting room. She turned and bent down to the girls, "What are your names?"

"Lucy."

"That's a pretty name and..."

"I'm Isabel."

"Yes, and I'm Chris."

"Well, now that we know one another, we are going to have some fun and draw some pictures. But, we're going to go into that room over there," pointing to the room through the large glass windows, "...and Mummy is going to sit out here."

Helen took Lucy and Isabel by the hand. "We won't be long." She looked over at Allison, "Mrs Brownley, the children are going to do some drawing, one at a time. We will work with them separately. So, please take a seat." She pointed to a small waiting area and Allison sat there, wondering what she had done. She had acted so quickly. *Were the children able to deal with this interrogation?* she thought. A young man with a ponytail came in and took Chris into another soundproof room.

Allison picked up a magazine, and gazed at the first page. A girl, a famous celebrity, in a beautiful wedding dress, floating on clear waters in a canoe, with flowers draped over her, on a Pacific Island. She smiled at the camera, her pretty face spelling out joy and happiness. *What a contrast to my life.* Allison fumbled with the pages, her imagination adrift with the ocean image. She looked up, out of a dream, to Isabel's voice, "We had fun, Mummy. The lady got us to draw you and Daddy in bed, and me in bed, and Lucy."

Helen interrupted, "Mrs Brownley, sorry. Are you okay now?"

"Yes."

"We will write a report to you."

"Thank you. Is there anything wrong?"

Helen shook her head, repeated that she would get in touch, and they left the room.

"Can you dub Lucy? Mum, I have to get to a practice," said Chris, walking on ahead. "That was a waste of time, if you ask me."

"Go, it's fine."

Chris ran on down the stairs and Allison took Lucy's hand. Isabel went on in front of them, back down the old staircase. It was more treacherous going down than coming up. "Here, don't you let go of my hand," Allison said.

"But I want to catch up to Isabel, where are we going?"

"You're going to hop on my bike, and Isabel and I are going to go back over there across the bridge, and around the park. But we're going to cross the park and go to see Nana."

"Yes, please," said Lucy, wriggling around on the bike, with Allison steadying it. The ride towards her mother's place was much cooler, the sun having taken a turn behind the clouds. Her mother lived near the City, and Allison was glad to ride up their pathway.

"What happened to your skirt?" Mattie asked as she watched Allison getting off her bike.

"Mummy had an accident and we did some drawing," Lucy said hopping down off the bicycle and running inside to join Isabel.

"Oh, it's the usual disaster. Don't worry. I overdid it. I took the kids into that counsellor we talked about. I didn't want to worry you, so I went ahead myself."

"Come in and tell me."

They settled the children, gave them some afternoon tea, and sat down in the lounge.

"It's nothing really but a test done by drawings, and a couple of counsellors questioning in a way that they can tell if anything is wrong. I won't know until they send in their report, but I've done my best and now I feel guilty."

"Why? Because you're afraid to speak out? Is that a reason to feel guilty, Allison?"

Allison shrugged and didn't answer.

Mattie went on, "You say one thing and do another. Both Bob and I have noticed that."

"Hang on a minute. Haven't I done a lot? And, God knows what's happened to Ed?" She followed Mattie into the kitchen. "I found some papers with '*molestation*' and strange formulas and chemical symbols on it. I thought I'd go and get this sorted and now you're angry with me?"

"No, you're just confused right now," said Mattie, running the water in the kitchen for a cup of tea.

"You know what?" Allison started to cry, "What I'd really like to do?"

"And what's that, dear?"

"I'd like to go and see America. These papers. I'll go and I'll face Jack, damn it... find out more."

"That's too dangerous, I told you to stay out of it. You shouldn't go."

"Always protecting me, Mother, just because I'm an only child. It is what I have always wanted to do. Go and see Randy. Find out. Face my dream." Mattie's eyes narrowed at her comment, as it hit a raw edge, and she turned her back to pour hot water into the teapot. Allison realized she'd said too much, Mattie knew more than she let on...

There were tears in Mattie's eyes.

Chapter 7

The sophistication of the Holiday Inn Hotel in Chicago suited Jack. He arrived almost to a hero's welcome when he was greeted at the airport by the team for his assignment. But he preferred to discreetly mingle with the local staff, where he enjoyed the glamour of his newfound fame as 'the man from Downunder.'

"How do you like the wine? Oyster Bay Chardonnay - it's a New Zealand vintage," he said as he licked his lips from the cool rim of the wine glass. He narrowed his gaze at his female companion across the table.

"Hmmm...Sexy," smiled his companion. Jack took another sip and leaned towards her, gently pressing his knee against her thigh.

"Shall we have another, upstairs?" She looked coy and pushed back her seat, rising tall and elegant as she stood up and walked over to the counter.

"I've a lunch time appointment. Can you cancel that client you have booked in for one o'clock? I'll be back in time for my three o'clock," she winked at the receptionist and left the dining room. Jack nodded to the receptionist to book it to his room, casually walking behind her. He moved to a separate exit, and took the lift to his room. He opened his apartment door quietly and he felt a soft breath, whisper in his ear.

"Hey, Mister Downunder, you're my next appointment."

"Shsss, don't let my roommate hear, shsssss."

"Who gives a shit?"

"I do." Jack closed the door. "Listen Molly," as he pushed her inside. "We have to be careful. I have work to do... to catch up." He paused, "My wife's decided to come."

"What? You told me you two were no good anymore! That's why you're here... ain't it?" she pulled him towards the bed.

"I know," said Jack. "Listen, you've got to trust me."

He looked straight into her eyes, jerked her forward, bent down and slid his tongue inside her mouth, deep into her throat. Molly struggled trying to catch her breath, but Jack was too strong and liked the resistance. He forced his thick fingers between her long luscious thighs, edging them outwards.

"Stop it. I want to know."

"You're gonna make me mad," said Jack, his hands groping at her stockings and pushing them down her thighs.

"Y'all still want me to visit down there, to that place you have?" she repeated, staring up at him in her best Southern accent.

"Shsss. What I want is for you to stop talking and give me some juicy pussy."

Molly struggled to control the conversation. But Jack's hands did the talking and he grabbed at her breasts and pulled them up, cupping them in his hands and bit her delicate nipple through the fabric of her blouse. Molly yelled.

"Quiet."

"Why shoot fire, Jack... your wife...you treat your wife this way?"

"Don't bring her into this," Jack said easing her panties off slowly, and keeping his gaze directly into her eyes. "She's not sexy like you. She's got a face like a rat, who'd fuck a rat? She acts like one, sniffing around." He pretended to sniff into her neck, laughing. "Yes, snooping where she's not meant to snoop."

He stopped and bent down to stroke her thighs, pushing against her, he mumbled into her labia. "She's not worldly like you," as he licked her ivory thighs, "and... you KNOW how to put fire into a man... don't you?"

Molly sighed, taking in a deep breath. Jack jumped up suddenly, rolled her over and smacked her bare buttocks. "I like my women half-dressed. Here... over here." He got up and pulled her off the bed, "and cut my hair like you're supposed to be doing."

He sat in a chair in front of the long mirror, by the bed, and put his arms out to touch her. "Yes, half-dressed, you do the cutting, I'll do the feeling, and then we'll play." Jack pulled down his pants and allowed his massive tumescence to ease inside her as she sat on his lap.

Jack had met Molly soon after he arrived, in the hotel dining room. He watched her slide past him, the click of her stilettos on the marble floor. Her tight skirt waved those beautiful round buttocks at him, sending shockwaves direct to his penis. Molly was the hotel's hairdresser, a vast contrast to the professional women in his group. She was cheap and common, someone he could have his way with and control. Molly, with her slow southern drawl, was just what he needed after his absence from Josh.

"Damn, that meddling bitch of a wife." He had told her she'd get more than she bargained for. Now Josh had to suffer. *I'll fix that when I get back*! He pissed in the toilet and slammed the lid down, clicked the door shut and walked on down the passageway. It was going to be a long drive to the airport.

Chapter 8

Allison hugged her mother and the girls, telling them Sarah was going to look after them part of the time she was away in America.

"I hate that boy," said Isabelle.

"Don't be so silly and take care of your sister."

Sarah was such a good friend, helping her mother with the girls.

Allison waved goodbye and settled back, ready for the long flight across the endless ocean. It gave her time to reflect on the reasons why she had made her choice to finally face her American dream. Writing to Randy had made it come true. She was secretly excited at the chance to meet. The hours passed, and finally an announcement was made. Breakfast would be served, followed by the gradual descent into Los Angeles. Allison squinted through the thick glass plane window at the rolling brown hills stretching for miles. It was strange to see such so much land. Everywhere, networks of traffic below, and then the buildings, spreading like octopus arms, filling every space imaginable.

They touched down on American soil.

Allison followed the masses of people into the terminal building, and slowly made her way across to her connecting flight. She took her seat bound for Chicago, sat back and let the roar of the engine drown out any fears of reuniting with Jack. Upon arrival, Allison integrated into the crowds of passengers, her knees feeling numb from the long trip, and anxious to spot Jack. She caught sight of him leaning against a post.

Jack saw her also and with a slight smile of recognition, moved towards her. He was his usual self - calm, polite, asking her how was her trip.

He gave her no reason to complain. He was so plausible walking towards the baggage claim.

When Allison's bag finally appeared, Jack stacked them onto a trolley and they left the airport, and finally arrived at the Holiday Inn Skokie, North Chicago.

Stopping outside the lobby, she gasped at the entranceway. The lobby was filled with lights. Crystal chandeliers hung down to almost touch her. She stood and marveled at the marble floors and walls of hanging variegated ivy, tastefully circling the entire walls above her, with concealed lighting. She followed Jack past the reception and into the lift to the floor where Jack slipped the card through the slot and it clicked green.

"You'll be getting one of these. I just haven't arranged it yet. It's simple to use." He pushed it open and let her in.

Allison, stood by the long mirror, letting her handbag fall onto the bed. She looked around the roomful of glamourous couches and a small desk, *a place to write*, she thought, *Jack lives like a King*. The bathroom had beautiful lights all around the mirror - it felt like the Hollywood that Allison imagined. She was in America and her dreams were already coming true.

The water was soothing and she turned against it to let it run down her face and hair. When she came out, her hair in a towel, Jack had made her a cup of tea, and was stirring the sugar as she sat down.

"That feels better," still rubbing her hair and taking a sip of tea. "Oh, this is just like we're at home."

"How's the kids?"

"They're fine. You know Sarah?"

Jack sat down and nodded, tapping his knee under the table, opposite her, trying to temporarily repress his memories of how many times his hard penis had slipped into juicy Sarah.

Allison told Jack that Sarah was helping with the kids, but he didn't seem interested.

Jack got up, "I might go down and grab a bite to eat, what about you?"

"I'm not hungry," Allison said, going over to where Jack had prepared her cup. "I'll be fine. I just want some sleep. I'll see you soon." She collapsed into the soft covers of the neatly arranged bed. She just couldn't confront him. She didn't have enough energy right now to go on.

Allison woke in the morning to the loud gush of water in the bathroom. Sitting up, she looked around, rubbing her eyes. The memory of her glamorous surroundings came rushing back to her, and she sprang out of bed, taking a look at herself in the mirror.

Jack yelled at her, screaming they were late for breakfast and to get ready.

Allison ran the shower and quickly dressed, brushed her teeth and smeared some lipstick into her dry lips, fumbling with her make-up bag.

For a moment, Allison felt she was being controlled, possessed, the role of who she had become suddenly awash over her. They entered the huge dining room and voices. American accents filled the room.

"Well... Hello there, so this is your lady. Introduce us," said the man.

"Allison...," Jack put a hand out. "This is Steve. He's our next door neighbor."

"It's a pleasure, Ma'am. Allison is a lovely name," smiling as he talked, "My wife's coming in tomorrow. You ladies can go shopping together."

"Nice to meet you, too." His handshake was friendly, his eyes smiling.

"Yes, I'd love that." He had a thick crop of blonde, untidy hair, with a wide face and round glasses. He looked young and outgoing. He didn't seem to quite fit the mold of their surroundings.

The breakfast was as grandiose as the dining room itself. They ate and retired to their room. Allison sat down at the small dining table, and watched Jack hurrying to fit papers into his briefcase... her gaze fixed on the briefcase.

"Is there something wrong?" Jack looked over at her.

"Huh? Oh no, no. Where are you going?"

"Well... I have work to do. I'll meet you back in the dining room downstairs for lunch."

"Can I use the phone?" asked Allison.

"I've already called home, while you were asleep, if that's what you mean."

"Well, I just wanted to..."

"Look, save it," he banged the door and left her sitting there, still wondering if he knew the papers were missing.

Maybe that's the reason for his curtness. She thought about Mark Fenton. She looked at the telephone, the instructions to dial out. She couldn't understand.

Standing up, she went into the bathroom and looked into the bright mirror. Signs of tired, dry skin showed. Her complexion had a reddish tinge – a result of jet lag, which had a nasty habit of returning. She collapsed back on the bed. Her eyelids stung, everything ached, even her urine had stung, and she closed her eyes. The quiet rumble of the heater lulled her to sleep and she woke to the sound of the telephone ringing. She picked it up. A woman answered, Allison couldn't quite understand her.

"Can you repeat that please? Is this room service?" The voice didn't respond. She looked at the time. It was noon. She'd been sleeping for hours. She ran cold water over her flushed face and brushed her hair. Her clothes felt disheveled and she tugged to straighten them. There was no time. She pulled the door closed and headed for the dining room. A cluster of people were bent over steaming hot vessels of meat and vegetable dishes alongside displays of different breads and fruits. Jack's laugh rang out and he beckoned her to join him, "This is Allison, everybody."

Allison nodded, as many faces smiled back at her, carrying their plates around the table.

Allison felt so tired that the rest of the day was uneventful. The next morning they met Steve with a pretty woman, as they left their room.

"Well, how's that for timing… Allison, meet my princess, Sharon," said Steve, tucking, an arm under hers, as he introduced her.

"I heard Steve say you were coming," she said, giving Allison a hug. "A gal from New Zealand. Won't this be fun! We can go shopping together."

"That'll be great," said Allison as they walked down the passageway, and entered the breakfast room.

"How about after breakfast? There's shops across the road. A big toy shop. I'm not doing anything. It'll be a great way to get to know each other."

"I'd love that."

After breakfast, Allison waited for Sharon down in the lobby. Sharon had a confident stride when she came into sight, wearing a pair of jeans, snug into her figure, her blonde hair tied back in a ponytail, and a pair of large sunglasses on top of her head. She broke into a smile as she came towards Allison.

"Have you been waiting long?"

"No," said Allison and Sharon took her arm and, together, they dashed across the busy road and through the doors of Toys "R" Us.

"Where would you like to start? Take your time," said Sharon.

"I have never seen so many toys in one place in all my life. I guess the girl's toys, if that's okay with you."

"Why, sure, it's a pleasant change for me."

Allison stopped at the Barbie dolls and picked up a bust of Barbie, sitting in a makeup tray. Allison turned the doll's head towards her. "For goodness sake, look at this. It's Barbie's head," Allison said to Sharon, stroking the blonde hair. "It's a good size and you can make her up, with all these clips and eye shadows and lipsticks. It's like a beauty parlor. Isabel will love this," and she placed it in her shopping cart and they moved to the Strawberry Shortcake section. Allison picked up a battery operated sewing machine with a big strawberry on the arm of the machine. "Lucy loves all the strawberry shortcake toys but I've never seen a sewing machine." She had been teaching the girls to sew their doll's clothes.

"That didn't take you long" said Sharon, half glancing at all the different items and following Allison.

"I know. It's easy to get the first thing you see," replied Allison.

"We're spoiled for choice here," said Sharon. She had twin boys and didn't have any idea what little girls liked. They moved over to the boy's section, but there was nothing for Chris except a toy football. "Now, that I can help you with. What age is he?"

"Sixteen."

"It's a bit small, but he should get a kick out of it."

"That's funny," said Allison, and Sharon laughed and nudged her.

"My Steve loves visiting these shops. He dresses up as Santa and tricks our boys. It's so funny, honestly, I wish you were here for Christmas. You'd have a blast."

After a good look at everything, they left for the hotel in time for lunch.

"Would you like to take your shopping up to your room?" said Sharon.

"Yes, but I don't have a card." She set her shopping down by the table, and walked across to the reception.

A man looked up, "Can I help you, Ma'am?"

"Well, yes. I am in room 224 and I need a card for my room." Out of the corner of her eye, she noticed a tall blonde leaning against the counter. "Oh, and I'd like to know how to make a domestic phone call, please."

"Your card, Ma'am, can be obtained at the lobby… the counter where you first checked in."

"Oh, my husband checked in."

The blonde left, and the receptionist went on, "There's simple instructions to follow on the phone in your room. Call me back if you can't understand them."

Allison nodded and walked over to Sharon, standing by her shopping, waiting for her.

"Is everything alright?" Sharon asked.

"Oh yes. I just want to make a local call. I have a pen friend I want to contact."

"Sounds like fun. I can help you with that. Come up to my room after lunch."

"That would be great. I feel sometimes a bit out of place here."

"Been buying already, I see," said Jack, appearing out of nowhere. "I'll take your shopping up to our room."

"Say, what's all this?" Steve interrupted. "Shopping started already? How about some more this afternoon?"

"Great," said Jack before Allison could reply.

Jack slipped the huge toy bag inside the room and slammed the door shut, muttering to himself, *Damantion! She's buying the whole fuckin' town in one day! God damn it!*

He hurried into the dining room and pretended to be helping himself to the buffet when he came up behind Molly, pinching her soft butt. She jumped and turned around, "Well, where did you come from so soon?"

"My room, same time," he said quietly, before moving off.

Jack looked across the room at Molly sitting at the next table, thinking about how hard it was going to be, leaving and not taking her with him. He chewed into a piece of meat, pretending it was Molly. He chewed slowly.

"Jack."

Jack felt a tap on his shoulder, and was immediately aware of what he was up to when he looked around, relieved at who it was.

"Steve!" exclaimed Jack.

Jack told him he would meet the girls outside. *What a goddamn relief,* he thought. Swallowing the piece of meat almost whole, he sprang up, threw his napkin on the table and stormed out of the dining room. He beeped the green signal, pushed the door open, and went into the bathroom to spray on some aftershave. That damn woman. Why the hell did she have to come? There was a knock at the door. He walked over and opened it.

His raging temper faded into his trousers at the sight of Molly standing there. She had wiggled her uniform top down and loosened a button, "How did we get so lucky?"

"My hair appointment, remember?" he said, closing the door, and grabbed her, pulling her up against the wall.

"Jack I need you. Don't leave me. Take me with you."

He tossed her away from him. She skidded against the table and one of her stilettos bounced off as she hit the floor.

"Why are you like this?"

"Because I'm pissed. Of course it's you I want. But that stupid meddling idiot woman had to come, and now she's out there buying up the town. It's our last evening tomorrow night. I can't even give you a farewell screw, not without her in here. I have to get a key… we can't be here anymore. Fuck. I'm pissed off."

"She's so sweet."

"Who?" Jack looked at her.

"Allison, who else?"

"When did you see her?"

"At the counter when she was asking about using the phone."

"A phone call to who? Where?"

"Nowhere. Just a local call for God's sake."

"What do you mean, a local call?"

"Jack, stop… stop shaking me. I don't know where. What's she done now? You treat her bad. Is that how you treat your women?"

"Don't you dare question me." He ripped open her top, and pushed her over onto the table, bent down, and bit-licked her breast.

"That hurts. Be nice… big boy."

"Shut up for Christ's sake, and he turned her over to face the table. "A good butt fuck will put you right," as he spit onto her ass and pushed into her.

"Yeeoww," and she gripped the table. Her hairdressing bag sprawled to the floor and she wrestled against him, scrambling to pick up her tools as weapons. "I'm not staying here with you in this mood. I'm not Allison. Leave me be or I'll scream like bloody thunder."

He turned her around and put his hand over her mouth. "Shuss, you do as I say. Do you hear? You won't be coming with me." Jack liked to bribe and she let go of his arm. She stood there staring at him, suddenly turned, and straightened her clothes. Buttoning up her blouse, she limped out of the room.

Jack stormed over to the phone and called Josh, "The fuckin' papers. What did you do with them?"

"Wait a minute. They're in your briefcase right… the formulas for the dope?"

"Well, last time I looked. I wouldn't leave anything like that back home for Christ's sake."

"Why don't you try looking around your room? Who comes into your room, eh Buddy? Been screwing eh? Sticking your dick where it doesn't belong? Who knows? Who's been in your things? Don't call me up and bag my ass."

Josh put the phone down and thought of Mark's comments. This was going to be fun.

Jack threw the phone down.

"Fuckin' wife. She better not be fooling with me. He stared into his briefcase. He'd checked just before he left for the airport back at the lab. He made another call...

The dial tone came on, the number was unlisted. Jack smiled. She won't be seeing that bastard. Pittsburgh is not on the list.

Chapter 9

Allison's continuing enthusiasm about all that she saw, brought a new aspect to the never-ending grind of city life. Steve had driven them along the main streets. The city bordered on the Great Lakes, a spectacular view. High above them loomed Sears Tower. She craned her neck to find its peak.

"Gosh Sharon, I can't believe how tall it is."

"Yes, it's tall I guess. Come on, let's find your outfit. Do you have anything in mind?"

"I don't think so. I'll know when I see it."

Walking along, they could see the train racing across the overhead bridge. The lights became brighter as darkness set in. Allison stopped at a shop window to admire an oyster-colored jumpsuit, falling in folds with a huge belt of matching material.

"That's it… That's what I'd love."

"Well, take your time." Sharon strolled in and asked the assistant to find a size 6. In the change room, Allison pulled off her tight top and trousers, and slipped into the soft, silk folds, pushed open the door to show Sharon.

"Wow, look at you. It shows off your amazing hourglass figure, doesn't it?" She turned to the assistant.

"Does it?" said Allison. Minutes later, she handed the jumpsuit to the assistant to wrap. They left the store with jubilant smiles and strolled around, until meeting Steve. Allison couldn't wait to tell Jack when they got back to the hotel, but he was nowhere around. Steve went down to the lobby and Sharon invited Allison up to her room for a coffee.

"So tell me more about the country you live in," asked Sharon.

"Well, it's very small. Compared to your country of course... but it's very pretty and doesn't have all your crowds of people. There's lots of parks and beaches everywhere. You can go from east to west coasts in a day. The country is so narrow but quite tall... about the same as your West coast from Mexico to Canada."

"I bet that's nice. Nice for the kids, huh?"

"For everyone really, especially the tourists - they get to see so much. It's because we are two islands, with a tremendous latitude and climate change. One minute you're driving through flat plateaus, next minute you're amongst mountains. It's very dramatic." said Allison, stirring her coffee and smiling as she said it.

"We'll have to come sometime."

"You should." Allison took a long sip of coffee, pleased she had impressed Sharon. "By the way, about my pen friend, he's from Pittsburgh. We're going there and I'd like to see him."

"How long have you been writing to him?"

"We wrote way back in our teenage years, and he found my letters only just recently, and wondered if we'd ever meet. I guess New Zealand has always been an interesting place to learn about."

"Well, how about that, and you of course," Sharon winked at her. "Jack will think that's cool."

Allison went on, "I need to call him."

"So... call."

"Can I call on your phone?"

"Why sure. Here, give me the number, I'll dial it for you."

Allison handed it to her. Sharon clutched the phone in the crook of her neck and took a sip of coffee, waiting for the dial tone. She shook her head, "The number is unlisted."

The door opened and Jack was standing there with Steve.

"The girls have had a ball," said Steve.

"Yes, and Allison got her outfit. It looks wicked on her, Jack." said Sharon.

"Yes, well we better go and see it on," said Jack moving towards the door, and they returned to their room.

"You'll be happy now, won't you?" he said, and placed his briefcase down by the table and opened it.

"Yes of course… why?"

"You better tell me what you have been doing snooping in my briefcase?" Jack flicked through his papers. Parts of his papers he was looking for were tucked up towards the back.

"When was this?"

"You tell me." He threw the briefcase down and made a grab at her. "You put them back. You came all the way over here just to put them back."

"Stop it. I don't know what you're talking about." She shook herself free. "I'm not well…, I need see a doctor. You're hurting me and I don't know what you're talking about. I haven't even been with you."

Jack threw her back across the table.

"What's this about a doctor?"

"I'm finding a sting in my urine and I'm all itchy, and there's your function tomorrow night and…."

Jack thumped the table so hard it bounced into the air. "What have you been up to while I've been away?"

"What do you mean? I've been home."

"Don't give me that innocent stare. I know what you've been up to, and I know what you've planned coming over here… chasing some stupid pen friend. Yes, your stupid little game. You think you can come over here and look up an old mate for some quick nooky… telling everyone, about some stupid pen friend."

"You bastard. You're the one that's so naïve. Grow up."

"*How dare you.*" He grabbed her, shoving her against the door. Allison pounded the door. "Don't you dare say anything to anyone. *Do you hear me?*"

Allison shook her head.

Jack let her go and left the room.

She stood there stunned. He knew about the briefcase. She bit her bottom lip and wondered how she was going to solve this. She tapped on Sharon's door, "Can I come in again?"

"Are you okay? You look pale. Did you knock?"

"Only now on your door. I have to see a doctor, something's wrong with my woman parts."

"You might have thrush? Every woman gets that on a long plane ride," she put her arm around her. "Listen, I can drop you off to get some medication. You can use my hair rollers when you get back, and catch us all up at the preview before the graduation starts."

"But I don't want to impose on you."

"Don't be so silly. You can get an appointment."

Sharon drove Allison over to a huge Medical Centre, not far from the hotel. The only appointment Allison could get was mid-afternoon, so Sharon gave her instructions on how to return, and dropped Allison at the entrance of the Centre. She walked into the main foyer and went over to the receptionist. "Excuse me, I have an appointment at three o'clock."

"Name please," said the woman not looking up.

"Allison Brownley."

"Fill these out."

The receptionist put the forms on the counter and Allison sat down in the waiting area. Minutes turned into hours before she was ushered into a sterile room.

"Mrs Brownley?' said a woman in a white uniform. "Please take all your clothes off and put this gown on, and knock when you're ready."

Allison slipped off her clothes, put the gown on with the buttons fastened up the front, and knocked on the door.

The woman came in, "Now we just slip you into this chair. You put your feet up on these stirrups and the Doctor will be in shortly."

Allison lay there, her feet in the stirrups, staring at the blank wall. She wiped a tear out of her eye. Panic loomed inside her at how she was going to get out of here and back to the hotel, when the door opened and a man swished into the room.

"Good afternoon, Mrs Brownley, I'm Dr Miles. I am going to have to do an internal examination," he said, pulling on a glove. His bland expression hit her as he bent over her and thrust a gloved hand up into her vagina.

"Ouch."

"Hold still please, Ma'am. This is a swab to test, as well. We'll send you the results."

Allison squeezed her eyes shut. "I'm just visiting, I'm at the hotel down the road."

"We'll send them out." She winced as the cold metal claws brought a sudden rush of pain.

"Please wait for the initial report before getting dressed. The other results take a couple of days." He released the stirrups, pulled off his gloves and left the room.

Allison was directed back to her cubicle

"Ma'am?" said the woman in the white uniform, knocking on her cubicle, "The doctor has given you a prescription for Candida... nothing to worry about it, it's a yeast infection. Go down to the lobby and pay for this prescription."

Allison dressed and took the lift down to the counter.

"That will be two hundred dollars ma'am," said the receptionist. Allison didn't look up but opened her purse, took out all her traveler's checks she'd been saving, and signed them.

"Can I use your phone? I need to get back to my hotel."

"No ma'am, the pay phones are through the doors over there."

Allison walked out the doors to the phone booths and stared at the instructions. A man approached her.

"Mrs Brownley?"

"Yes."

"You need a ride back to your hotel?"

"Who are you?"

"A friend of your husband. He asked me to stop by. You better get in." He gripped her elbow firmly, and pushed her into the car, closing the door.

Allison's eyes widened when another man, seated next to her, spoke. He reached into his pocket and pulled out a New Zealand passport.

They sped down the long highway. Allison was too afraid to look at the man next to her but the driver was black, tall and looked mean. The car skidded into the parking area and the man next to her, opened the door, shoved Allison out and, without comment, they sped away, as she stumbled into the hotel lobby. She swiped the card that Jack had finally given her, and let herself in.

She tipped everything out of her handbag in a mad panic, but thank God, she still had her passport. Sharon's rollers were in the bathroom. Quickly plugging them in, she walked into the bedroom. A red signal blinked on the telephone. She picked up the phone but decided it would have to wait. She took a shower, and washed her panties. She realized she was too frightened to answer the message. The men must have the room number. She'd have to tell Jack. She dressed, tightening the belt of her jumpsuit, and fumbled with the rollers. Her fingers stuck in her tangled hair. She was late. She finally pinned the last roller and grabbed her make-up bag. The foundation disguised her dehydration and she looked like a ghost. Once again, she went back to the phone and read the instructions. 'Dial number 9'. *Maybe from Randy*? She had told him she would be at the Holiday Inn. Her hair must have been set by now. Panicking, she raced to pull out the rollers, turned once more to look at herself. She loved the feel of the soft silk and did a little smile in the mirror, and ran out the door.

She stepped out of the lift into the foyer to the sounds of laughter. Men were in their dinner suits, and women wore colorful evening dresses. The tall blonde Allison had seen out of the corner of her eye at the counter - she sipped a glass of wine talking to Jack. Jack listened. He looked up to see Allison approaching, and walked over to her. He took her arm, and pulled her away from the crowd.

"You turn up late like this after your little adventure. You whore. If this pussy sickness gets around, I'll never live it down. Already the next door neighbors know. Who else have you told?"

"I was late getting back. Some men brought me back… they said they know you,"

"I said who else have you told?" Jack looked worried.

"No one."

"Then I don't want to hear another word come out of your mouth. You have just ruined the only important night of my life. Everyone's talking about you and your doctor visit. Find your own way around, but don't follow me," he turned away and moved back into the crowd.

"I see my rollers worked. You look great. Where's Jack?" Sharon said.

"He's busy. He came over, but he's busy."

"Are you okay?"

Allison nodded.

"Then hang out with us."

Her fragrance matched her glowing complexion, and Allison decided that Jack wasn't going to spoil the evening, nor her new friendship.

When the formal speeches began, Jack took his seat beside Allison. Supper was served and he sipped, or more like gulped, his wine. He kept his gaze to a subtle level across the table. As the evening came to a close, Allison left the function and opened the door of their room. The light was still beeping so she lifted the receiver and listened to the instructions of the operator.

'Press nine for recorded messages.'

"Allison are you there, can you give me a call?"

Allison sat down on the bed and stared at the phone. Mother sounded so upset - what is wrong? She looked at the time and knew it was too early to call New Zealand.

CHAPTER 10

When Allison opened her eyes and looked around - she was still in the hotel. She couldn't remember if she'd dreamed the phone had rung, or anything about the day before. She threw the bed sheets back and went to the shower. The running water on her face helped her think. As she stepped out, she heard the door open.

"Is that you?"

"Yes, who else? You were asleep, so I went out for breakfast."

"I've had some bad news," she said, wrapping herself with the towel. "I have to go home."

"What's brought this on, all of a sudden?"

"My father," she came out of the bathroom. "He's not well, I have to go home."

"I'll take you to the airport." Jack was sitting down. He looked untidy.

"No. I'll get a cab. I just need to change my ticket. Oh and can you buy another suitcase?"

"What for?"

"I can't fit the toys in. You told me to bring just a small bag."

"Well, how did I know you were going back? I'll see."

"Thanks. I can't get those kind of toys in New Zealand."

"I know, I know, you don't have to go on."

"There's something else."

"What?"

"I got a ride back to the hotel yesterday with some men who said they knew you."

"From who?" Jack rose as he looked up at her.

"Well they said my name. They knew who I was."

"They said your name? So you got in the car? You're even more stupid than I thought you were. *Fuck it*, I give up with you. Do you know there are con men out there who know who books into these hotels? Next thing you know… you're dead." He put a finger to his head.

"They had New Zealand passports."

"So…, fake. You're thick. You and that stupid Detective. Next thing you know you'll get had up for murder."

"What Detective are you talking about?"

"The one you hired. You didn't come all these miles to see me. You're up to something. You're the one in trouble. I can prove it."

"Prove what?" Allison stood facing him, her neck pulsing in a rage.

"Get to the airport yourself. Fuck your bloody toys."

Jack left her standing there, slamming the door behind him.

•   •   •   •   •

A car pulled up outside the hotel and Jack got in.

"Why did you contact my wife?"

"Why did you involve her? You know what happens when you don't follow instructions. Someone gets hurt."

The man driving kept his eye on Jack through the rear vision mirror.

"She's leaving today. She stumbled onto some of my papers by accident. She hired a detective to get me for a divorce, and he found out things, but he's not talkin' anymore. She's nothing to worry about. I'm working on the deal. I've got what I want, and I need to be left alone. I'm only a consultant. Damn you."

"Don't dictate to us. We give the orders." He turned around to face Jack. "Is that clear? We have a deal. Your money will be in the Caymans when you perform and produce the new process and it is tested. Your head's been so far up your ass, you haven't been paying attention to business. You're going on a joy ride."

The car sped into a backstreet and into a garage. It was pitch black inside. The car door opened and Jack felt a strong hand grip him, and haul him out of the car. He could hear echoes, like they were in a cave.

"Your mouth's been running… you're so good at what you do. Is that right Mr Brownley? Fuck the Kiwi Mob. Bring us results and we'll pay you more. Bring us grief and we'll put you through that hammermill outside your shed."

"Not this way. I'm just a research chemist developing a new process."

"You think you're so smart. You need to be reminded what we want from you."

There was silence. Jack strained to adjust his eyes to the darkness. He could smell rotten weed and flesh. It smelled like a dead animal kept as bait for the rats.

"*Listen*! I'm on to it. I have the formula," Jack screamed. "I'll get it concealed. Tell me when to drop it off. Money in the Caymans, and we're sweet."

Jack choked. A thump to his chest. Coughing and spluttering, with blood pouring out of his mouth, Jack took another thump, and another, until he lay in a heap, motionless.

He woke to the sound of the engine and footsteps. The lift of the hotel jerked, and next he knew, he was in his hotel bed, covered in blood.

Chapter 11

Allison sat in her cab. All she could think of was her mother's upset voice, and the news of her father lying in a coma.

Landing in Christchurch, she hurried into the terminal building. Mattie's face lit up instantly as soon as their eyes met.

"Oh dear," said Mattie falling into Allison's arms.

"I can't believe it," Allison said. Tears rolled down her cheeks as their faces touched. They clung to each other, walking towards the baggage claim. Mattie drew out a handkerchief to blow her nose and Allison took her arm.

"He just fell out of bed early on Tuesday morning, and I couldn't get him back in bed. I called the ambulance, and when they got there... they said he'd had a stroke."

"A stroke?" Allison picked up her bag and they left the airport. "And what happened then?"

"Well, they took him to the hospital, he's..." she started to cry again. Allison put her arm around her mother, and they crossed the road towards the car without saying any more.

Allison drove out of the airport and Mattie went on, "He's still in a coma."

"Oh, no. What's going to happen?"

"That's what we don't know... nobody knows with a coma. He'd been complaining about a terrible headache, but I thought nothing of it."

"You can't blame yourself."

The rattle of the stones echoed up the familiar driveway - but there was no Bob with his smiling face to greet them. Later, inside the house, the sun streamed into the lounge, warming them, but it was a lonesome warmth.

"When can we see him?" asked Allison, putting her bags into the spare room and closing the door.

"I'll have to call."

"I'll make some tea and go for the girls. How's Chris taking it?"

"No good... he's lost. He doesn't understand," Mattie followed her into the kitchen and started getting the cups out. They worked well together and it was a good to be back, even though it was a worrying time. They sat together. Bob's quiet, unassuming presence somehow still drifted through the room, in spite of the emptiness without him.

Allison drove to pick the girls up. She passed their house and wondered how bad the situation was going to be with her father. He may wake and everything would be back to the way it was. She got out of the car, to see Isabel jumping up and down and calling out at Lucy.

"Mummy, Mummy," she raced over and hugged her with Lucy tripping behind.

"Girls! You'll fall! Isabel, be careful of Lucy."

"Mummy, Isabel's hurting me."

"Oh, give us a hug. Have you been good girls?"

"Yes, but not at Sarah's," said Isabel. Allison got them into the car.

"Now what does that mean?" said Allison.

"I hated it. Sarah's - that boy."

"Well he might not like you either."

"He does, he tried to kiss me," she giggled.

"Yeah, and I saw," said Lucy.

"You shut up," and Isabel thumped Lucy with her school bag.

"Yee - Ouch, you hurt me."

"Here stop that, with your Grandad sick in hospital."

"Can we go and see him?" asked Isabel.

"I don't know dear, we'll have to see," said Allison, pulling out from the curb.

"We did some watering for you, Mummy. Do you want to go and see?" said Isabel.

"No, dear. We'll go in on the way to school tomorrow."

They turned into the driveway and Allison got out, opening the door for the girls.

"Does that mean we're staying at Nana's?" said Isabel, scrambling out of the car before Lucy.

"For a while, yes."

"But when does Daddy get back? Why didn't he come back?"

"No. Daddy is working in America still. He can't come home yet. Too many questions, Miss Isabel," said Allison, following the girls into the house.

Mattie was on the phone to the hospital. "Allison didn't like her expression, when she put the phone down, and said, "I'll ask Emily if she'll mind the girls."

"Mummy, what did you bring us?" Isabel said racing after Allison, to look for Allison's bags.

"I might have something for you, but it's only small."

Allison went off into the kitchen with Isabel and Lucy following her. Isabel put her head down and began to cry. Lucy had found the cakes Mattie had placed on the kitchen table. Mattie loved buying cakes of all sorts. Bob's favourite cake was called Fly's Breakfast." It had sultanas mixed with cinnamon sauce in a square of pastry.

"Mummy, I'm sorry. Poor Grandad. He's not here to have his favourite cake, and we've missed you." She burst into tears again.

"I know dear, it's not fair. Grandad is resting and Nana and I are going to go and see him," she helped her up to the old kitchen table with its checkered table cloth. Lucy quietly waited for Isabel to wipe her eyes and take one of the cakes.

In a moment of quiet, Allison picked up the phone and called Emily. But Emily was no help or support, she only wanted to probe for gossip.

Allison sighed and sat at the old kitchen table, putting her head in her hands, "Emily is going to see to the girls."

"That's good."

"She mentioned the business with Jack. Poor lady, she felt embarrassed that she'd interfered."

"Good thing she did." replied Mattie.

The ride to the hospital was slow. They walked along the corridors; the familiar smell reminded Allison of her brief nursing career, cut short when she found herself pregnant with Chris. All those arguments with her father seemed futile now, as they entered the room where he lay. The sun faded outside the window and his frail form was lifeless, his eyes closed and sunken. Chris took a seat, staring aimlessly, looking for life from his beloved mentor. Nobody moved. The trickle of instant tears brought everyone into reality that his time was almost over.

CHAPTER 12

Inevitably, Bob did not wake. They were left with just his memories. At least they had each other. As each day passed, Allison could plan what she had to do before Jack's return.

"Mark," said Allison.

"Yes, speaking."

"It's Allison Brownley here. I had a message to call you."

"Yes, you did. A result came in from the autopsy, on my partner Ed Marshall," he paused. "You had better come in."

"Can you tell me what this is about?"

"Not on the phone. When can you come in?"

"I can come as soon as you like."

"Then shall we say 10 o'clock tomorrow morning?"

"Yes, that would be fine." She replaced the receiver slowly, and ran to find her mother.

Allison whistled like her mother always whistled. The return whistle came from the back door. Allison opened it; Mattie had been cutting some roses and was shaking her jacket from a shower of rain.

"Mark Fenton wants me in his office. What have I done?" queried Allison.

"You haven't done anything. There you go again, blaming yourself for all this. You look terrible. Now stop that and pull yourself together," responded Mattie.

"But, those papers..."

"All you have to remember is, Ed was instructed by you to investigate Jack." Mattie went on trimming the leaves off the roses, hammering the ends of the stems with Bob's old tack hammer. "How about we go out around the shops? We always find something to look at. Some new spring fabric has just come into Fabric House."

Mattie placed the roses in a pewter vase and put them on the dining table, their perfume filling the room. Allison was never alone with her worries when Mattie was there. The two of them drove off into town.

Next morning, Allison knocked at the glass pane door of Mark Fenton's office.

"Good Morning, do you wish to be called Mrs Brownley or Allison?" said Mark, opening the door for her.

"Allison," she said - stepping into Mark's office. The smell of tobacco filled the room.

"Take a seat," he went to sit at his desk. "Do you mind my pipe?"

"No."

"The Police have the results of the autopsy. He had acute corrosive changes in the GI tract with edema of the glottis and emphysema of the lungs. There has never been any evidence that I know of him suffering from emphysema." He stopped. "Would you know anything?"

"How would I know his health problems? He never said."

"It also bothers me that you were visiting here, when you knew Ed was not here. Can you explain that to me?"

"I, err I ...I wasn't getting an answer on the phone."

"I'm not sure I follow."

"I came in to his office - because I couldn't get an answer to my phone calls."

"I saw you place a file back on the desk. Do you have any of Ed's papers?"

"I ...I knew about the formulas, and some weird chemicals. I think maybe to do with cough syrup."

"What do you mean cough syrup?"

"I think I recognized one of the names from the ingredients on a cough syrup bottle."

"I'm not sure I believe you. Were these formulas to do with your husband's work?"

"I don't know." She stood up and went on, "I employed Ed and he was working for me. I came into your office and looked around. I saw your name. I thought I was in the wrong room."

"Yes, but you weren't," Mark stood up to join her.

"How do I know what's inside that file?"

"Didn't you look?"

Allison stood there staring at him. She didn't answer.

"I will have to pass on this. I don't feel there is any more need for us to continue." He threw a folder to one side, kicked the chair back, and moved towards the door.

"What happens now?" asked Allison.

"You will be contacted," he opened the door and tilted his head in a gesture of courtesy, and Allison left the building.

• • • • •

Mark reached for the phone.

"She's got those papers. We need to go after her." Mark sucked on his pipe.

"How do you know?" said Josh.

"Copper's instinct."

Chapter 13

Allison sat in the open foyer of the airport. It was a Saturday, and the girls were excited, watching the different planes arriving on the tarmac.

"Is Daddy coming to stay at Nana's?" asked Isabel, leaving the window and sitting next to Allison.

"Yes. I haven't asked him but I'm sure he will."

Jack's flight was announced and the girls ran towards him. He bent down to greet these cherubs as they ran to meet him.

"Hello, girls. Haven't you grown," and he took both their hands.

"Did you bring some presents?"

"No, sorry, I didn't get time."

"But Mummy said…"

Jack walked over to the baggage department with Isabelle running behind him.

"Mummy said you had some presents."

"Well maybe later, we'll see."

"You can stay with us at Nana's,' said Isabelle.

"Yes Daddy, it's fun. Nana has lots of cakes," said Lucy dancing up and down, pulling on Jack's hand.

"What's this about?" said Jack, looking at Allison.

"You know… it has been hard with my Father passing."

"Of course, how did all that go?"

"Sad. We can sleep in the outhouse." Allison bit her bottom lip, and walked on ahead. She didn't know what to think about the toys.

•   •   •   •   •

Jack was glad to be alone back at his house. He threw his two suitcases on the bed and picked up the phone.

"Just got in. I found some of my papers, but there's still some missing."

"Come on up," replied Josh.

"I want to know."

"Just get here."

Jack parked his car on the street, walked up the driveway, and tapped on Josh's door. Raunchy music was playing, and men's laughter rang out from the kitchen.

"Here's my favourite buddy, home from Yankee land," and he gave him a swift ass hug. "Cheers to Mr Downunder. Isn't that what they called you?' He took a swig of his wine. "Come on in, you old bastard." He shoved a glass in Jack's hand and whispered, "I got your favourite wine."

Jack looked at the men surrounding the table in the kitchen. He recognized the one with the scar.

Josh took another sip of his wine and flopped down on a chair. "Grab a seat. This is Harry, Victor, Mark and you know Motley here."

Harry was built like brick shit-house, with a beard and furtive eyes that pierced through Jack as he sat opposite him. Victor was tall with black, oily hair, swished back, and tinted glasses... looking like a possum on steroids... and he wore a Rolex, which he constantly touched.

"You want to know where the rest of the papers are," said Josh, looking around the group.

"Don't play games. You know I can't complete the deal without them," said Jack.

"Well you should have thought of that when you went out screwing," said Mark, sucking on his pipe.

"What do you mean?"

"Over in Yankee land."

"Mind your own fuckin' business, rat face. One rat's enough of a screw, without you showing up."

Mark stabbed Jack's hand down with his pipe. Jack snatched his hand away.

"Enough!" said Victor, blowing out smoke over Jack. "We have the rest of your papers and your next pay off. We need a drop off time. I need proof this shit's going to be clean."

"You'll have the proof when I see those papers." Jack pushed his chair away. He was sure he'd seen the old rat before. "It's been a long day. I have to go water the horses," and he walked down the passageway towards the toilet, but opened Josh's bedroom door instead. He knew his way around. Quickly, he went to Josh's filing cabinet, and opened it. He caught sight of photo copies. Ed's hand writing. Footsteps interrupted him.

Motley was standing at the doorway, staring at Jack. "Did ya get lost?"

Jack closed the lid and shoved past him, sauntering down the hallway. He stuck his head around the corner of the kitchen.

"I'll see myself out." Jack noticed a woman standing staring at him, as he closed the door. *Nosy old bag, nothing else to do*, he thought. *What else is new? Everyone's out to screw me.*

Next day, Jack drove to the plant out in the country. Josh's car was parked around the back.

"Looks like you've been in the shit. Who the hell were those thugs last night?" Jack said, arriving down the dirt track and looking at what Josh had constructed. "Are they, you know… from…?"

"Yeh, well, you already met Motley. It's your bloody deal. Leaving me here to teach those pricks. I told them you'd arrange their pay-off when you got back. I thought like you… they'd wanted to meet you," Josh laughed.

"You cunning bastard."

"How did you fix up the accident?" asked Jack.

"Never you mind. I was only covering my tracks. But you're so stupid! You've got all the town involved. Everyone knows what we're doing."

"It's not me… It's you."

"It's not you is it? You fuckin' pencil dick slime bag." Jack gripped him, swinging him up against the wall of the shed.

"It's your Missus and the bloody detective, you stupid bastard. The cops want to question you." Josh shook himself. "Don't fuck with me. They were snooping around at work when you left... in the basement."

"What did you tell them?"

"I told them nothing. We were at a function."

Jack dropped him in the dust, and walked over to turn on the conveyor belt. It squealed like a stuck pig. The head pulley took hold and the beets paraded up the conveyor, dropping to the waiting hammermill, disintegrating to pulp and juice at the other end. Jack nodded in approval.

"Looks like the start of an Ethanol plant to me. Did you get the air conditioner compressors?"

"Yep, but I haven't done any more than the Teflon paint in the cylinders."

"We'll have to keep quiet if some cop is snooping around. Did you get a look at him?"

"They all look the same to me. Oversized pig, shifty eyed, writing notes all the time."

"We've got to get this dope ready. I'd say we have just months before we're screwed. We'll meet here every other weekend... not to arouse suspicion."

"Why so long?"

"I have some other plans that have cropped up."

"Like what?"

"You'll see." Jack left the plant, half-smiling to himself at the thought of Molly's arrival.

CHAPTER 14

It was Monday morning, and Jack had arrived to stay at Mattie's. He went inside the house to have his shower and give his favorite thing a good scrub. It was his and he could wash it as fast as he wanted.

"Can we come in, Mummy?" asked Isabel, tiptoeing up the steps, with Lucy.

The floor of the room had a definite tilt to it. It was all part of the charm, and when Lucy pushed Isabel across the sloping floor, they both fell onto the bed, knocking over Jack's briefcase. Allison was busy stuffing clothes into the old closet.

"What are you doing Mummy?" asked Lucy, jumping up against Isabel.

"Oh, putting things away, trying to tidy. Don't knock Daddy's things over. I've just made the bed."

"It's heavy Mummy."

Allison turned around and took the briefcase from Lucy, then placed it back beside the bed.

"Come on girls. It's time for some breakfast," and they hurried to the kitchen. After breakfast, Jack joined Allison outside.

"It's time your mother moved out of here," said Jack, tying his shoe laces.

"I know, but it's hard."

"What's hard, leaving all this useless shit?" he said, looking out at the mosaic pathway that led to the garden. "All this needs is a bulldozer."

"Don't say that, Jack. Not to my mother," cautioned Allison.

"She needs to move on. While I was away, an old house on a large section, came up for sale."

"Where's this?"

"It's actually across the park from where we live, in that blind street. Your mother could move in there more or less right away. I'll take the house off someday and build two townhouses. She can have one of the townhouses."

"Then... when can we have a look?"

"I'll make the arrangements," Jack looked at his watch. "I had better finish getting to work, and I'll make a call to the land agent."

Jack was inside the main house, when Allison noticed the briefcase was still open. She glanced at it and could not help but look inside. There were a bunch of keys beside a large letter. Allison paused and picked it up. It was addressed to Bellamy Labs. The stamp was from America. Allison felt the weight of it, but had no time to read it. She looked at the wardrobe. Should she hide it there? She sat staring at it.

"Interesting... isn't it?" Allison jumped and looked up. "It's not what you think. I have a colleague coming to stay. Actually, I was going to tell you anyway, but you have to stick your nose into everyone's business."

"Who's coming to stay?"

"You'll see. You won't need your detective for this event. Now... if you'll excuse me, I'll finish getting ready for work."

He closed the case, and reached inside the wardrobe for a tie.

"Nothing I do satisfies you. You want this house for your mother? Then stop looking at stuff that doesn't belong to you." He snapped the lock on the briefcase and left.

Allison stared outside the window. How could she be so stupid? Nothing has changed. Nothing. He'd even found out about Ed. She got up and walked to the kitchen.

"What's wrong?' asked Mattie, coming out of her bedroom in her dressing gown, her hairnet still on, carrying an empty cup.

"It's Jack. I'm so stupid... I'm so stupid." Allison sat crying in the alcove.

Kimmy brushed up against her legs, meowing softly as if to comfort her. She bent down to stroke him and looked up at Mattie, "I found a letter in Jack's briefcase. It was from America. I didn't tell you, but I think I saw him with a lady in America. He said someone was coming to stay with us at our house."

"Did he say who it was?" asked Mattie.

"Yes, he said it was a colleague, from when he was working at the laboratory."

"What? How is this going to happen?"

"It just is," and she started to cry again.

Mattie brought a steaming coffee, sitting beside her with Kimmy's wagging tail, brushing against them.

"I don't think you should worry. It may not be what you think. How could he be so blatant, anyway?" queried Mattie.

"You might be right," Allison perked up and wiped her eyes. "Jack has seen a house. Would you ever think of moving?"

Mattie didn't answer but looked down and took a sip of coffee. The sun fell on their feet, and she stroked the old cat. He meowed, broadcasting a foul stench as his stale teeth reeked of decay.

"We'll go and look, there's no harm done," said Mattie.

"I know it's hard. You weren't prepared for this. I'll give Jack a call," Allison got up and left Mattie sitting in the sun.

Allison went inside and called Jack.

"Your mother doesn't realize that this is an opportunity. I have plans with this all done. She'll be in a brand new townhouse before she knows it."

"I know, you don't have to tell me, but it's just hard for her."

"Well, tell her to get over it. Listen... I'll see you at one o'clock."

Allison joined Mattie returning from the mailbox with a letter in her hand. Smiling, she handed her the letter.

"What's this... from Randy?"

She tore open the letter and began to read. "Something's not right. He's sorry he missed me."

Mattie sat down to join her. "It's useless trying, Allison. It's like this house."

"You're always right, Mother. I guess that's with living and learning." She gave her mother a long, deep hug.

It was an easy drive past Allison's house and around the corner into the little blind lane overlooking the park. Mattie turned the engine off and they both gazed across the open spaces of the park.

Jack pulled up beside them and he got out with a woman carrying a folder. "This is Marjory Hays."

"How do you do, ladies? I'm the agent acting for this property," she spoke with an English accent and handed them her card. "I just want to say that this is a unique opportunity. It's a deceased estate, so it is the first time offered in forty years."

They walked up the old pathway and stepped onto the fake green turf covering the steps.

"Who lived here?" asked Allison.

"An old lady," Marjory swept across the unglued pieces of fake turf with her stiletto. "This plastic grass was for her, so she wouldn't slip." She opened the glass front door, to a rush of stale odors.

The first thing Allison noticed were the rounded corner walls in the passageway. Brown mottled carpet, like brown slime, covered a fabulous hidden hardwood floor throughout the house. Every door was domed with dark brown varnish. Allison caught Mattie's expression.

"The lounge is quite bright," said Marjory, walking over to pull at the old Holland blinds, which clapped upward with a loud bang, spurting dust into the sunlight.

"Here, I'll fix that," said Jack leaning over her.

"It's a dream of a section, don't you think, Mrs Smith?" Marjory looked at Mattie over Jack's shoulder. "If you look out these windows, you can see the beautiful park from here, but you don't have to mow it."

The main bedroom ran off the lounge and then a door opened to the next bedroom. Back out to the passageway, another bedroom featured at the end of it. The bathroom, old shower and laundry were all dismal. A roller door opened out to a large garden, where a mass of untidy wire netting failed to control rows of raspberry bushes.

"The old girl must have liked her raspberries." said Jack.

"Don't worry they can be pulled out, but just look at the section," said Marjory.

"Well, that's what we're here for," said Jack.

"Then why don't we go back inside? I'd like to show you these plans I have."

Back in the kitchen, Marjory pulled another Holland blind, which seemed to roll up at an easier pace. The sunlight brightened the area, and she laid the plans out on the flecked Formica bench top.

"Here we have a sketch of how two townhouses can sit on this land," she looked at Mattie.

"You wouldn't need to get too comfortable here. We can take this off in the summer, no problem," said Jack staring out into the park.

"It's all very nice, but we'll have to think about it. Come on Allison, I think I'll leave it, just to talk it over."

"Thanks for your time, Marjory," said Allison. They opened the front door, returning to the car, facing the house.

"So what do you think, Mother?"

"What do you think?" said Mattie turning the ignition key.

Mattie, like Allison, was trapped. A lost soul saying goodbye to the old garden, the quaint walls of the house that had given her so much pleasure for such a short time. It was like saying goodbye to Bob. Reality was, it was old, like her, and unable to care for itself.

There was nowhere else to turn. She said goodbye.

She said one more goodbye to Kimmy, the old cat, who didn't know his fate. He meowed for his last meal and a stroke of his coat. Allison then helped Mattie box him up and take him to the vet for his unfortunate sudden demise.

Allison admired Jack for his tenacity. There was nothing manual Jack couldn't handle. Allison helped him load a lifetime's accumulation of property. Bob's tools, arranged on garage walls hanging on cut-outs of hammers, saws, tools and garden utensils. Jack moved Mattie's belongings across the park with little trauma, and Chris was only too happy to join her and boasting to his mates about having his own bedroom.

Jack had his family back to normal.

While Jack mowed the lawns one day, Allison saw the chance she needed. Sneaking into the garage she opened the car door. Jack's keys hung in the ignition. She slipped them out, went towards her car and called out to Jack, "I'm going to help Mother."

There was a lot of lawn to mow on their corner section and he nodded as she sped away.

She parked the car outside Bellamy Labs. She knew which key fitted the side door of the building. She opened the door and raced up the stairs to Jack's office, knowing no one would be around. She went in, heading straight to the top drawer of Jack's desk, her fingers sliding over the different shapes of keys to fit the lock. The smallest key unlocked the drawer. She recognized the letter from the brief case. She grabbed it. A few pages were folded back into the envelope with the American postage stamp. It wasn't as heavy; some of it was missing. She opened the pages.

Dear Jack,

How does it feel being back with your family? How is your wife, now that you are home? Did you send me my ticket? ...All my love Molly.

Molly was that blonde woman with Jack in Chicago! Allison grabbed the letter and read it again. The hairdresser at the hotel! Without another thought, she flew back down the stairs with the letter, locked the door and raced to her car. With the engine roaring, her heart beating, half swallowing back gulps of tears, she fled up to the Russley Hotel where she used to work, and ran to the counter.

"Hi, I'd like this photo-copied, please urgently," the girl, half nodding to her in recognition, took the pages, ran the photo machine, and handed them back to her. Allison raced back to Jack's office and returned the letter, and quickly sped home.

She placed the car keys back where they belonged and closed Jack's car door. The sound of the mower was more distant. *Jack must be over the other side of the property*, she thought. She walked casually inside and went to look for Sharon's number. She had it somewhere. She must call her. It was urgent she find out. She sat in the dining room, watching Jack and listening to the long dial tone. A woman's voice, it was Sharon.

"Why, if it isn't Allison? Is that you?"

"Yes, it's me. It's so nice to hear your voice. I miss you."

"Me too. Listen, Steve told me about your Dad. I missed giving you a hug. I'm so sorry."

"I know, I miss him. I hate this," and she began to cry.

"What's up baby?"

"It's Jack. I didn't tell you everything, but he's having another affair. Did you see a blonde woman with him?"

"Listen, Honey. It's not for me to say. I think it should come from you. You know what I mean. My telling you what I know, will only influence your decision."

Allison kept sobbing but listened.

"Honey, don't cry. You are a beautiful person. You'll make the right decision. Now you stay in touch, and look after those kids."

Allison put down the phone. "That son of a bitch." She missed her father. She paced around the room, waiting for Jack to finish his lawns. This bitch wasn't going to come, not now, not ever.

The drone of the mower stopped, and Allison banged on the window, "Jack, I want to talk to you. Are you finished?"

He continued wiping the mower, running water through the catcher.

Allison went outside and stood amongst the wet grass gushing from the mower. "I need to talk to you."

"Can't you see I'm busy?"

"No, it can't wait. I've waited too long and it's over," Allison responded. Now she was abrupt and determined.

He stood up, straightening his back after stooping, "What shit are you on about now?"

"Your visitor. That woman, when is she coming?"

"Shit, what brought this on all of a sudden?"

"Well, now that Mother has moved over to the park, I thought I might move over and let you have your visitor to yourself." Allison's eyes drilled into his with fire inside.

Jack threw the rag down and moved towards her, "Now listen here. Nobody's going anywhere they don't belong. Do you hear me? Nobody. As for my visitor, what would everybody say around here if you moved out, eh? Trouble with you, is you don't think." He put his forefinger up to his head and jabbed it hard against his head, knocking it several times, "Only trouble is... you have nothing up here." He pushed past her. "Do the cleaning up yourself," and went inside.

CHAPTER 15

Jack wasn't in the mood for the phone call from the Police department. He parked on Montreal Street, outside the Police Station, and entered the building. It was cold, one of Christchurch's early spring mornings and winter hadn't let up. He reported at the desk.

"Good morning," said a tall officer, dressed in plain clothes, as he walked past him.

Jack sat down in the cubicle, tapping his knee. A policeman called him into a side room.

"Mr Brownley? Good morning, I'm Constable Keats, and I just need to ask some questions." He had an official form in front of him and began filling it out.

"Where were you on the night of September the twentieth? Can you tell us your movements, please?"

"I was at Bellamy Laboratories for an award dinner. I had a speech to do. I was getting ready to leave on a work program. I don't know… what's this about?"

"Well there has been an inquiry about a Detective, Edward Marshall, who was there at the function. The autopsy shows damage to his bronchial tubes. We are looking into this, as we're not satisfied he just died of an accident."

"What are you trying to say?" Jack stood up.

"Did you leave the function at any time?"

"I have rights, and I'm certainly not saying anything more until I contact my lawyer. Can I go?" He walked out past the policeman and turned, "You'll be hearing from my lawyer."

"Not so fast, Mr Brownley. There's more to this. Your wife has filed a complaint with the court on your conduct with your children."

"She what?"

"Looks like you will need a lawyer."

"It was her that hired the detective. You can go after her. She's the one."

"We will, sir."

"Then I can leave?"

"We will be in touch."

Jack left the building.

•   •   •   •   •

The letter from the Court finally arrived. The report indicated there was a hint of fear, and went on to say she could take legal action. Allison dialed the Police department.

"I want to ask for some help on getting a protection order."

"Whom am I speaking with, please?"

"Allison Brownley... it's not for me, but for my friend."

"Well then, tell your friend she has to sign a statement. All these acts have to be documented."

"Thank you, have there been any messages? The name is Allison Brownley."

"What was this connected to?"

"The accident of Ed Marshall."

"Someone will call you back."

She put down the phone, and packed the car with a few belongings; soon the girls would be home from school.

"Why are we going to Nana's?" asked Isabel, stuffing her favourite things in the car.

"Nana needs the company right now."

"But what about Dad?"

"He's busy working. He won't mind if we stay away for a bit. Now help Lucy pack what she wants."

When they were finished packing, Allison ran the engine and backed slowly out of the driveway with Isabel and Lucy, surrounded by their chosen belongings. It was late in the day when they rounded the corner. Mattie was waiting for them at the front door. She opened it and a gush of smoke came out.

"Sorry about the smoke, I'm having trouble with the old fireplace," she said, waving her arm around as if to move the smoke away. "I think we need a chimney sweep." She helped Allison in with her things.

"It's cold, Mummy. I don't like it here," said Isabel, stumbling inside with her bags.

"Put some extra clothes on, and don't complain. We'll get some heat going, when we fix the fire."

"Come on, girls. Nana has a nice dinner for you, and there's lots of places to explore around here," said Mattie, putting her arm around Isabel.

The dimness of the walls, the cold, the smell of smoke, was all too much for both Isabel and Lucy. Allison let the bundle of clothes fall onto the spare chair in the sunroom to the left of the front door. It was now her bedroom.

The night was closing in, and Jack would be returning from work. It felt strange somehow, the first night without him. She helped the girls settle. Mattie had made a pot of stew, with gravy, mashed potatoes, topped with carrots and parsnips. She was good at preparing tasty, wholesome meals, and the little kitchen smelled delicious. Allison and Mattie carried the steaming plates to the old dining room table in the lounge. With the fire now crackling properly, they felt warm and safe.

The phone rang. Allison went to her mother's room, and picked it up.

"What the fuck are you up to?" Jack's voice roared into the receiver.

"I didn't want to tell you."

"Tell me what?"

"I want to have a break and help my mother."

"Fuckin' like hell, you do. I'll give you until tomorrow to come to your senses and I'm coming over there to drag you out, and get my girls."

"Listen… you're not listening…"

"Fuck I'm not. Look… I warned you before. My lawyer will be on to you. I know what you've been up to. I'll be over tomorrow night."

"Mummy who were you talking to?" called out Isabel from the girl's bedroom.

Allison got up to tell her, standing at the open door, "Oh, just Daddy."

"Is everything alright Mummy?"

"Yes dear. Now don't you both look cozy in here?"

"Are you coming in to read us a story?"

"Of course," Allison replied as she sat down on Isabel's bed. "And you've got Grandad's lamp to keep you company. See the monkeys?"

Allison reached over to take a closer look at the porcelain monkeys, sitting on the wooden base, and touched their faces. "I used to love this lamp… when I was a little girl," she sighed, squeezing the tears out of her eyes. "Grandad would tell me the story of the three monkeys."

"What are the monkeys doing?" asked Isabel.

"Well, one monkey has his hands over its eyes, like this." Allison covered her eyes. "Now you try."

"What do you think that means?" said Isabel, covering her eyes.

"They're blind."

"I can't see," Lucy called out.

"I know you can't. Now, put your hands over your ears," said Allison. Lucy made a mumbling sound.

"And now over your mouth. See no evil, hear no evil and speak no evil."

Isabel and Lucy looked with fascination at their mother and the lamp. Allison started to open one of the books.

"I like that game!" screamed Lucy.

"The message is a proverb, not a game Lucy."

"What's a proverb, mommy?" asked Lucy.

"A proverb is a lesson on how to live your life in a good way, and treat others how you'd like to be treated. These monkey statues were discovered in Japan hundreds of years ago.

"Wow, are those monkeys that old?" said Lucy, leaning over to take a closer look.

Allison smiled and wagged her finger. "We mind our own business, and we keep away from bad things. We don't say bad things, or tell on people, or listen to things you shouldn't."

"Like when you and Daddy shout at each other?" asked Isabel.

"Kind of like that."

"I don't like it when you shout at Daddy… and where's "Tigger in the Long Grass?" asked Lucy, reaching for one of the books.

"I want that one. Did you bring that one, Mummy?" asked Lucy. "We like that one. It reminds us of Kimmy. He's a ginger cat like Tigger."

"No dear, I didn't. But we have "Cat in the Hat with Ham and Eggs, I am, I said," Allison replied as she turned the large pages of the book.

"He's so funny, "Green eggs and ham," Lucy and Isabel giggled.

"Now cozy up. I'll leave the light on," said Allison, tucking them in.

"I loved Grandad. I miss him. Now I can watch the monkeys, and think of him," Isabel turned towards the old lamp, snuggling into her pillow, and smiled up at Allison.

"Goodnight, dears. Mummy loves you, and so does Daddy."

"And Nana," they both said.

Allison closed the door and joined her mother in the lounge. Mattie sat close to the fire, peeling apples and throwing the skins into the flames.

"We'll call a chimney sweep in the morning. I know it's late in the season but we've no choice," said Allison, taking a seat. "That was Jack. He's mad as always. He's coming over here tomorrow to get me."

"He can't do that. Didn't you say you'd called the Police?"

"Yes I did. I got the feeling I was one amongst millions of callers."

"What about that old chap, Mark Fenton?" Mattie asked as she handed her an apple slice on the point of the knife.

Allison crunched into the crisp flesh of the apple, "I could call him, I suppose."

CHAPTER 16

Jack didn't waste any time in contacting his lawyer. He burst into the office late morning demanding to see him. His secretary rose from her desk, knocked on his door and disappeared inside. Jack was almost ready to open the door when she opened it and a thin faced man with a grim expression beckoned him inside.

"It's not looking good for you, is it Jack?" He sat behind his desk, tapping his two index fingers. "You better tell me if you were involved in any homicide."

"Look, my wife's the one who hired Detective Marshall. Before that I had never heard of him. She's crazy. She's calling me a pervert. She's deserted me. Walked out with the kids. She says I'm having an affair with my work partner. I had an important job to do in America and she comes over there with some sexual disease. I've got evidence from the hospital she went to for treatment. I'm telling you. I'm worried about her. I think she needs to be committed."

Jack sat down and buried his head in his hands. He looked up at Colin Kirk with watery eyes, "I've had just about as much as any man can stand."

Colin responded, "We'll take it to Court and sue her for defamation of character. Keep any evidence we can use against her. Don't worry... I'll handle it. You'll come out a rich man. And with full custody of your children... if she does anything silly. We'll get our own detective and catch her with her pants down. She walked out?"

"Yes."

"And arrived in America with the clap?"

"Yes. And we can prove that."

"Then we've got her."

"Good, just what I needed to hear." Jack responded and stepped out of Colin's office, raging mad.

Everything was going wrong for Jack, and Molly was coming to town. He needed fresh pussy. Good tight pussy. He didn't have time for all this shit. He drove into work to show his face and go over some notes for his briefing on the trip. There was a message from Josh.

Jack dialed Josh's home number.

"What's happened?" asked Jack.

"I got busted. Someone ransacked my place and everything's gone. The cops are here."

"What's gone?"

"You should know."

"What do you mean?"

"You were in my desk... that night you were over here. You have a habit of leaving little trail marks."

"You're crazy. What would I want with your stuff anyway?"

"Motley saw you, you damn liar. They were photo copies. I took those before you left. You knew that."

Jack flung the phone down. He hated being wrong – or worse, being tricked.

•   •   •   •   •

Allison walked the girls across the road with their bicycles, waved goodbye to them at the front entrance of the school, and walked back to her mother's. *That crusty old bugger, Mark. He hates me*, she thought, as she went inside to dial his number.

"Hello. It's Allison Brownley. I need to speak with you," she said after a recorded greeting. There was no answer.

She decided to drive to Mark's office. She walked straight past the woman at the desk and knocked at his door. No response. She tried the handle, but it was locked. She went back and asked the woman if she could leave a message. She wrote on the piece of paper that it was urgent, and handed it to the woman.

Jack drove out of the car park at Bellamy Labs, thinking on his way to Josh's. He went back in his mind, tracing Josh's words. The fuckin' neighbor, he'd have to deal with her. He drove past Hereford Street and noticed Allison's car coming out of the building area where the detective's office was. His car tires squealed around the corner, and into the building parking area. The receptionist was typing and calmly looked up over her glasses at Jack standing by the counter.

"Look, my wife was in here, Allison Brownley." He hesitated. "Sorry, I'm Jack Brownley and here is my card. I work down the road at Bellamy Labs. I just missed her." He smiled at her and winked.

"Oh yes, Mr Brownley. She was in a hurry, but I have a note from her for Detective Fenton. He's working on a case." She looked at Allison's note and smiled back at Jack. "No doubt you know what this is about?"

"Oh yes, of course, my wife and I have been away, and we had some business here with Detective Ed Marshall."

"Oh, his partner? He was such a nice man… pity all that smoke. Those two men, they do nothing but smoke and ruin their lungs."

"Yes, it's no good for the lungs," Jack responded, smiling at her.

"I told them constantly to stop smoking," she went on typing, "shall I keep the note?"

"Ar, yes, better not interfere with Police evidence."

Jack smiled again, backed out into the open air and leaped into his car. He went back to his office and wrote to Molly. He'd tell her the bad news. Fuck that bitch wife. What's she doing going back into that office? He'd have to pay Detective Fenton a visit someday. Fuck Josh, stupid cuntman involving the bloody cops.

CHAPTER 17

Allison went back to Jack's house, her old home, and unlocked the front door. She had some time before fetching the girls. She stood, facing the dreaded passageway. The sun lit up the girl's room, and their remaining toys lay undisturbed. Big ted and small brown teddy sat on Isabel's bed and one of Lucy's Strawberry Shortcake Dolls was on Lucy's bed. Allison left some toys behind. She wasn't sure what was going to happen with Jack. She took a deep breath and started looking for the book, "Tigger" and other favorites. Gathering up the books, she was about to close the front door, when the phone rang.

"Is that Mrs Brownley?"

"Yes."

"I have been calling this number, but got no answer. I didn't want to leave a message."

"What's this about?"

"I need to meet with you. When is a good time?"

"Who am I meeting with?"

"It's about your police inquiry. I will identify myself when we meet tomorrow morning."

"Oh, I see." Allison went cold. "Tomorrow morning, where?" her voice went shaky.

"Your local library. I will be carrying a blue folder and wearing a raincoat. Make it nine o'clock."

"Okay," Allison was hesitant. "That will be fine."

"Oh, and by the way, if I don't show in fifteen minutes, I will call you to reschedule."

"Please, don't call here again," Allison was afraid of Jack's interception. She panicked and hung up, running to the car, clutching the handful of books. She was late for the girls.

That evening, when the girls were ready for bed, Isabel ran to Allison.

"Look Mummy, it's Daddy's car outside."

"Isabel," Allison bent down to her. "Remember what I told you last night. It's not what you think you see." She turned around and Jack was already standing at the front door. Allison opened it before he could knock.

"Are we going home?" asked Isabel.

Jack looked at Allison.

"See what you've started?" said Jack, stepping inside, and walking the girls down the passageway. "Come on girls, Daddy wants some time with you. I'll read you a story. Go on into your bedroom." He put his hand on Isabelle's shoulder, and gestured her to take Lucy and wait for him. He smiled at her, closed their door and turned to face Allison, "I've been to my lawyer today and you have twenty-four hours to make up your mind what to do."

"Keep your voice down... you will frighten the girls."

"You'd better listen to me."

"What do you mean?"

"Just that," he went into the girl's room, closing the door in her face.

Allison stood staring at the dark wooden door, listening to the cheerful sound of his voice when he spoke to the girls. She walked back into the kitchen.

Mattie was doing the dishes and spoke without looking up, "You don't have to take that, Allison. He can't threaten you."

"I know... I know. I just want peace when the girls are around. I'll figure something out. I might get my old job back at the hotel."

"Isn't that a bit soon?"

"No, I'm worried. I might need extra money. Listen...," Allison spoke quietly, looking behind her. "I haven't had time to tell you, but I'm meeting someone tomorrow morning."

"Oh, when did you arrange that?"

Allison took a tea towel, and wiped the draining dishes. Her eyes rested on the swaying branches outside the tiny window. "When I was over at the house... I was really scared."

"Wait... before you panic," cautioned Mattie.

"Jack has to have access to the girls. He called his lawyer. Maybe it's a lawyer, and you know how much they cost. He's got something planned, he's...," Jack's footsteps rounded the hall corner.

"Come here!" Jack yelled at Allison. "Whatever it is you're up to, it's not going to do you any good. I'll be back tomorrow night," he slammed the door.

•   •   •   •   •

Allison walked a block down from the school. The library opened at nine o'clock and it was time to find the man who called. In the library, she walked past the main counter across to her aisles of favourite books. Her mother had encouraged her to read widely from a young age. Picking up a book by a female author, who was also an artist, she began to read the jacket illustrated with a painting by the author. From her peripheral vision, a tall man in a raincoat brushed past her. He stopped and looked back at Allison.

"Hello... are you Allison?"

"Yes."

"Bring your book and we'll sit over here." He pointed to one of the tables. He put down his blue folder and the books he had gathered onto the table, and put out his hand.

"My name is Tom Briggs." His large hand gripped hers.

"You're not from the Police department?" asked Allison, taking a seat.

"Well, in a way yes. Constable Keats is not going to see you. I am the acting Investigator."

"Why do you need to see me?"

"I was working for Ed Marshall… and it was your husband I was investigating."

"That's right. Now I know who you are."

"Yes. I've had a hard job trying to contact you." He opened his folder and started to write. He reminded her of Ed, although he was a whole head and shoulders taller. He had curly dark hair, his eyes were brown and had a warm shine to them.

"Allison, what do you know about your husband's activities? What are the real reasons for your hiring Ed?"

"Well, I don't know where to start. I thought you were the Police."

"Why would that bother you? Have they contacted you?"

"No. Mark Fenton said they were going to."

"Have you met Mark Fenton, the Inspector?"

"Yes."

"What did he request?"

"Oh, he said I had some papers of Ed's. He said Ed's death… was no accident. Is that what this is about?"

"Let me put it this way. Mark Fenton is not to be trusted."

"I left him a message, a note. I said it was urgent."

Tom's face remained expressionless as he listened intently.

Allison continued, "I have some…"

"Allison, if you have anything that might help, then I need to know.

"Mark went on about emphysema, very technical, sounded like a chemical poisoning."

"I think he's working for someone and something is going on. He's out to scare you."

"How do I know all this is true? I don't know who to believe." She put her head down and began to cry. "I'm scared. I don't know what he's up to."

"Hey listen," he stretched out his large hand. "I can help you."

"Jack has threatened me. He is coming over tonight to get me. Take my girls. The lawyer says he can," she began to sob. "I thought you were the lawyer coming to get me."

"Jack's lawyer?" Tom shook his head.

"Yes… I can't stand this. It's no good for my mother. It's not fair." She took out her handkerchief and blew her nose. "I don't want to go back to Jack's house." She started crying again.

Tom stood up, looked around, sat down again next to her and said in a low voice, "Listen, you probably heard this from Ed too, but don't listen to his threats."

"I have some papers. Jack must be looking for them. I don't know what to do with them."

"Would you let me look at them?"

Allison stopped crying and took a breath. She looked at the card Tom handed her with the title Tom Briggs, Private Investigator.

"Thank you," she looked at him with blurry vision. "With everything… it's been hard to know who to trust."

"Have you got a good lawyer?"

"My mother has someone in the Church. It is a friend's son. Should I call him?"

"You need to, Allison, otherwise you can find yourself in a very vulnerable position, especially with Jack."

"I know. I'm thinking of going back to work as a waitress. It might help me."

"I think that's a good idea. The more people you mix with, the better you will feel. Like I said, not so vulnerable," he smiled at her.

Allison looked again into his kindly eyes for a moment. She felt as if she had known him all her life. He pushed back his chair, leaving the books on the table and turned to shake Allison's hand again. "I am sure for both our sakes, we will get to the bottom of this," he gripped Allison's hand firmly as she stood up to join him.

"I do need someone to help me."

They parted company at the library door. Allison walked back to her mother's, thinking about Mark Fenton. Who was he working for?

Mattie was sitting in the lounge reading the paper.

"Any interesting news?" asked Allison, closing the front door.

"You have to look hard. Otherwise it's all the same, like Ed's news. I only saw that by chance," she looked up over her glasses. "How did you get on?"

"You know that undercover agent Ed told us about? It was him. He wants to look at the papers."

"I bet he does."

"Well mother... what else am I supposed to do?"

"You can call the lawyer I told you about. I'm going to see Emily today. Her daughter that put you on to Ed... maybe she might know this Tom Briggs."

"Here's his card. I can only do so much at a time," Allison handed it to Mattie, who laid it on the side table and continued reading the paper.

Allison went into her room and sat on the couch in the sun by her bed. She looked for the friend's number she had scribbled in a small notepad, and dialed Julie's number. Julie had organized her a waitressing job at the Russley Hotel a few years back, before moving to the White Heron by the airport, opposite the American Deep Freeze Base.

"Julie, have you got a moment to talk?"

"A quick moment. How's everything?"

"Yes. I'm just going through hell right now." Allison squeezed her eyes to fight back the tears, "...is that job still available?"

"Yes, when can you start?"

"Well I'm not sure yet."

"Look, when you've made your mind up, call me. What's the matter with you? You dither with everything."

"No I don't."

"Like hell you don't. Have you left him yet?"

"Yes... sort of."

"That's a bit of a weak answer. You call me when you've really decided. Sorry, I've got to go."

Allison went back into the lounge and took the card back. She hated what her friend Julie had said. She was right, she did dither, damn it.

"What's the name of that lawyer?" asked Allison.

Mattie put the paper down. "Lloyd James. You could tell him you're Mattie Smith's daughter."

Allison looked up his name and dialed the number.

"Hello, it's Lloyd James here. How can I help?"

"Hello, I'm Allison Brownley. I am staying with my mother, Mattie Smith. She knows your father from the Church. I have left my husband and I'd like some advice."

"You need to come in and make some statements. I can write to your husband's lawyer. I'll put you back to my secretary for an appointment."

"I made an appointment," said Allison, putting the phone down and calling out to her mother. Allison went into the lounge to join Mattie.

"I'm afraid it's a process you can't avoid," cautioned Mattie.

"But, what if I'm wrong?" Allison leaned back in the old swivel chair and stared out the small window. "I hate this," she put her head in her hands. "I need proof."

"Proof for what?" Mattie threw her paper down. "That he's a liar? Can't you see the signs? When are you going to learn?"

"Oh, stop it Mother. You're always telling me what to do. I can't stand it."

Allison got up and left the room.

The day slipped by into the evening and Jack hadn't called or come around, so Allison decided it was time to follow up with Tom. She dialed his number.

"Hello, it's Allison. I've been thinking, I'd like to meet again."

"Have you heard from Jack?"

"No."

"Did you call a lawyer?"

"Yes, I did."

"Good. Then let's meet around the corner this time, at the coffee shop in the mall, same time. Meantime, if he comes over, don't answer the door."

Allison put the phone down and went around the house checking the old black blinds, making sure there was no chink opening anywhere. She double-checked the locks on the doors and went to bed. It was a long sleepless night as she listened to the whisper of the wind. Her mind played tricks on her. Afraid, she peeped through her blind, peering across the park for any strange movements. She felt their house was an easy target for any attack. Jack had been cunning, luring them into this property. They were vulnerable. Allison gripped her nightgown around her and shivered.

The next morning, after the girls crossed the road for school, Allison walked around to the local shops. Inside the coffee shop, Tom was seated at one of the tables. He got up when Allison came towards him. He looked somehow different without his raincoat. His long legs suited his blue jeans. His yellow jersey set off his olive skin. But his eyes looked distant, as he managed a smile.

"How do you take your coffee?"

"Same as you," and she looked across at his cup half-empty, a teaspoon fallen off the saucer, and a packet of cigarettes beside the cup.

"I like your choice of color."

"What?" said Tom, looking down at his jersey. "This old thing... it's probably the Maori in me... brings out my olive skin."

"Oh, so was this from your mother's side or your father?" Allison sat down.

"My grandfather was Scottish. He met my grandmother over on the Peninsula... there's quite a settlement of Maoris over there. I guess they got together, probably because she was stunning... beauty like a golden sunset. Anyway, enough about me. How did you get on?"

"I don't know where to start," said Allison, sitting down and taking out the mangled papers from the file. She thanked the waitress for the coffee, stirred in some sugar and took a sip.

"Ed must have been probing into the situation with the children," said Tom, ordering another coffee, and lighting a cigarette. Mind if I smoke?" He studied the paper with the word "molestation" highlighted on it.

"No, that's fine," said Allison, looking serious. "I took the children to see a counselor."

"I know," he inhaled deeply, and slowly exhaled the smoke upwards into the air.

"How?"

"I contacted Jack's lawyer. Jack had been informed."

"Oh no! Now what?"

"He's not harassing you, is he?"

"He didn't come over last night. But the people at the Council buildings told me Jack's behavior wasn't bad enough to restrict him."

"That's right, but don't underestimate him," said Tom, scouring the mangled papers. "How did these get so torn?"

"I found them under our bed. They almost got vacuumed up."

He looked up at her, with a whimsical smile. "They look like government stamps. Do you understand them?"

"Sort of."

He looked straight at her. Their eyes met. "Have you got that job yet?"

"No, but I will."

"That's good to hear. And your children, how are they?" He went on turning the pages.

"Oh, they love their bedroom. I brought some Pears prints from America, and Isabel is in charge of decorating. I had to clear that doubt about the girls, even if it meant facing Jack. I did it so that nothing could go wrong. Now I feel when he takes them... that I have done my best."

"Yes, you have. It was a very brave move."

"Really?"

"Yes. You stood up to him. Now keep it up, and I'll get back to you about these papers. Let's get them copied."

They left the coffee shop. Tom handed her back the copies, and said goodbye. When Allison returned to the house, she went straight to the phone to call Julie.

"Julie, it's me, Allison. Listen, is that job still available?'

"Yes of course.'

"Can I start with lunch-times?"

"That would be fine for now, but with the coming season, it gets busy round here, and we'll need you at night-times."

"That's fine."

"So, shall we start you... end of this week? Give you a chance to get a uniform, okay? You'll be fine. You've done it before. Get you out of the house."

Allison put down the phone and turned to Mattie, "I'm doing some shifts up at the White Heron."

"Isn't that where all the Americans go?"

"Yes, Mother, and I know what you're thinking; but I'm only working up there."

"How was the meeting this morning with that agent?"

"I showed him the papers."

"Do you know where I put those shoes I used to wear for waitressing?" Allison looked at her mother.

"Go and look in the cupboard. It's a bit of a mess."

Allison crawled into the deep recessed hall closet she and Mattie shared. Both Allison's and Mattie's shoes were scattered and buried around the dark corner. Her waitressing shoes must be at Jack's house.

She raced out to cross the park, skipping across the green. She hardly stopped for traffic, her feet dancing on the pavements, until she turned the corner. A tall figure slipped behind the trees by the front gate and stopped to unclip the bolt of the gate. Allison took a sudden dive into the corner bushes. It was Tom carrying his blue folder, coming out of her house. His yellow jersey was easy to spot from the bushes. She watched him as he drove away.

Chapter 18

It was the afternoon when Allison drove around Hagley Park, lined with cherry trees, their pale pink blossoms blowing in the gusts of wind, looking like a white Christmas. She thought about Sharon's Steve, how different it could be. She parked outside the old clock tower building, a Christchurch landmark commemorating the Jubilee of Queen Victoria. Allison gazed at its splendor.

She couldn't get Tom out of her mind, as she made her way towards the staircase of the adjacent building. What was he doing at her house? She climbed the stairs to the third floor. The architecture held a sense of ancient decay. Narrow passageways, wooden doors with brass plaques abounded. She finally found, "Lloyd James, Barrister and Solicitor', and opened the door. A woman sat at a desk, scratching her head with a pencil. "Hello, can I help you?"

"I'm Allison Brownley."

"Please take a seat, I'll let Mr James know you're here." She sat back at her desk and looked over at Allison, "Is this your first time seeing a lawyer?"

"Yes."

"Don't worry, I'm sure he will be able to help you."

Allison nodded back at her and kept her gaze towards the floor.

A tall man opened his office door, introduced himself as Lloyd James, and invited her to sit down. Through the window she could see the trees from Hagley Park waving in the breeze. She felt nervous relaying everything to this man. He seemed so professional, writing everything down and not looking into her eyes, not like Tom. She wished it were Tom giving her all these instructions about having to file for a separation. She didn't like him, swiveling around in his huge chair. He was abrupt, just like Jack. But she had to proceed if she were going to be free. It was the law.

Finally, Lloyd James responded, "I will write to your husband's lawyer. We will contact the Family Court and action the counseling sessions for both you and your husband. It's current procedure. Once all this has been documented, you are protected."

"But I hired a detective, and now he's dead… and I'll be next."

"Look, I'm not sure I'd go that far," he gave a bit of a cough. "I am not a detective and I certainly can't get involved in any homicide… attempted or otherwise. I don't do criminal law." He swung back on his chair. "Your husband will probably cut your allowance off, and you will have to apply for a Domestic Purposes Benefit."

Allison sat watching his huge glasses moving up and down on his huge nose, as he rattled off his speech. He didn't seem the friendly sort. She looked past him, through the window, trying to offset his personality with the view of Hagley Park, but his voice went on. "What I need to do is contact Legal Aid, and then you won't receive a bill. I'll get my secretary to show you out. Nice to meet you, Allison. I'll be in touch." He got up and moved over to the door, and shook her hand again. Allison left his office, walking through the maze of narrow corridors.

•   •   •   •   •

Jack stood at the kitchen window eating his take-away pizza. Damn crust is tough as my old shoe. Damn that woman, she couldn't cook much anyway, except a bloody tough roast. It'd be better than this shit. He spat out a piece of dry crust and tossed back his beer can. Beer dribbled down his chin. He crumpled the empty tin can into the palm of his hand. Fuck her, she stopped

Molly from coming for now. Fuck her. Where the fuck's Josh? He'd better get his ass over here.

He threw the can out into the hallway, opened the fridge door, took out another and with a click of the lid, he leaned back against the kitchen bench to let the brew flow, drinking steadily.

"You took your time gettin' here." Jack glared at Josh, as he walked into the kitchen.

"There's a lot going on right now. Don't get your tits in a tangle," he giggled, and threw his jacket down on the kitchen table to catch the beer Jack flung at him.

"Here, get this down you," and they left the kitchen to sit on their favourite couch in the dark hallway. Josh took a swig of beer and stretched his legs out in front of Jack. "What are you looking so smug about?"

"Me, I'm just over here, drinking your beer and waiting on instructions." He took a swig of beer. "Didn't you say we need to get on... now you're here with the formula?"

"Well now your place got done, we'll have to retrace everything."

"That fuckin' neighbor."

"Oh, I meant to tell you. The night of the bust, she's had a heart attack, she's alive... had a stroke and can't talk."

"How do you know all this?"

"I live there, the cops wanted to know everything. I think they thought I'd given her a bloody heart attack, for Christ's sake."

"Well, who did?"

"Mind you own fuckin' business." Josh smiled at Jack. "Anyway, I've got the originals. Ed ratted too much."

Jack turned in fury and grabbed Josh by the neck. "Hey, not so fast fuckhead. I'm the one in charge now." Josh knew too much. Jack scowled.

Josh threw him off. "You go see that wife of yours. She's sure left you running. I hear she's left you."

Jack turned around and thumped him, "Fuck her."

"Hey, she's your problem, not mine."

"I know, but I'm not finished with her. She has a whole pile of shit coming right down on her pointed, rat-face head." Jack stopped suddenly, "I didn't tell you that. How did you hear?"

Josh only smiled and shrugged his shoulders.

•   •   •   •   •

The evenings were getting lighter now that it was spring. Allison started her part-time job at the White Heron, clearing tables. Easy work, but long hours. Julie had wanted her to fill in for someone at night-time. It was late when Allison pulled into the driveway and turned off the lights. She usually parked her car outside. Mattie's car was in the single garage, locked away. Allison walked up the steps towards the front door and turned suddenly when she heard a familiar mocking voice.

"So we've been out for a screw, have we?"

"I've been at work. I'm not talking to you. You're drunk."

"Don't you back-chat me, you whore." He lunged at her and she fell down on the steps. Jack picked her up, and dragged her around to the back of the house.

"One word out of you and I'll snap your head off." His breath smelled of stale alcohol. The blood rose thick in his cheeks and his eyes blazed red/white like a jackal. He thrust her up against the wall. "You've ruined my life. Everything I've worked for."

"You frighten me. I can't live like this," Allison screamed.

"Like hell you can't. You just up and left. Damn you," Jack growled.

He threw her. She fell on the concrete and hit her head against the side of the garage. Jack grabbed her again. Allison screamed out and he put his hand over her mouth to stop her from yelling.

"Shut up. Shut up. If that mother of yours shows her ugly face out here, I'll cut it off. And yours too, you bloody rat face."

"You never treated me any good. It was always Josh. Josh this, Josh that," she mumbled half through his hand on her mouth.

"Well fuck you. You'll never see him again." He flung her away from him.

"What's Josh done? Where is he?"

"It's not what you think. How could you accuse me of fucking Josh for Christ's sake? Where do you get such sick ideas?"

Jack started to cry. He sank down the side of the old garage wall and sat there, tears dripping down on his collar. "Everything I've done, I've done for you. You and the children."

"But you were never around. You never told me how you felt. I only watched you. Yes... watched you with Josh and now that woman, Molly."

"How do you know her name? You've been snooping again haven't you?"

He got up, finding his rage erupting again, and took a swipe at her but missed and fell against the wall.

"You can have your sick little shithouse over here, but you won't have my girls. No you won't. I'm coming back over. They'll be packing their sick little back-packs and saying goodbye to their sick little mother and your sick fuckin' mother, who's the cause of all this."

He lunged again at her.

"I didn't snoop, you told me. You wanted me to share the house with her. How could you?"

Allison felt strangely powerful as she watched him stagger off slowly into the darkness.

Allison picked herself up and ran back around the house, opening the front door, and locking it behind her. Gasping for air, she fell into her room.

She cried herself to sleep, only to wake the next morning to the same reality. She quickly found the number of Lloyd James and asked the secretary for him to call. Then she dialed the number of the Court House. Why had she not done this before? Her life was catching up on her. She gave the Court her address to process the counselor.

Lloyd James called and carefully explained, in his monotonous tone of voice, that he would write another letter to Jack's lawyer to arrange for custody, and settlement process of the matrimonial property. Lloyd saw only the legalities and without any heart-filled gestures, he laid out what was next for Allison to do.

When Allison arrived for her first meeting with the Court appointed counselor, Jack was already inside.

"Good day Mrs Brownley. I am your selected counselor. My name is George Geoffrey." He put his hand out to greet Allison. He was a tall, well-built man, with a full head of white hair that sprung out in every direction.

"Please take a seat." He sat down, his face expressionless.

"Allison, it appears you are the initiator of this marriage break-up. Would you mind explaining this to Jack?"

He sat next to Jack and looked across at Allison.

"I feel this is all my fault." She sat facing them, clutching at her handbag and blinking the tears out of her eyes.

"Why do say that Allison?" He shuffled his feet and then crossed them and leaned back against his chair.

"Jack has never loved me. I am nothing to him," said Allison, looking across at Jack.

"Hey... wait a minute! What the hell have I been working for all this time?" interrupted Jack.

"Now, wait." George put his hand up like a stop signal and sat forward.

"I want a direct answer. Allison, you say Jack has never shown you love. And you say, Jack, that you have shown actions."

"Like bloody right I have."

"Have you ever used any words of love to her, Jack?"

"Oh, she's always prattling on about this and that... you'd never get a word in."

"Is that true, Allison?"

"I... I want to discuss my feelings. Jack doesn't say much, who else can I talk to?" Allison lamented.

"Jack, you want to comment?" and George looked across at him.

Jack shrugged his shoulders and grunted, "This is total made-up bullshit."

"In what role do you see yourself in your marriage, Allison?"

"A Mother."

"What about a wife?" said George, writing notes.

Allison sunk her head into her lap and started to sob.

"I've had enough of this crap... I'll just get my girls back," said Jack, getting up to leave.

"Now, wait a minute. Mr Brownley, having custody of your girls is not the problem."

"Isn't it? She almost had me up for molesting my own children." He pointed a finger at Allison.

"Jack, you will stop right there. You are to have shared custody. A letter was sent out to you and Allison. Please do not aggravate the situation. You will get reasonable access." He looked at Allison and stopped for a moment.

"Are you alright Allison?"

"Yes, I'm fine. Jack and I will do our best with the girls." She wiped her nose with her handkerchief. "I need time." She looked up at Jack who was still standing. "It's me. I need time to absorb all this."

George continued, "What I'd like to see the two of you do to start with, is to be civil towards one another. Allison, you'll have to look at what it is you want. And you, Jack, let Allison have some space."

George got up to join Jack. Allison wobbled the chair out from under her and moved towards the door. They left the rooms, and walked out of the building. Jack had his car parked outside.

"Get in... I'll drop you back."

Allison sat beside him, still wiping her nose. They drove along the familiar roads and turned up the long street past their house, and around the corner. Jack turned the ignition off and sat staring out the car window at the moving trees in the park.

"You didn't have to do this... go this far. We could have worked it out."

Allison fell silent and then spoke softly with tears in her eyes, "I know."

"Why didn't you tell me how you were feeling?" Jack looked at her.

"I couldn't." She took a gulp and sat still. There was only silence.

"Get out then." Jack pulled away from the curb and left her standing there.

Chapter 19

It was Jack's turn to have the girls, and Allison had her nights of work. Allison said goodbye to Mattie and drove out past the rhododendron bush, with its brilliant spray of apricot flowers always swaying to greet or farewell.

It was beginning to get busy at the White Heron, and she parked the car, rushing in to join her friend, Julie.

"Glad you're here. There's all these tables to set. We have a new flight in from the Antarctica Air Base." She stood reading her list. She was a sharp-minded woman from England, and preferred working to co-parenting her four children with her ex-husband.

Allison raced over to the drawers and began piling silverware onto her tray. She grabbed the napkins and started folding, pleating them like a fan. She could hear the American voices, booming out from the nearby bar. Several women were sitting in armchairs, along from the restaurant, with their legs crossed, skirts hiked up a bit, and ankles bobbing a welcome.

"Allison, have you made sure we have seating for tables of fours and two's?"

Allison, in her fluster, had only grouped the tables in long settings. Julie shook her head and rushed over to move the tables.

"The men don't want to sit with other people. You should know that by now. Wake up, girl. Where's your head these days?" Julie kicked the chairs in place. The tables were easy to separate. It was time, and not a good look to be moving tables when the restaurant was about to open. "You need a good stiff drink." Julie remarked to Allison.

"But I'm driving."

"Oh! Take a cab! Get a life, for Christ's sake." Julie chewed her gum and spat it out in the bin. She was a heavy smoker. "After work? I'm off for the next few days. Sarah's in charge."

"Okay, I'll stay for a bit." Allison went on placing the napkins. The restaurant soon filled. It was Friday night and already the buzz was on. The Officers from the flight came in separate groups. Many looked tired. Their flight uniforms were a deep khaki green. The fabric was shiny with fur trim on the collar and the United States flag on their shoulders. It gave an instant look of respect and stand-offish charm.

Allison didn't look at their faces. With Julie watching, she kept on with her work, taking orders and going back and forth to the kitchen. It was an exhausting night and her feet were swollen and hot. She could feel the flush rising in her cheeks, and almost fell with a heavy tray when a voice said, "Here... I'll help you."

She was bent over, picking up the cutlery, when she looked into the eyes of a stranger.

"No, no really it's okay," replied Allison.

"Can't a guy help a pretty gal?" with that American accent and wide toothy grin, he looked straight into her eyes.

She brushed her apron and gathered up the dirty cutlery, smiled at the stranger and left, going backwards through the big swing doors to the kitchen. She put her tray down, opened the swing doors, and peeped into the restaurant at the stranger. He was sitting, looking in her direction. By the time she had unloaded her tray and swung the big doors open again, the stranger was gone. All she could remember was his beautiful eyes. Or was it his face? The broad cheek bones, the olive skin, the dark head of hair, the eyes, soft brown, and inviting images raced through her head.

"Here, finish clearing those tables and we'll leave the rest to the other girls. We're going for that drink," said Julie, interrupting her thoughts.

Allison finished clearing the last of the plates and the usual debris on each table. She often wondered how people could be so rude. They even left their napkins stuck in their unfinished drinks. The dye from the serviettes spilled out onto the starched white tablecloths. She went to pull the tablecloth off.

"Here, leave that for the night shift," called Julie.

Julie had combed her hair and her dangling green earrings glistened in the light. She was an attractive blonde, with huge self-esteem. Allison admired her. She liked being around her, watching how she coped.

"Come on, you've worked hard. I'll buy you a drink."

Allison asked for a gin and tonic and sat down, and Julie went to the bar. Allison didn't want to appear conspicuous in her uniform, so she shrank into the big lounge chairs and quietly scanned the room.

"Here get this down you," Julie pulled up a chair and lit a cigarette. She blew the smoke into the air and took a sip of her drink. She had a long cocktail, with an umbrella hanging to one side. She undid the umbrella and flung the piece of cut up orange into her ashtray. Allison leaned forward to rescue the tiny umbrella and Julie smiled at her.

"Always thinking of those kids," she tapped her cigarette on the ash tray. "How's single life without Jack?"

"I'm getting there. I haven't thought about it much. There's been so much going on with my father passing, and moving in with my mother."

"You need to watch that," Julie took another puff, blowing the smoke away into the room.

"What do you mean?"

"Just that. You have your own life, now that Jack is out of it. You have to move on. Not be so dependent on your mother."

"I know, but your husband didn't cheat on you." Allison looked at Julie with her legs and stiletto shoes, spread out to one side of the chair. She reminded her of the woman, Molly.

Julie cautioned, "Yes, but it's no excuse to hide yourself away, now is it?"

"No, but I'm taking it slowly, which means I really have to get back now."

"You're no fun."

"Well I'm not dressed for this and I did promise my mother I would be home."

Julie's eyes narrowed.

Allison finished her drink and put it down on the table, reached for her bag, and stood up to go. "See you next shift."

Julie got up and wiggled over to the bar, crowded with hungry Americans.

Allison drove back down the quiet street, and turned into the driveway. The shadows of the trees danced their eerie parade in the windy night. She got out. She was certain she saw a figure move away from behind the huge Macrocarpa tree growing directly opposite their driveway. No, it was only a shadow, and the sound of leaves rattling on the driveway distracted her. She closed the glass front door and was glad Mattie had pulled down the blind. She tiptoed in to see if her mother was still awake, but no, she stood for a moment watching her mother sleep. How lucky she was to have such a companion. She didn't care what Julie had said, she loved being with her mother. She was the best mother in the world.

CHAPTER 20

Sarah had been on holiday with her family, and was glad to be back at work. She was another capable woman whom Allison had gravitated towards. She often called in, and Isabelle was glad she never brought her boys. She pulled up outside Allison's door and gave a quick knock on the glass pane.

"Yahoo... anyone home?"

Allison opened the door.

"Hey, I won't stop, but wanted to tell you. It's Halloween this weekend at the base."

"Sounds exciting. Do we dress up?'

"I'm not, but knowing you," Sarah laughed. "Shall we go?" she stood rattling her car keys in her hand.

"How about after work?"

"Yep. Good excuse for me. I don't have to say where I am."

"Do you want to come in?" asked Allison.

"No, I've got to go pick the boys up from cricket practice... see you Saturday night," she waved as she got back into her car. Sarah's dark hair never looked a mess. Everything about her was immaculate. Allison closed the door smiling to herself. She went straight to her mother's cedar trunk box, and opened the lid. What could she find in the way of material? She knelt down and picked up some off-cuts of ballet costumes she'd made for the girls. She held up a large piece of tulle. It could make a petticoat. Allison already had black stockings and a long black polo tee shirt. Now all she needed was the red and white spots. At the secondhand shop, not far from where she lived, in the rack, was an old fashioned red and white spotted dress, waiting to be pulled apart to make a gathered skirt. Black fabric ears and white gloves and she was ready to be transformed into Minnie Mouse.

Work that night led up to a frenzy of untidy tables, with a few of the Navy personnel leaving early to dash off to the party. Dirty dishes and dirty glasses faced her. She was relieved to see how many costumes there were, going into the hotel bar. Sarah was adding up the takings and making sure everyone had completed their duties. When her work was finished, Allison rushed into the rest room to change into her outfit, throwing off her uniform. Stuffing her things into a bag, she rolled on her black stockings, pulled on her black long-sleeved, crew neck top, and took out the red and white spotted skirt with the matching braces. It was fun. Changed into her outfit, with a last look in the mirror, Allison pursed her lips and painted them bright red. She patted the bouncy spotted skirt, and leaned closer to the mirror to pin on the black ears and the large red and white spotted bow into her hair. Sarah burst into the restroom, just as she was finishing drawing black whiskers on her cheeks.

"Wow! Don't you look fun? I can be a bad fairy for the night," Sarah said, pulling out a pair of large silver earrings. "Look... what do you think?" She slipped them into her ear lobes. Her brown eyes sparkled as she looked into the mirror across at Allison. They hung in three glorious silver balls, a real statement with her short brown hair.

"Don't you look gorgeous!" exclaimed Allison with a toothy smile.

"Come on, who cares what we look like? Let's go."

Sarah took Allison's arm and they ran across the road, screaming and laughing as they climbed under the fence and into the grounds of the American Deep Freeze Base.

"Watch those ears," laughed Sarah, holding up the wire of the fence, so the two of them could slip underneath. The base was directly opposite the White Heron, and they raced inside the main entrance, swaying to the sounds of funky American music.

"All ladies welcome. It's Halloween," a man dressed in drag shouted above the music. "You have to sign in," and handed them the registry and a pen.

Allison signed, wearing her white gloves, while Sarah giggled. Beside the registry, figures dressed in black robes handed out wands and feathered masks. Sarah took one of each, and pushed her way through the crowd with Allison trying to keep up, as they dodged mocked cobwebs, and bumped into jostling costumed bodies. It was a wild spectacle, full of disguised figures gyrating to the thumping music on the dance floor.

"Come on. Get to the bar before the music stops. We'll miss out," shouted Sarah in Allison's ear.

They moved with difficulty through the crowded room, towards the bar. Allison couldn't resist staring at the costumes. She stood close to the bar, when a dark figure appeared next to her with a box of strobe lights flashing on its chest. Eyes stared at her through a black helmet. Darth Vader swished his robe around him, and rushed away into the crowd.

"Here, grab your drink," said Sarah, and they made for a nearby table. The huge hall had side entrances opening out to pool tables and rooms with even more tables. The main attraction was the dance floor, crowded with bump and grind people in fancy dress.

"I'll get the next one," Allison called out to Sarah above the noise. They sipped at a colorful cocktail and stood by their table, watching the crowd moving simultaneously in lines dancing the Electric Slide. Allison was so excited. She'd never seen line dancing before and started to shuffle her feet, smiling back at Sarah.

"Go on. You're crazy enough. Join in,' Sarah shoved her towards the dance floor. "Here, I'll watch. Have a go... I'll take your drink. Go on.... Dance!"

"But I don't know the moves," Allison went to pick up her drink again.

"Oh don't be such a baby. Here, put that down. Now get your beautiful ass out there." Sarah gave her an extra shove, swinging her earrings and laughing into the crowd.

"Hey, Minnie Mouse, come join us," said a tall Arab, dancing across in front of her.

Allison had danced all her life, until she met Jack. She had liked the fact he played in a band, but she only got to watch the dancers. Her body craved for movement. Did she still have the rhythm? She poised... and with a smile that spelled magic - Minnie Mouse was alive. The style of dance was easy and natural, and she quickly picked up the repetitive beat. Some remained dancing in lines and others broke off in couples. A swish of black fabric engulfed her. She turned around to face the masked man in black, the eyes of a stranger staring through the mask. They danced opposite each other, never speaking, but the attraction even disguised by costume, sent a thrill right through her, down to her connective vibes. The music stopped and Allison rushed back over to Sarah.

"You don't have to stop. You're a laugh. You look good. Go on back. They're announcing the winner of the best costume. You might win it."

"Don't be silly."

"Don't *you* be silly. Now go on... wiggle that perfect ass!"

The music stopped and the microphone squeaked. "Sorry folks, technical error," said the announcer, tapping the microphone. We have a winner for this year's Halloween and it's... Where is she? It's Minnie Mouse."

Allison put her white gloves up to her face and bent over, squealing with delight.

"No! No not me," she kept shaking her head and moving towards the stage.

"Come on pretty mouse, and get your prize," said the announcer. "And where are you from?"

"I live here in Christchurch," Allison still half-stifling her voice with her raised gloved hand over her mouth.

"Did you make your costume?"

"Yes I did," she smiled with pleasure.

"Well ain't that grand folks. A full round of applause for Minnie Mouse... from New Zealand." Everyone cheered and whistled. "You've won a crate of wine. Who's gonna help this pretty gal drink this?"

"Yehhhhh, whoo-eee," yelled the crowd, as Allison stepped down from the stage and looked back at the announcer. "Someone else will help you with that later. Enjoy... you did a great job," and he beckoned someone in the crowd to come forward.

The music began to play, and hundreds of balloons fell from a huge net in the ceiling. Black and red balloons, popping and dancing up into the ceiling and back down again among the dancers' feet. Allison saw the dark figure carry her crate across the room and stand by the door. Sarah winked at Allison, and grabbed their handbags as they moved towards the door.

"Well aren't you savvy tonight, girl? Who's the hunk?"

"I only danced with him, but he's helping with the crate. Are you ready to go?" asked Allison.

"Yes. I better get back home. Hey, not too fast with that crate, Mister," said Sarah attempting to take it.

"It's heavy, ma'am. Where's your car? I'm happy to carry this out for you." said the stranger, looking at Sarah.

"I bet you are and drink it too," said Sarah pushing against him in the crowd. "No really the two of us can manage," Sarah tried to take it from him, but it was too heavy.

"I have my car over in the hotel parking lot, over the road. I can drive over." said Allison.

"I'll wait here," said Sarah.

Allison left Sarah standing by the doorway, laughing with the stranger. She drove her car into the narrow driveway of the Deep Freeze Base, packed with cars. She drove slowly, trying to dodge the line of cars coming towards her. She saw Sarah wave at her, and Allison pulled up by the front door.

The dark figure bent down into her car, and placed the crate in the back seat, "I'll be seeing you."

"Oh really?" Allison gave him a wide smile and blushed. "Thanks for helping."

"My pleasure, ma'am."

Allison drove off back to the hotel parking area to wait for Sarah. She sat in the brightly lit parking area, looking back occasionally at the case of wine, shaking her head in disbelief.

Sarah knocked on the window of the car, "I gave him your number."

"You did what?"

"I gave him your number, silly. If I can't, you as sure can. Didn't you see the way he followed you around? Don't be such a chicken," she banged on the side of the car. She stuck her head in the window. "Let me know if this dreamboat calls."

Sarah walked over to her own car.

Allison waved goodbye and drove down Memorial Drive with zing in her heart, her fingers still tapping the steering wheel.

The next morning, as Mattie got out of bed, Allison burst into the room, bubbling like a geyser gush of steam.

"Mother! Oh my goodness! You'll never guess!"

Mattie smiled at her daughter, and reached into her closet for her robe.

"I met a man."

"You what?"

"Yes... I just have a good feeling. I really do."

"What does he look like?"

"Oh, he was dressed up like Darth Vader. And I won the prize for best costume... Minnie Mouse!" Allison hugged her mother, and danced around the bedroom. "Oh my God, I can't believe how much fun I had. I danced, and danced." She took Mattie's arms and went to swing her around the room.

"Hey, slow down. How do you know what he looks like?"

"I've seen him before. It was his eyes."

"Oh, Allison. You're such a dreamer. You can't go by eyes."

"Look. Haven't you always told me? *Go by instinct*," as she danced around the bedroom, and stopped suddenly turning to Mattie. "Didn't you fall in love on the tram?"

"I know dear, but back then it was different," Mattie looked away. How well she remembered like it were yesterday. Charlie's eyes were the first thing she saw as he stepped on that tram - that fateful day that changed her life. Their eyes locked and never diverted. Mattie never told anyone how deeply she fell in love.

It was Sunday, and Allison was looking forward to getting the girls back and telling them about her costume.

Jack slowly steamed up the driveway. As usual he did not get out of the car, he just looked at Allison, nodded and backed down the driveway.

"Girls. Mummy won a prize."

"We know."

"How do you know?"

Isabel looked blank. "Cause... Sarah told us," putting her things into her bedroom drawers. They had a perfect routine of unpacking their clothes when they re-occupied their room.

"Where was Sarah?"

"At Dad's," said Lucy.

"Shut up Lucy. You're not supposed to say, remember."

Isabelle didn't look at her mother.

"Don't worry girls, Sarah is a friend of Daddy's too," and she went on helping them tidy up and put the overnight bags under the bed.

The phone rang. Mattie was close by and picked it up. Her facial expression changed and she handed the phone to Allison.

"Who is it?"

"The American."

"Hello," said the voice. It was deep and slow. "Is this the number of Minnie Mouse?"

Allison smiled into the phone and answered, "Yes."

"Well aren't I lucky... finding you?"

Allison giggled and the voice went on.

"Is that all you can say?"

"No... but thank you for helping my friend and I."

"Yes. Your friend was nice enough to give me your phone number. She said you needed some help with your prize. I'd like to take you out." There was silence for a moment. "Are you still there?"

"Yes, I'm here."

"Where would you like to go? Dinner? We could take a bottle of wine? Is there a problem?"

"No. I have to see. I have children."

"Well then, bring them along. We could go somewhere the children might like. I'd like to meet them."

"That would be nice. Maybe you could come and visit?"

"Why don't I? Listen, if you tell me your address, I'll cycle down and meet y'all."

Allison gave him directions to her house and put down the phone to face Mattie.

"He's coming. He's coming. Oh my God. I'm so excited." It was time for the girls to go to bed, when there was a knock on the door.

"I'll get it," shouted Isabel.

She opened the door. "Daddy! Mummy... Daddy's here."

Allison went to the door. Jack took a step into the house.

"I saw some creep trying to ride in here," he watched Allison. "I chased him down the road and gave him a shove off his bike and sent him into the stream." Jack's tennis shoes were wet and covered in grass clippings. "I told him... if he shows his face over here, I'll have him up for trespassing."

"What about you, trespassing?"

"What about me? Now listen here," he raised his voice and Allison shoved him outside, following him, closing the door behind her. She ran into the driveway towards the stream. Jack ran after her, and pulled her back.

"Nobody's going to come between me and my wife and my children," he blazed at her and shook her. "I told you the other night. Any screwing and I'll have you up for foul play. You won't see those girls again. Do you hear me?" He threw her into the rhododendron bush and ran off.

Isabel came screaming out to her mother, "Mummy, why's Daddy so mad?"

Allison, hauling herself out of the rhododendron bush, wiped the tears away quickly and hurried Isabel into the house with her arm around her shoulders, still looking back towards the stream.

"Daddy thought he saw a burglar. He made a mistake."

It was a nice man coming to visit, Isabel." Allison led her back. "The three monkeys, remember, tell us there is nothing wrong."

"But he pushed you."

"He was upset because he thought we were in danger."

Isabel shrugged, sighed and skipped back inside.

"Here, let's get Nana to read you a story tonight, eh?' Allison went to Mattie waiting out in the kitchen. They nodded at each other and Mattie followed the girls into their room. Allison reached inside the kitchen cupboards, her fingers moving fast, pushing aside cleaning bottles, to find the flashlight. She opened the old drawers and fumbled through all the clutter wondering at the amount they had accumulated since moving.

She ran down the hallway and poked her head into the girl's room, "Have you seen the flashlight?"

Mattie looked up over her glasses, finger to lips and whispered, "Shhhhh."

Allison closed the door and walked back, trying to remember where she'd last seen the flashlight, when Mattie came out of the door and followed her back into the kitchen.

"You mustn't get upset in front of the girls."

"I know, but I'm sick of Jack."

"Yes, but he doesn't see it your way."

"What? That he can do as he pleases, but I can't?"

Allison banged the drawer back in place and turned to Mattie, "*Look!*... Okay, I'll get that separation and I'll get a new life. That's it. I've had it. This is just all I need to get out."

"Okay, calm down. The wheels of the law are slow and you shouldn't do anything that will jeopardize your custody of those girls," Mattie put her arms around Allison and drew her close.

"But Mother, I want to be loved," she spoke into Mattie's soft hair, leaning against her neck. "I want to find that man. What if he is lying somewhere out in the stream, hurt?" She broke away from Mattie and stared out the window, "What did you do with the flashlight?"

"It's in my room. I keep it by my bed."

Allison rushed into Mattie's bedroom, picked up the flashlight and waited in the lounge for darkness to set in.

"Where are you going? I'm worried about you." Mattie sat down and picked up the newspaper.

"Shhhhh Mother. I can take care of myself. I'm just going for a walk, that's all."

She closed the sliding door, made her way across the bridge, and along the narrow path while pointing the flashlight to guide the way. The thick, clumpy, exposed roots from the trees caught in her shoe, and tripping, she landed on the soft dirt. The flashlight flew out of her hand and fell into the stream. She leaned into the stream to reach for it. Its beam lit the stream bed as she reached into the water. She noticed something odd - a bicycle with one wheel in the water, balancing on a large rock in the middle of the stream. It had been badly damaged and was missing the other wheel.

She stood up and brushed at her clothes in the darkness. Clinging to the trunks of trees, she made her way back to the pathway carrying the dying flashlight, and walked towards the light of the park. She walked back across the road to Jack's house. If the garage was open, she could sneak in and get another flashlight off the bench. Jack always kept a couple. She crept into the property and hid amongst the old garden. A light came from the passageway, but nothing else was visible. She could hear voices, and laughter coming from around the other side of the garden and the hum of the old spa pool. Jack must have been busy fixing up the old spa. It sat on the other side of the property under a dilapidated canopy, on the far side of the garage. A couple of people could ease into it quite comfortably. By the front porch, she waited for the next burst of laughter, and moved closer to listen. Jack's laughter rang out above the hum of the jets of the spa.

"Yes. I did it," Jack's voice rang out. Allison could hear another voice, a muffled woman's voice.

Allison sprang back when Josh peeked his head out of the spa pool and reached for a towel propped up on the canopy, "Yes, and what happens now, you old bastard?" He shook at the towel. "You better watch those Navy guys. They are mean motherfuckers." He stepped out with the steam rising off his skin. He wrapped the towel around his waist, and knelt back down into the pool. The woman's voice stopped.

Allison moved closer, not seeing the garden rake propped against the wall. She stepped on the outward prongs, and the wooden handle sprang back and knocked her hard on her forehead. It clattered on the concrete path as it fell. Stunned, she half fell against the dead flowers, her head throbbing. She could see Josh's toweled figure looking out into the garden and going back shaking his head. She lay there, watching. Lights came on in the house but a tiny hint of light flickered through the thick velvet curtains.

Holding her head, she stumbled home in the dark.

Chapter 21

It was awkward sitting opposite George Geoffrey and Jack. They had completed only half of their sessions. Allison decided not to reveal her discovery. Jack would only deny it. "So Allison, you have signed the separation papers? Where do you see your marriage going now?"

"I still need time. I need to discover and think about what I want in life. I had to sign those papers. Jack wouldn't."

"I see," said George looking at Jack. "Jack, what have you got to say about how you feel?"

"Ohhh... she just thinks she can do as she pleases. What do I feel...nothing."

"Who are you talking to, your wife?"

Jack just shrugged. He did not want to glorify Allison's tactics with any comments.

"I think, if I may intervene here, part of your problem, Jack, is you don't address your wife by name. Everyone one has a name... whoever they are."

"Oh, what a load of crap! Don't you lecture me," Jack shifted in his seat. "Look... I haven't time to sit here and play dumb school class. Who the shit do you think you are?"

Jack's teeth sprayed out over the thick lips, like a piranha sensing with its jillion taste buds whether this prey was worth eating or perhaps a predator. He loved taunting people, and even George didn't stand a chance with Jack. Jack stood up and threw his chair against the wall.

"No! Fuck all this bullshit. The lot of ya. I've had it. She... yes SHE signed the fuckin' papers. You get your stupid papers out and write that horseshit down. But I tell you this...," and he leaned into both of them, "I," and he pointed into himself, "Get my girls. She's been screwing around."

Allison leaped from her chair, "No, you've been screwing. Yes! You and Josh and some woman in the spa bath. I saw. Look at this bruise. It was me that made that noise."

"What the fuck are you on about, whore?"

"Wait, the both of you. What's going on?" George put his hand on Jack's shoulder.

Jack brushed it off. "Don't you dare fuckin' touch me!" and he stormed out of the room.

Allison sat sobbing into her hands. George stared out the window, speaking slowly to Allison. "There is so much anger and revenge inside of both of you. Nothing will get resolved in this heat. I suggest you take some time off."

There was silence in the room.

Allison swallowed back her tears and left. She thought about her outburst on the way home, wondering how all this would be solved. She sighed to herself, and went about her daily chores, getting ready for her evening shift.

That night, she slowly drove out the driveway. The birds proudly offered their evening melody through the open window of the car.

Allison walked into the main lounge of the hotel and looked around. It was empty, silent but for the quiet hum of the refrigeration behind the bar. The empty chairs looked ghostly, in rows of circles, like a circus with no audience. She went into the restaurant, tucked her handbag behind the counter, and tied her apron. She did not know the maître d'. She prepared the tables, pleased that it was quiet. The maître d' had said nothing about the large bruise on her forehead, *or perhaps hadn't noticed*, she thought. It was a Tuesday evening and business was usually slow at the beginning of the week. When Allison finished, and walked out to the car, she heard a voice in the background.

"Allison. It is Allison isn't it?"

She turned around and stood against her car, looking into the eyes of a stranger.

"Allow me to introduce myself. I'm Chuck." He put his hand up to her face, gently touched her bruise. "What happened to you?" he asked.

Allison stood motionless. His touch. That instant feeling triggered her woman zone.

"May I ask the same question?" replied Allison.

"Me? Oh, just got into a fight. It's nothing," he hesitated. Still caressing her forehead, in his slow American accent, he went on, "I want to know what happened to you? Did someone do this to you?"

"Oh, a garden rake. I was walking where I shouldn't have been." She looked down, "I'm stupid. I stood on one end, and the other end flicked up and hit my head." Allison looked again into his eyes. She could see kindness in those chestnut eyes.

"No, you are not stupid. You know, I came to see you. Someone sprang onto me, and my bicycle went flying."

She nodded and began to cry. Allison brushed the tears out of her eyes, but they fell down her cheeks before she could catch them. She could feel his warm breath on her face as he drew her closer.

"Hey, don't cry. I didn't mean to do that," he backed away, still holding her shoulders.

"No, sorry. I just wasn't expecting to see you again. I errr... I..."

"Look," he drew her in against him and patted her back. They stood there for a while, both absorbing each other's presence. Then he let her go. "I know we're strangers, but I feel we know each other. There's something about you. Don't worry about me. Some jerk did this to me, but I'm not put off."

"It wasn't just anybody. It was my husband," she wiped her nose on her handkerchief from her pocket. "I have to go home now. How will you come down if your bike's gone?"

"How did you know that?"

"I went looking for you that night and I found it in the stream."

"Well, aren't you a little beauty? You'd go out looking for me?"

"Yes, well why not?"

"You must really care about people," he drew her back into him. She could feel his heart racing and the warmth of his body.

They stared into each other's eyes. Both hungry, both lonely, both vulnerable. Chuck's eyes moistened, like soft raindrops on a lily pad. His lips parted slightly as he leaned closer. His soft lips touched hers and they kissed. The passion seemed to come from nowhere.

Allison stood, wet with desire against her car, like a tramp in the night - struck down by flames of desire she never knew existed. She clung to this stranger, his aroma overpowering her senses. She let all her defenses go.

He cocked her leg up against him, and pushed her gently against the car. Stroking her, his gentle breath still pounding, Allison couldn't resist his fingers, the gentle pathway they made up against her leg. So tender, so extremely tender. Nothing had prepared her for this moment.

"Oh my God, stop."

He stopped caressing her and looked down at her.

"I don't even know you. I'm sorry. You caught me off guard. I have to go," she pulled away, and looked down at the ground for a moment to catch her breath.

He opened the car door for her and she got in.

"I'll call you," he whispered, and blew a kiss.

She sat back in the driver's seat, wound the window down, and looked up at him as she turned the ignition. They gazed into each other's eyes for a moment more. She drove away. Her heart didn't stop pounding until she was inside her home. She threw herself down on her bed and wept. She wept for all she'd wanted. She wept for that day on the bridge. She wept that same way, but she never knew why. To wake, and see her dream come true, in the eyes of a stranger? She lay back, thinking, and hugged herself and smiled through her tears. "Chuck," she said his name. She turned away and drew her knees close to her chest in the fetal position, and fell asleep.

The next morning, it all came back to her. No, it was not a dream. It was real. She put her hand up to her mouth. The kiss. So simple a gesture, but so powerful. She scrunched down in her bed and giggled and giggled, and then sat up to pull back the curtain beside her bed. The trees suddenly sprang out at her. Their giant branches like arms waving at her in adoration that she had joined their jubilation in the glory of a new day. "I'm alive. I'm alive," she jumped out of bed and opened her mother's bedroom door.

"You'll never guess."

"Hello dear. Never guess what?"

"I met the American man last night, for real." Allison's eyes were wide with vivid memories as she went and sat next to Mattie. "Oh my God, he is so gorgeous."

"What's he like? Do you know this time?" Mattie lay back on the pillows, took off her hairnet and put her reading glasses down.

"Well," said Allison, turning her head towards Mattie and squirming. "He's kind of average build, but very muscular. He's got big biceps." Allison squeezed her upper arm.

"I don't want to know about his muscles. Come on, what's he really like... this hunk?"

Allison could not wait to continue, "Yes, I think you'd say he looks kind of like your Charlie. Olive skin, dark brown hair... oh, and a fabulous smile."

Mattie's heart missed a beat at the word Charlie and what he meant to her, and how she had to leave from New Zealand - how he had another mission he couldn't talk about. *How cruel*, Mattie thought. She let her daughter bathe in the sunlight of romance, and went on listening.

"He's going to call me, but we have to be careful. I won't bring him here. He's the one that Jack pushed off his bike into our stream."

"Have you signed that separation paper?"

"Yes, Mother." Allison lay back across the bed. "Isn't it exciting?"

"Yes dear, but you don't know anything about this new man."

"I know." Allison leaned over next to Mattie and kissed her soft cheek. "You're such a great listener. I knew you'd understand." Allison left Mattie sitting up in bed. She sensed that the telephone was about to ring close to her in the old kitchen. When it did, she pounced on the receiver immediately.

"Did you get home okay last night?" his voice echoed slow and calm reverberations, reminding Allison of his kind and reassuring manner.

"Yes."

"Did the bed bugs bite?"

"No, but I wish something else did. Allison couldn't help but be the tease."

"Ohhhh, aren't you the gal, eh? Hey I was thinking. How would you like to go dancing tonight?"

"Yes, but how?" Allison stood there, transfixed to the phone.

"Well," he said and paused, "Can you get your car up here and say you're going to work?"

"I suppose I could."

"I don't want another punch-up."

"No, I know. I'll wear my uniform and bring a change of clothes."

"See you tonight."

Allison put down the phone and began to dance, "Mother, it's true!" She ran back into Mattie's room. She spun around hugging herself and opened the closet to look for some clothes. "I'm not wearing them. I'm taking them with me."

She paused, "Is it okay if you look after the girls for me just this once... please! Sarah's on tonight... I can't wait to tell her.

"You be careful of her. She'll tell Jack."

"Oh, Mother she's my friend. Why would she do that?"

"A number of reasons. You're too inexperienced and too trusting, and you don't even know this man."

Allison shook her head and left the room. She could hardly wait until it was time to go. She turned the volume up in her car, and backed out the driveway with her favourite dancing music booming. Nothing was going to stop her. "I can't get you off my mind," she hummed to herself and swished into the driveway of the hotel. She slammed her car door and raced into the lobby to look for Sarah. Poking her head into the restaurant, she caught Sarah's eye.

Sarah closed the drawer of the cash register and came over to Allison, "So what's up?"

"I'm going out with Darth Vader."

"You're what?" Sarah was shaking her head. "Told ya, it wouldn't take you long. You bitch." She gave her a nudge. "Where's *my* date?"

"Stop it," Allison clutched at her bag. "I have to change. Can you cover for me... if anyone calls?"

"Sure, just go and have a good time."

"Thanks, I'll tell you all about it tomorrow."

Sarah winked at her and turned back into the restaurant. Allison went into the lady's toilet area. Sarah cared about her and Allison trusted her. *Why shouldn't she trust her?* Allison thought. Just because she likes Jack doesn't make her a bad person.

She looked at her watch as she went to change. Time was near. She looked into the mirror with half-closed eyes to admire her clever turquoise eye makeup, which complimented her turquoise outfit. She leaned closer, tousled her hair, and placed some simple pearl earrings in her ears. She stepped back for that last look, grabbed her purse, and walked to her car. The sun had gone down and darkness of the night helped to calm her nerves. A figure dressed in white stood out against the dusk. Chuck walked towards her, smiling and holding out his hand.

"Wow, you look like a princess."

Allison remembered Steve's words, smiled, and looked away.

"Don't be shy. Why shouldn't I say that? It's the truth," he smiled again, and opened the car door. "Mind if I drive? I can drive on your side of the road."

"I'm sure you can. Where are we going?"

"Let's make it a surprise." His huge thighs filled the seat, and as they moved down the road she felt like they were flying on a magic carpet.

Allison couldn't resist watching him out of the corner of her eye, his strong arm, his hand on the gear stick. He smiled back at her, as if he knew what she was thinking; his brilliant white teeth shined in the dim light. His moustache, and his wide cheekbones reminded her of male models in foreign magazines. She'd seen faces like his, on stage in the performances of the Russian ballet. Mattie loved the ballet and Allison remembered her Mother billeting the dancers when they came to town. Chuck filled a theatrical role in her mind.

"What are you thinking about? You're staring at me," he put his hand on her knee.

"Oh I'm fascinated with you. That's all. Do you like the ballet?"

"Funny question, but yes. I love going to the orchestra, opera, ballet… whatever. All that high-brow stuff. We have a lot to learn about each other."

Allison smiled at him and they drove on in silence, until they came to a huge hall with people standing outside. It looked a busy place and Chuck pulled into the parking area and helped Allison out of the car.

"You don't know this place?" asked Chuck.

"No… I haven't been out in a while."

"It's called 'The Fire House.' It used to be a firehouse, but it's been turned into a dine and dance. We hear about these places. Come on, I'll buy you dinner. Are you hungry?"

"Starved," replied Allison.

Chuck took her by the hand, and they passed the door attendant at the entranceway. The whole floor glistened in the lighting with people bouncing under the huge rotating disco ball that hung from the ceiling. The colored rays caught her eye, as they walked past the dance floor and slid into a booth.

"What would you like to drink?" asked Chuck, as he helped her take a seat.

"I'll have a glass of white wine. I don't mind which one, as long as it's cold," she smiled up at Chuck, who beckoned a waiter and ordered their best Chardonnay and a beer for himself.

"We Yanks love your cold beer. Steinlager's my favourite," he slid into the seat opposite and took both her hands.

"Now tell me, little Miss Madame… what else do you do besides throw cutlery on the floor?" he started to laugh and shake his shoulders. "Just kidding."

"Well, I'm a mother."

"Well that's the best job in the world. What are your children's names?"

"I have a son, Chris, and he's sixteen."

"Wow, you must have started young." Their drinks arrived, and Chuck tipped up his glass to Allison's. "Cheers to the youngest mother on the planet." They both laughed. Chuck took a long sip and licked the froth from his moustache.

"It always gets in my moustache. It grows so fast. We have to watch that in the military."

"So what do you do in the military?"

"Hang on, we haven't finished with your story first. What about the other two, don't tell me...," he paused and sat back, "Let me guess."

"I actually got remarried and then I had my two daughters. Isabel is seven and Lucy five years old." Allison took a sip of her wine.

"Are they pretty like their Mom?"

"Both Chris and Isabel have auburn hair, and Lucy has more strawberry blond-colored hair." Allison smiled and flushed at the compliment.

"Wow, a honey blonde eh? Come on, tell me more about them."

"I don't want to bore you."

"You're not. I love children."

"Do you have any of your own?" Allison asked.

"No. Hey, I'll have to meet them. Take them out on a picnic. I have odd days off, but I can arrange something." He finished his beer and called the waiter for another. "This is thirsty work."

Allison sat fiddling with the stem of her wine glass, "Chris plays a lot of sport. Like right now... it's cricket season."

"That's right, it's an English game. I keep forgetting your culture down here is very English. We play baseball. It's still with a bat, different sort of bat, different rules. That's great, and what do the girls do?"

"Oh," Allison smiled, "They're into their dolls. I'm getting them the latest craze, the Cabbage Patch Dolls. You adopt them and they each have their own name. Kind of ugly, soft little creatures. Oh, and I've made matching clothes for them and the girls, too." Allison's face lit up with pleasure and Chuck squeezed her hand.

"Good on you, gal. So you can sew, eh?"

"Yes, my mother taught me."

"You sound like you have a really great family," Chuck hesitated. "Now, you want to know a bit about myself. No, I haven't had time for children. I fly the big birds down to the ice. They're my children. The C130's, big iron birds of the sky. It's seasonal, so now's the time we have to kick ass, and push for flights. The Antarctic ice is only right for so long. Then winter sets in and it's far too cold to operate an aircraft, other than refueling it in the air. Most of the people are set to stay down there until it warms again."

"How long are you here for?"

"Depends," he looked at her. "Why?" He smiled and thanked the waiter for his beer. "What would you like to eat? Waiter, could we have menus please?"

"Listen, I know what you must be thinking and I'll say it for you. You are not a one night stand." He shifted in his seat and looked at her. He wasn't smiling when he said it.

"I'm not saying that," replied Allison.

"Shhhhh. Don't cry on me. Come on, I think you need to be happy." He slid out from his side of the booth and held out his hand to help her out. She stood up next to him. He was a head and shoulders taller than her. His strong body was poured into a well-treasured pair of white pants with a matching, tight fitting, short-sleeved, meshed top, unbuttoned to reveal a gold chain.

Allison wondered who gave him the chain.

Chuck ran out onto the dance floor. He turned to face her, and began to twist his black shiny shoes on the wooden floor to the beat of the music.

Allison remembered the night she danced across from him. His gaze now - the same familiar gaze through the mask of Darth Vader. Their eyes met - they looked so familiar and welcome. He put his hands out to her to pull her closer to him. He leaned towards her and swayed rhythmically into her movements. Allison loved dancing, wriggling and twisting her hips, seductively encouraging him. She moved to his style; they didn't need to touch. They moved in a pattern, their bodies synchronized, dancing as one. Only the moving lights joined their ecstasy. They wanted to dance to every bit of music, as if the music were their life.

They ate dinner and danced until it was closing time. Allison skipped her way out to the car, laughing and hugging her dancing partner.

Chuck drove back to the Base, and got out of the car, promising again to call her. He kept his distance, but blew her a kiss. Allison drove home, down Memorial Avenue's long, straight road, with the beat of the music firmly fixed in her heart. In her mind she danced all the way home. The kitchen light was on. When she opened the front door, Mattie was standing in the kitchen waiting.

"You're late. Where did you go?"

"Oh... it was fabulous. We went dancing. We danced all night," Allison stopped and paused. "You don't look well. Is there something wrong?"

"It was quite a bit of trouble after you left, when a knock came on the front door," Mattie paused, looking pale. "I didn't want to open the front door alone in the house. It made me nervous. I looked around the corner and a man was standing there saying he was from the Police." Mattie went into the lounge and sat down. She put her hand up to her head.

"Go on Mother, who was he?" Allison asked.

"Look, it's got nothing to do with who he was, but everything to do with what you are doing," Mattie cautioned.

"I don't understand, Mother. What harm am I doing? I just want to be happy."

"But you can't. At least not while I'm here. I can't take this anymore."

"Who was the man?' Allison sat down with Mattie, putting her arm around her, stroking her back.

Mattie looked over at Allison, "It was that Tom Briggs... said he had some information on some papers."

"Sounds odd, at such a late time of the night?"

"I know. I didn't ask him in. He showed me his badge. He apologized for the lateness, but he said it was urgent," replied Mattie.

"Where did you say I was? At work?"

"What else could I say?" Mattie looked down at the brown carpet.

"You could have said I'd gone to bed."

"And where's your car? And what if he demanded to see you? Look, I'm not lying for you. You can't go out with that man anymore. After all, he's only here for a short time, and he'll be gone. They all go away."

Allison stared into the empty fireplace and stood up. "I'm not like you Mother. I'm going to pursue my dream. This man is real and I am going to see him again. Even if it means we have to hide. He needs me… as much as I need him." Tears welled up in Allison's eyes, "Yes, I have never felt so sure… so fast. You either help me, or I leave. I mean it."

Mattie shook her head, got up, and shut her bedroom door.

Allison went into the bathroom, and ran cold water over her burning face, wiping away the falling tears. She knew she had said words she didn't mean. She heaved a huge sigh and went to bed.

The next day it was all both Mattie and Allison could do, but to say sorry.

Mattie entered her room, and announced in a soft voice "I'm sorry for how you feel. I don't mind if you bring your friend down here. This is my property and I can say who comes on it. I'll call Lloyd James and have an order made out. I've been thinking and I've decided I'll do that."

"That would be wonderful, Mother. Why should we be victims for Jack? I'll call Tom and see what he wanted, but I'll be careful. Don't worry, I'm learning how to be careful."

Allison got up out of bed and hugged Mattie. Their small, silent tears ebbed down their cheeks.

Allison called Tom. His recording came on and she left a message. She put the phone down and it rang again. The American voice took her by surprise.

"Well, that was quick. Are you that keen for a call?"

"I just happened by the phone, smarty," replied Allison.

"Hey come on, kidder, what are you doing later?"

"Can you come down here?"

"What, and get molested again?" Chuck laughed. "What did you have in mind?"

"Well, my mother would like to meet you and it might be best, if you come by later."

"I know what you mean. Sneak in when it's dark, so big bad boys don't get me. It's fine with me. I'll come down and surprise you." He hung up.

The rest of the day went by without a word from Tom. Allison didn't understand, but night was falling and her anxious heart took control, when a gentle knock came from the window. Allison peeped out and Chuck was waiting back in the garden. She opened the door and he laughed, giving her a hug and lifting her up into the air.

"I love this mystery meeting. Do you have someone hiding in a closet that's gonna pounce on me?" Chuck put her down, bent over, and dropped his body with hanging hands and clenched fists like a frame of an ape, "Come and get me, Princess."

"Shhhhhh, you'll wake the girls."

"But I wanted to meet them."

"No, first you have to meet my mother. Her name's Mattie," she took him by the hand and opened the lounge door. Mattie looked up from her paper, and stood up to come over to shake hands with Chuck.

"Don't get up, Ma'am. It's a pleasure to meet you, Mattie."

Mattie's face went pale.

"Have I said something to upset you, Mattie?"

"No, it's just a long-ago memory, that's all."

Chuck sat down next to her, and Allison left the room to go and make some tea. She knew he had come into their life for a reason. He fitted in, somehow. When she went back into the lounge, Chuck was sitting reading part of the paper. He put it down when she walked in.

"Mattie and I share an interest. We like the newspaper."

Mattie smiled at him, "It's been nice meeting you, Chuck. I'll let you both have the lounge."

"Oh, don't let me spoil your evening. I'm only getting to know you." Chuck said getting up to face Mattie.

"No, it's fine... another time," she looked over at Allison. "I'm going to bed. I don't mind. I love to read. I have a good book, so goodnight and I hope to see you again, Chuck."

"Goodnight, Ma'am. You will," he nodded, and Mattie left the room, carrying her cup of tea.

"Your mother is as pretty as you. What was that she was talking about, earlier? I hope I didn't upset her."

"Oh you didn't," Allison walked across the room, placed a cup of tea next to Chuck and took a seat next to him. "During the war, you know, the Americans came here."

Chuck nodded gazing into her eyes with his full attention, and took an obligatory sip of tea.

Allison went on, "Mother was working in Auckland as a hairdresser, and met an American. Quite by accident as it were, while she was going to the movies on the tram. She loves to tell me the story."

"Wow, what an episode! What happened?"

"That's it... a six-month raging love affair and then nothing but years of letters. He was a Navy Diver," Allison stopped and sighed. "I don't know much about it. All I know is she came back from America...." Allison stopped and sat in silence.

Chuck reached over, and pulled her across him, onto his knee. He hugged her tightly. After a while he spoke, still hugging her, "It's tough being in the military. I did my time in the Philippines. Never a day off... working long hours in the filthy heat. We were onboard a ship, stationed there." He sighed and looked away, "Now I just fly the skies. I never know where I'll be posted after this." He turned her around to face him, and looked into her eyes. His voice was serious. "You're too nice... too good for me, Allison. I can't offer you anything." His eyes had that dreamy glistening look again. "I shouldn't be doing this to you."

"But why?" Allison leaned close to him and hugged him. "I've just found you. I don't want to let you go. These moments are ours to experience and remember. This is *our* precious time!" Allison felt her eyes brimming full.

"Shhhh, baby. Shhhh, I don't want your tears... silly gal." He pulled out his handkerchief for her, stood up and led her into her bedroom. "Here, lay down where it's more comfortable. I want to massage you. Make you feel wanted. Poor Baby. No one has cared for you properly. No wonder you cry. You are starved for love." He began to stroke her. He knelt down beside her and continued to rub her back.

Allison let out a huge sigh and closed her eyes. When she felt the silence, she opened them, but Chuck had gone.

Chapter 22

Allison jumped out of bed to grab it before its ring stopped, her heart pounding for the sound of Chuck, when Tom Briggs' loud voice rang in her ear, "Allison, is that you?"

"Yes, I left you a message. You gave my mother a fright the other night."

"It was urgent. I'm sorry, but I was under orders to contact you," responded Tom Briggs.

"Why?" Allison's voice was shaky.

"It's about Josh Somerville."

"Do you want to meet?" asked Allison carefully.

"Yes, I think we should. How about lunch? There's a nice place in the same mall as before… about late morning?" He hung up.

Allison raced to get the girls ready for school. She kept herself busy, slowly regaining her thoughts. At the small restaurant next to the bank, she caught sight of Tom, already seated. He stood up, when she walked in. He wore a grey business suit, a lavish gold watch, and his blue folder lay on the table.

"Allison," he put his hand out to take hers. "I'm a bit over-dressed. I've just come from the Courthouse." He looked at her kindly.

The gaze felt familiar somehow. Allison sat down and smiled back at him across the table. There was something in his eyes that reminded her of their first meeting, and the trust she felt whenever she was around him.

"I've taken the liberty of ordering a glass of white wine for you. Do you mind?" queried Tom.

"No," responded Allison.

The wine arrived.

Tom picked up his glass and continued, "Yes. Josh's place got done over and reports came in... a bit more to dig up. And I also owe you an explanation about those papers. Cheers." He clicked at her glass and they took a sip. "I'm sorry, but the papers have been taken as evidence. That's where I've been this morning."

"Ohh... I never heard about Josh." Allison kept her gaze on her glass. "Does that mean I'll be questioned?"

"You could be... and I wanted to warn you. Josh's news might help. I only got word myself late yesterday. Your mother said you were at work. Did you get that job?"

Allison sipped her wine and looked up quickly at Tom. "Yes, I was at work for a while," she hesitated. "My mother was upset when you came to our home."

"I'm sorry about that." He got out the menu. "You work that late?"

Allison buried her face in her menu, "My hours vary from lunchtime to nighttime."

"Listen, I know it must be hard... with Jack and all." Tom put a hand on hers.

"It is. Jack attacked me after work. I waited until it was too late to come home." She knew it was a lie and said, "I'll have the Caesar salad. I'm not all that hungry, but thank you."

"I'll have the same," responded Tom to the waiter.

Tom then brought out his blue folder and wrote down her answers and the date and flipped it shut. "There was evidence in Ed's blood reports, but sometimes the Police can't present that, so the case may go nowhere. I just wanted to prepare you. Let you know those papers are being held."

"You still have those papers, don't you?" Allison hoped she'd catch him out.

"Of course I do."

"And you would pass them over as evidence?"

"If I had to, yes, of course."

"Did you give them back to Jack?"

Tom looked at his watch. "Sorry, my time's running out. I don't think Jack is who you need to worry about." He stood up and went over to the counter to pay. Allison joined him and they walked back outside into the bright sunlight.

"I get the feeling something is not right," remarked Allison.

"I do too," responded Tom.

"Welcome to the party." Allison left him and walked back to the house.

"You had a phone call while you were out," said Mattie when Allison arrived home.

"Was it Chuck?"

Mattie smiled, "I like just hearing my name called out by an American. Yes, he's going to call back."

Allison sat down watching Mattie get ready in front of her dressing table.

"Tom apologized for upsetting you. He asked me where I was... again."

"I told you."

"He bought me lunch and some wine." Allison stared at Mattie. "I hate these detectives. They want to catch you off guard... and I think he is a natural born liar."

"That's their job, but the wine is a bit odd. Wasn't he on duty?"

"No. He said he was finished for the day. He'd been to Court," responded Allison.

Mattie shrugged and said nothing. Combing her hair, she got up to look for a jacket in the closet. Calling out to Allison, "How would you like to go out?"

"But I want to wait for Chuck."

"Ohh, silly girl. You're too obvious. Make him wait."

Allison sat limply on Mattie's bed, half-lying back, still feeling the effects of the wine and stalling for time. She got up and started to get ready. The phone rang.

"Now, not so fast," said Mattie. "Remember, don't be eager."

"Is that my pretty lady?"

Allison loved hearing his voice, comparing it to Tom's, and responded, "Hello. You left quickly. I didn't get to say good night."

"I know, I wanted you to relax," he paused. "I just rang on the off-chance I can get a day off, and thought we could all go for a picnic. Bring Mattie too. How would you like that?"

"I would, but the girl's Dad would freak."

"Hey, no mention about him. I am not inviting him... I'm asking you."

Allison thought about it, "Yes, when is your day off?"

"It's one day next week. Your children will be on school break, so it won't matter."

"No, that's right... it won't matter."

"Hey, I've got to go. I'll come down in a couple of nights. I have to do another run to the ice. I'll surprise you." Chuck hung up.

Allison wanted to stop him. She wanted more of his company. It frustrated her, but she knew she had to face the problems she had created. Mattie was making the coffee and they sat together in the lounge.

It was hard for Allison to stifle the feelings that Chuck had aroused, and sometimes she found herself in a romantic daydream. One evening, as she was half-listening to the television in the lounge, she heard the same knock at the window beside her. She sprang up, drawing back the curtains. Chuck was coming up the steps. She opened the door and he instantly picked her up.

"I've missed you like crazy," Allison smiled consciously like a Cheshire cat.

"I know, so have I. I feel lost without you," he bent down and kissed her.

"Mummy," Isabel stopped in the hallway and stared at Chuck. Chuck made a sound like Donald Duck, and Isabel went running back into her room and peered out - this time with Lucy. Chris opened his door next to the girl's room and stood there. Allison brought Chuck down the hallway.

"Chris, I want you to meet Chuck."

Chris, in his new found boy's deep voice said, "Pleased to meet you." He put his hand out to greet him.

"You're the cricket player, I hear?" responded Chuck.

"What's Mum been telling you?"

"That you're pretty good with that cricket bat and mitt."

"Yea, it's a great sport."

"You're Donald Duck," called out Lucy and shut her door. Chuck opened it, said something in Duck talk, and closed it again. There was a squeal of delight, followed by giggles.

"Anyway, good luck Chuck. You've got your hands full with those two," Chris smiled and closed his door. Chris was polite when he had to be. The muffled sounds of his music rang out from Chris's room, as Allison opened the girl's door.

"One of you is going to get their fingers mashed. You don't play with doors."

"He started it, the Duck man," said Isabel jumping on her bed.

"Isabel, Lucy, this is Chuck."

"No he's not… he's Donald Duck," said Lucy poking her tongue out at him.

"Boy, you have a long tongue. How many lies have you told?" responded Chuck.

Lucy stared at him. Isabel grabbed one of her books and opened it.

"What have you got there?" said Chuck taking a closer look. "Do you mind if I look?"

Isabel shook her head and passed it to him. Chuck turned to the front cover.

"The Little Red Engine… I remember this story," he sat on the bed to read it to them and Lucy came over to sit next to him. Allison crept away back down the hall, and peeked into the lounge. Mattie looked over her glasses and smiled back at Allison.

Next morning, Allison dug out the old picnic basket from the closet in the laundry. It brought back memories of her childhood, when her father loved taking them to the beach. Mattie kept an old thermos under the kitchen bench, and was filling it with boiling water when the phone rang.

"Good morning, Ma'am," said Chuck respectfully.

"Hello there. You picked a nice day for a drive," said Mattie.

"Yes… I wanted to let you know, I'm on my way."

"Well, you can't trust who you'll run into."

"No," he paused. "Tell Allison I'll be down in a bit, please."

Mattie put the phone down. "Yes, he'll be here soon," she said turning to Allison. "Oh, and tell the girls to get their sun hats out. It's going to be scorcher."

Chris appeared in his pajama pants with an old tee shirt, and opened the fridge door, standing in his usual manner, staring into the fridge to see what he could find.

"Want to come on a picnic?" asked Allison.

"What, with those two?" said Chris, pushing Isabel out of the way, as she raced into the kitchen.

"Why not?" asked Allison

"Cause, I got better things to do with my time," taking a piece of leftover pie, and spilling its contents onto the kitchen floor when he slammed the fridge door.

"You always say that. We never go out as a family. Chuck's taking us," replied Allison.

"Well he's out for brownie points isn't he?" Chris spoke with his mouth full and bending over to scoop up the food on the floor and drop into the bin.

"Don't be like that."

"Oh well. Don't know much about those Yanks up there at that Base, but I bet he is in this for points." Chris walked back down the passageway and into his room, turned up the volume of his sound system and closed his door. Allison could hear him singing to the tune of the music.

"Are we going swimming, Mummy?" asked Isabel.

"Yes. So hurry up and get a change of clothes picked out. You girls are good at that."

"What's Daddy going to say?"

"I'm separated from your father, and that means that I am allowed to see other men," said Allison, bending down to face her. Isabel shrugged and went back to her room to finish getting ready. They were interrupted by the sound of Mattie opening the front door. Chuck's voice gave a whistle.

"Wow, don't you look good today," he said to Mattie, still giving her a cat call, as Allison came to join her. Mattie smiled and went back to the kitchen.

"And daughter too," he gave Allison a hug and poked his head around the passageway to listen for the girls. "Everyone aboard…Toot Toot, the Little Red Engine is leaving for the beach."

They packed the picnic into Allison's car, and with Chuck at the wheel they drove out, leaving Christchurch City, turning into the tunnel to go west, towards Governor's Bay and around to Diamond Harbor.

"I've heard about a little beach around in Diamond Harbor. One of my colleagues went and raved about it. Does everyone want to try it?" asked Chuck.

"Can we go in and swim?" asked Isabel.

"Why sure."

"It sounds gorgeous," said Allison, smiling over at Chuck. "We live here, but we never somehow go to these places.

"Well, now's the time," and he gave her knee a little tap. "I spent a bit of time aboard ships back in the Philippines." Chuck cast his eye down at the huge old carrier ship, on the ocean ahead of them as they climbed the steep hill.

"Can we go on a boat?" asked Lucy, staring at the back of Chuck's head.

"No, not today, Lucy. You're going swimming. No time for sailing. We can do that another day."

Isabel and Lucy sat in the back seat with Mattie, and chattered. The drive took them through rolling countryside, until they finally wound their way up a steep slope. The car had managed to stay safely perched on the slope. It was a day they never forgot, swimming in the waves and Mattie sitting under the huge Pohutukawa trees that grazed the steep banks of many inlets throughout New Zealand - trees with their Christmas spiky flowers offering a stirring blanket of pink mist while they whiled away the day. They sang nursery rhythms all the way around the bays, until slowly the voices faded. Lucy and Isabel's eyes were shut, their heads flopped over against their Nana's shoulder. There was only the gentle rumble of the car tires, churning over the well-used roads, passing back through the countryside, into the tunnel and back along the flat roads home.

When they arrived home, Chuck left with Allison's car.

CHAPTER 23

It was New Year, and Allison was busy making plans when Sarah called, "What are you doing for New Year?"

"My friend Kate, from down south, called up and asked if I'd like to join them for New Year. Bring a friend she said. There's a big tent party at Lake Tekapo."

"Wow, how are you getting there?"

"My car, except it needs a really good tune-up. Chuck's offered to do an oil change and a tune-up at his work. They service the planes up there at the Base."

"What about the girls?"

"Mother thinks it might be okay to leave them with her this once. I'll see."

"Jack might find out. It's a bit risky."

"Not unless someone tells him."

"Well, I won't. God's honor. I never say what you do. Don't know where I'm going... still the same boring shit."

"I don't know what Jack's doing, but he said he didn't need the girls."

Allison put the phone down and went into the lounge. "That was Sarah on the phone. She didn't think I should go away with Chuck."

"No, I agree. But you'll do what you want to do."

"We've been over this before, Mother. I'd love to take Chuck down South or the West Coast. He's never seen those beautiful lakes. He loves scenic places and he's been so good to us... taking us around. Don't you think?"

"Yes. I'll agree there, but it's risky."

"Here's Chuck now, he's brought my car back. I better go. I'm taking him back to the Base." Allison closed the door and ran out to him.

"It's running like a bird. Hop in, I'll show you." They spun out the driveway and roared past the trees. "Engine sounds good doesn't it?"

"Mighty powerful! It's never sounded like that before. Thanks for doing that for me."

"It's a pleasure, ma'am. Listen, if you've got time I'd like to take you on a tour."

"Sounds great."

They drove past the main Base near the airport. "Do you know why that Totem pole sits here?"

Allison stared at it towering above them as they rounded the corner.

"See that thunderbird at the top of the pole? That's me every time I fly South."

"Oh come on, be serious."

"I am serious. It's always been like that. Back in... let me think," he cocked his head to one side. "I know, back in 1956, the first drop to the Antarctic was made. My grandfather, Chief Lelooska made it... from Oregon."

"Oh come on now, you're kidding me. Nobody can fly from Oregon to the South Pole!"

"No! I'm not kidding. I told you... I'm part Indian." He laughed and pulled up outside some grey iron gates. I want to show you where I work." Chuck stepped around to open the door for her in his usual respectful manner.

Allison got out, facing the barbed wire fences. She could see the enormous Hercules aircraft closer now. For the first time she gasped at their huge grey, aluminum wings drooping to the ground like weary albatrosses. The roar of their engines was deafening as huge plumes of exhaust drifted down the runway.

Chuck went on ahead towards the nearby building, past the barbed wire fence, and opened the small side door. Inside was a long, narrow corridor with offices featuring interior glazed cubicles. People were busy typing, all in military uniforms. They took no notice of Allison, as she followed Chuck out onto the huge runway. He stopped to speak with one of the security guards. Chuck's khaki pants flapped in the wind, and Allison caught hold of her hair as it swept across her face, blocking her view, and pushed her skirt down.

"Come on, pretty girl. I told you I'd show you one of my big birds," he took her hand, and they ran to the back of the plane. Its back ramp was let down onto the runway, so it was easy to hold onto the railing and step up inside its huge belly. It was empty of cargo. Chuck bent his head into the side of the cabin and called out to the engineer to turn off the engines they were testing.

"See these runway tracks. These are like a railway. They act like a guide and all the cargo is rolled on and off on these rails. The red netting at the sides holds cargo as well, but we also transport passengers. They sit in rows of four, cramped in. Bit of a thrill for the egghead scientists."

Allison nodded and stared at all the flashing lights and vibrating equipment.

Chuck beckoned her to follow, and went on up to the cockpit. "This is where I sit, hour after hour. It's a long flight down there and back. Usually it's too cold to stop our engines and spend the night."

Allison bent down, and peered out the window looking at all the instruments. "You must be very clever. It's amazing." She backed out, and slowly moved down past the equipment.

Chuck balanced easily across the railings, totally confident with his ability to maneuver amongst his gear, and jumped out first to offer his hand up to Allison. He signaled back to the engineers and raised his voice as the engines began to roar again.

"Now you can tell all your folks for New Year, you've been inside the United States Navy Hercules, huh? How many Kiwis get to do that?"

Allison smiled at him and they ran back across the tarmac towards the buildings. They followed the corridor inside.

"I'll come down later on my bicycle, okay? Better rush, I've some more work to do to finish up here." He waved goodbye and went back inside the building.

Allison turned her car around. The engine purred like never before. She thought about all that she'd seen, the fraternity of power, people and equipment - of another culture coming so close to her. She drove home with a smile on her face, pulled up outside the front door, and skipped inside. Allison changed into a pair of white three quarter shorts with a turquoise colored tee-shirt and a pink flower clip in her hair. She got out the old picnic basket, and helped Mattie with the dinner for the girls when the phone rang.

"Did you decide to go?" asked Sarah.

"Yes, it's just for the night, and we'll drive back tomorrow."

"That's a long way for one night."

"Well, we'll see," said Allison, trying to look for plates and silverware for the picnic. "Happy New Year. I'll give you a call when I get back."

"Yeah sure. You take care on those roads."

Allison put the phone down, and turned towards the refrigerator, thinking about what to take. Mattie was standing by the kitchen window when she drew her hand up to her face.

"I can see someone running. It looks a bit like Jack."

"What?" said Allison, closing the refrigerator door and going to join her at the window. "Oh my God. I don't like the way he's running."

"Neither do I."

Allison went down to the girls' room to see what they were doing. They were playing with their new Cabbage Patch Dolls and Isabel said, "Come and see what Roxanne's done to Lucy's Freda." The dolls were sitting having afternoon tea with the tea cups out on Isabel's bed.

"That's nice. I errrr… I," Allison ran down the hallway, and out the front door to Jack standing by the car.

"Give me the keys."

"But I need the car for the weekend."

"Give me the keys," he took a step up closer to Allison - enough for her to see his eyes blazing into hers.

She went inside and came back out with the keys. "Why do you need the car?"

"Because, I'm taking the girls for the weekend, and I need the car," he brushed past her and raced down into the girls' bedroom. Allison could hear Isabel scream and start to cry.

"No Daddy! Nana is looking after us."

Allison froze and stood there, wanting to hear the muffled words coming from their sobs. She flung the door open. Jack was standing, trying to pull Isabel out from underneath the bed. Cabbage Patch doll Roxanne was half-visible, tightly held by Isabel.

"Jack. Stop that at once. It's me you need to go for," screamed Allison.

"No… it's not! It's that bloody Yank. Where is he?" Jack lost his focus on the girls, forgot about them and stormed out of the room, slamming the door behind him. He got in Allison's car and roared out the driveway.

There was no way of warning Chuck.

CHAPTER 24

Jack turned the corner and switched off the engine. He sat staring into the rear vision mirror, slipping down in his seat. Cars rushed past him. He kept his eye on the passing cyclists. He gripped the steering wheel, his knuckles whitened as time ticked by, and beat at the steering wheel. Jack started the engine, turned around into the street towards the house, but kept back against the bank of the stream. It was steep there and no one would see him. He kept low in the seat until Chuck came into view, and he sprang out.

"Thought I'd catch you down here."

"Mr Brownley, is it?"

"Listen Yankee Doodle. Keep your fuckin' Dandee out of my wife," Jack grabbed the bike and flung it into the stream.

Chuck grabbed at Jack, clutching his shirt up to his neck and pushed him down the bank to the stream. "Listen Mister, don't mess with the United States Military," Chuck looked steadily into Jack's eyes. "If you've got a problem, bring it on man. Bring it on," Chuck kept clutching at Jack's clothes. He could sense the bully in Jack and repeated himself, "Come on, bully boy. What do you want from me?"

"You think you'll win this game. You won't." Jack struggled to push him off, gave Chuck his hardest shove, and stood back. "I've got my contacts up there at your dipshit Base. You'll be out of here before you know it. You've been messing with my wife."

Chuck took a step back. "Bullshit! That's a lie," Chuck took a swing at Jack and missed.

Jack fell back, got up and said, "One more trip down here and I'll have you up for adultery."

Chuck came at Jack again, not answering him but steadying his gaze.

"Don't come down here again, fuckin' with my wife," Jack mumbled.

"Give your best shot, you fish-lipped, faggot prick."

"You fucker...," Jack was up higher on the ridge of the stream and pushed Chuck, splitting his head. Chuck lay unconscious.

Jack drove off, back to his house, slammed the car door, and walked inside. He lay back on his bed and picked up the phone. "Happy New Year. You did well. I've got the car. Thanks Sarah."

"Oh, anytime. I hope I can help you. You're my kind of guy," replied Sarah.

Jack put the phone down and laughed. He popped opened a bottle of beer, walked down the passageway into the lounge, and sat down on his piano stool. He placed the beer on the table next to his piano, and began to play. Louder and louder he banged the keys, playing his favorite tunes. He slammed the lid down, walked outside towards Allison's car, and stood there for a while. He started the engine, listened, and then reversed it beside his car. It always sat next to Jack's car. He stared into the garage and got out to look for a funnel. "Yes, something's got to go... something's just got to go." He dipped into the ethanol he had from the plant and heated it carefully with sugar until it dissolved.

"Good old ethanol. Hello sugar-toasted valves, good-bye compression. Baby, your wings are gonna be clipped. Happy fuckin' New Year."

•   •   •   •   •

It was getting dark. Strangely, no one was answering up at the Base. Mattie had offered to lend Allison her car.

"But I'm trapped Mother… whichever way, I can't go. I don't know how to contact Kate down south. She'll think I've had an accident. If I go… we'll never get there, and besides what if Jack comes back and finds me gone."

Mattie sat, not offering a word, staring at nothing, then spoke, "I've said it all along. Nothing's going to work." She shook her head, "Nothing. You can take my car, but you'll drive into a trap."

Allison stood up from her seat next to Mattie, and went to get Mattie's keys. She squeezed them into her hand, walking up and down the hallway. The room was silent. Chris had gone out. The girls were fast asleep, and the late summer's light was fading across the lawn.

"Look at me, don't I look stupid?" She sat back down again, and started to weep. "Mother why am I so stupid?" asked Allison.

"You're not dear. You're not. You blame yourself for everything," Mattie continued to stare with her fixed gaze, this time into the empty fireplace. "Some things you can't change." She rocked to the motion of the swivel chair. "When you've lived as long as I have, you'll know the answer. You think you've got no time. You're impatient. You're unsure. You're too obvious." She looked over at Allison, "Look… if Chuck's the right one, he'll come back. He'll come back for you."

"Damn it, Mother. We've had this conversation before. You can't give advice."

Allison stood up dangling the keys, and threw off her shorts, went into the bedroom and changed into a satin slim-lined dress in her favorite turquoise tones with splashes of cerise pink flowers. She sat down in front of Mattie's mirror and brushed her hair. It fell into natural curls from the heated rollers she had earlier fastened in place. She stood up, and looked down at her feet. She was still wearing the light sandals for the trip. They still looked elegant, her dainty feet and her bright pink toenail polish were the finishing touches.

Allison came out of the bedroom, and spoke to Mattie, who had turned on the television, "Do you know what, Mother? I'm going to find him."

"You be careful. Jack is on a rampage."

Allison shut the door and opened the garage. She backed out, driving towards the Base. She pulled into the parking area, but all the parks were taken, so she drove down one of the nearby streets, and got out of the car. She walked into the hotel and Julie was there. It wasn't hard to recognize her laugh.

Julie's face lit up, when she saw Allison coming towards her, "Good timing, girl." She waved at Allison. "There's an open tab. Wine, white, isn't it? No come on, give her a White Russian, instead. This gal needs loosening."

"Who said anything about loose round here?" said an American voice.

"Oh," said Julie turning around to include the stranger, "this is Bealllll from North Carolina… he's a honey."

"Hello, my name's Beeaall. I talk reeaal slow."

"But he's not reeaal slow in the bedroom," Julie burst out laughing, and nearly fell off her barstool, pushing at Bill.

Allison took a sip of the new concoction and sputtered it everywhere.

Julie gave her a thump on the back. "Steady on, girl, plenty more where they came from. How come you're up here by yourself, anyway?"

"I met someone a while ago. His name's Chuck."

"There's lots of Chuck's up here," remarked Julie, taking puff of her cigarette.

Bill stood next to Julie staring at Allison. His huge feet were the first thing Allison noticed. The rest of him matched his feet. By the time Allison noticed his face, she was not inspired… he had a cold empty stare on a very handsome face. All she could think about was Chuck, her Chuck, the one that had made her life turn around. She looked out into the crowd.

"Listen, I have to go. I did have a date with Chuck. It was the guy in the restaurant that night."

"What night?'

"Remember, I dropped the silverware all over the floor."

"Oh, he's married… it can't be him."

Allison froze… slowly drinking the rest of her drink.

"Bill's not… are you Bill?"

"Me married? I'm too slow," he giggled.

Allison turned to look again into the room. "You must be mistaken. Chuck's not married. He never has been."

"Whatever, kiddo. After all, you're the new kid, so it seems," Julie laughed.

"What's that supposed to mean?"

"Nothing."

Allison knew it was time to go. It was past midnight when Allison opened the garage door and walked into the house. There was a note sitting on the kitchen bench, Mattie's familiar scribble read, *"Kate had called from the camping ground looking for you. I told her you couldn't come."* Allison was relieved, but nothing from Chuck.

She went to bed and fell into a dazed sleep. She dreamed about kissing Chuck at the beach in the moonlight, down in the little spot they had spent time at their picnic. It was real, the gentle tide washing in around their feet, rocking them as their bodies touched. Gentle, moist kisses.

She woke to knocking sound at her window. She sat up, her heart beating fast. "Oh no, not Jack at this hour." She slid herself under the curtains at the side of the window. She could see a shadow half-leaning up against the corner of the house. It was Chuck. She opened the door and he fell in.

"My God... what happened?"

Chuck picked himself up and limped into her bedroom.

"Here, you're bleeding... I'll get a cloth," Allison exclaimed.

"No fuss. I'm okay. I'm just stunned."

"Let me take you to the hospital."

"Hell no. That's the last place." He fell back down into the chair in her room.

Allison bent down and carefully wiped the dried blood off his forehead.

"Did you have an accident?"

Chuck eased himself back into the chair, still holding the cloth and wiping it himself. "You might say that. That old man of yours is crazy. US military guys are not allowed to fight civilians. I was at a disadvantage. He ambushed me again. It was better to let him think he got to me."

"But, I went looking for you. I went up to the Base. Julie was up there." Allison stopped.

"I was just sitting… fixing my bicycle and thinking about things."

Allison watched his eyes look away. She caught their sad expression. She sat beside him and stroked his hair. "What things?" She kept touching him, this time more tenderly. "What things do you mean?"

"That I am not good for you. I've caused you only unhappiness."

"Julie said you were married. Is that what this is all about?'

Chuck turned and stared into her eyes. "When did she say this?"

"Tonight," Allison felt her tears welling. "It's true, isn't it? It all makes sense now."

"No. You don't understand the full story. You never will," he looked down and wiped some more of his hair with the cloth. "I was in the Philippines and I met this woman. She was a lot older than me, with hair as dark as a raven, long and silky. She begged me to take her to America and save her four children from poverty. I was lonely. I loved children, and had never had a chance to have my own."

He paused and looked into Allison's eyes. "I'm not married. She left me, as soon as she got her green card." His eyes spelled mystery and misery, like the dream on the shoreline. His tongue slowly drifted across her lips wet with emotion. They came together; they kissed without further explanation. Chuck took her and held her, picked her up, and kissed her and gently laid her on her bed. He leaned down. It was his dream.

Allison wept. The sadness of the story touched her soul. She could see him for what he truly was.

He clung to her, raised himself above her and pressed down into her body.

CHAPTER 25

Jack woke with a splitting headache, his naked body twitching. A persistent housefly buzzed aimlessly against the window and back into the room, landing on Jack's nose. One swipe at the fly, and he sat up, threw the covers off, and went to the bathroom. He stood there; the unbearable throb in his head partly suspended his urine flow midstream. He reached across to the small cabinet above the hand basin to grab a couple of pain killers, and missed the toilet with his piss squirt. "Damn. Where's that woman? Now I'm swimming in piss." He threw the tablets down his throat and bent under the tap, gulping some water. His head throbbing, he threw the hand towel down on the piss puddle floor.

"Fuckin' New Year and nobody gives a damn. My life's fucked." He went back into the bedroom and sat on the side of the bed to dial Josh's number. "Where is that tight-ass bugger?"

The phone rang on and on for some time before Josh answered.

"About bloody time, ass-wipe." He could hear Josh yawning. "Where were you last night?" Jack lay back on his bed. "Can you come over?"

Jack put the phone down, and with the warmth of the sun, he fell asleep.

He woke to a knock on the bedroom door. "Come on, fancy pants. Whooeeee, look at you," Josh pulled Jack's feet down the bed.

"Where were you last night?" Jack sat up and frowned.

"Celebrating. What else would you do on New Year's Eve, eh big boy?" Josh stooped down to brush his hair to one side, looking in Allison's dressing room mirror. He turned to Jack, "Anyway, what happened to you?"

"I got pissed."

"Is it all back on?" queried Josh.

"What's back on?" asked Jack, pulling on a pair of shorts.

"You and Allison. Her car's here. I thought I'd walk in on you two."

"No, he was driving my car."

"What do you mean your car?"

"Well it's not hers, it's ours. He was driving it; he even had it up at his bloody work."

Jack walked out of the bedroom with Josh following. "I knocked him flying. Shagging my wife. He's probably dead for all I know."

"You're jealous, aren't you?" asked Josh.

"Jealous of that ugly mug? Hell no!" Jack opened the fridge door, grabbed a beer, threw Josh one, and sat on the couch in the passageway.

"Shit. You know how to knock them down." Josh tossed back his can and joined Jack. "First that detective, now the Military." Josh paused, "How are you going to cover up this shit?"

"Easy. I've got that bastard… he's bloody married," Jack sat on the passageway couch. "He'll be back over, and when he shows up, there's going to be a surprise waiting for him."

Jack sat, tapping his knee and looking out into the lounge. "I've dumped some ethanol in the gas tank. Fuckin loser, I'll get him." He could see sunlight stream in from where he was sitting. He turned to look at Josh.

"You have your life. You haven't lost your family. You don't know shit about nothing. You cover up your tracks and piss off, otherwise you'll never get any more lab work."

"Look… my apartment got ripped to bits. I'm being questioned for murder. That woman next door had a heart attack. God knows what happened there. What more do you want from me? Fuck you," Josh stared at Jack. "Any more questions from the cops and I'm not so sure I'll remember much."

Jack sprang to his feet and stared into Josh's face. "You'll remember every bit. There's no evidence. Relax," Jack shook his head. "And anyway, as for the neighbor, she's fuckin old, what do you expect? People her age go tits up it all the time."

Jack left Josh sitting in the passageway. He opened the fridge and came back carrying two more cans, and threw one at Josh. They sat on the couch and clicked open their cans, and turned to each other.

"Here's to the New Year." They tipped their cans and drank in worried silence.

After Josh left, Jack called Sarah and then called Allison.

"Sorry about last night…"

"Well it's upsetting for the girls. It doesn't matter about me," replied Allison.

"I thought I'd bring the car back and take the girls out. See what they say. Sarah's school is going swimming up at Pines Beach. They want us to come."

"I'll ask them, and call you back."

Allison put the phone down and went outside.

"Hey… where are you?" she called out. There was laughter coming from the big yellow-tipped Macrocarpa tree.

"Dad wants to go to the beach."

"Yeah, but what about…?" Isabelle appeared with Lucy close behind.

"Isabelle, remember what I said."

"We love Dad," said Lucy smiling.

"Oh, and Sarah's having the picnic."

"Oh no," said Isabel, walking away.

"Stop that. There will be lots of children there… don't worry about her boys. I'll call Dad. He's going to pick you up tomorrow."

Next day, Jack brought the car back, which gave Allison a sense of relief. She waved at them as they drove off, and thought how easy it was when she was under Jack's control. Sitting under the umbrella, gazing out at the view of the park and sipping tea with her favorite companion, her Mother, she tipped her tea up to Mattie, "Happy New Year, Mother Darling. I love you so much."

"And I love you," said Mattie.

When evening came, the phone rang. Allison wondered what sort of tragedy was next.

"Allison I have to see you. I'm coming down to talk to you," said Chuck.

"You sound upset."

"I'd rather talk to you."

Mattie was reading the paper when Chuck walked into the lounge.

"Happy New Year, Mattie."

"Every New Year's the same to me," said Mattie smiling at him from over her glasses.

"Well, it's been great to be here with you." He closed her door and walked across to Allison, who was waiting for him in her room and they sat together on the couch.

"Allison." Chuck looked serious. "I think we'll have to stop going out for a while."

"Why?"

"Isn't it obvious? I'm going to be in heaps of trouble with my work. Look at me. Getting into a fight at New Year's is kind of common, but messing around with someone else's wife is another story."

"Why has this suddenly been a problem?"

"I had this warning from one of the Lieutenants; somehow he got word I was seeing you and you were married."

"What? Jack! He wouldn't... that's not fair."

Allison clenched her fists, and repeated, "That's not fair."

"I know it's not fair. He obviously wants you back."

"Oh, for God's sake! You know what I've gone through?"

"I know... but I have to work and I have to fly. If we're patient, Jack will slowly give up, but not this way we are going."

Allison knew his words made sense, and he finally withdrew his hands from hers, and stood up to leave.

"I'll call you soon, okay?" he blew a kiss.

"Goodbye, Mattie" Chuck opened the lounge door, waved at her, left and rode out the driveway.

<h1 style="text-align:center">CHAPTER 26</h1>

It was 5:30am. Allison couldn't sleep. She had been unable to sleep much since Jack attacked Chuck. It frightened her, and she was glad it was back to a work day, and she could call her lawyer. Jack had promised to bring the girls back later that day. She got out of bed, and went into the kitchen to put on the jug for some hot water. Still deep in thought, she made two cups of tea, picked out some cookies from the pantry, and walked towards Mattie's bedroom door to peep in. Mattie stirred and looked over at her.

"Are you awake?" whispered Allison.

"Dozing," said Mattie, wiping her eyes and turning to one side to take the tea from Allison. Allison sat down next to Mattie, as always on Mattie's cedar trunk box. They both rested in silence, taking sips of tea, dipping favorite cookies into their tea.

"I miss Chuck," said Allison, and took another mouthful of tea.

"Yes, but you knew he'd do this."

"I can't live without him." Allison put the cup down on the floor, and put her hands up to her face and began to sob.

"You have to take control of yourself before it's too late. You have a responsibility to your children," replied Mattie.

"But I...," she went on crying. "I can't help myself. I just want him." Allison blew her nose into her handkerchief.

"You've always had what you wanted, Allison," cautioned Mattie.

"No I haven't. I had Jack, and that was supposed to be forever. But it was one betrayal after another. Now it's my turn to be happy."

"Is it?" asked Mattie, finishing most of her tea and swirling it. "You know… I've told you, you have to have patience. You're in too much of a hurry."

Allison stood up, bent over her Mother, and kissed her.

"You're probably right, Mother."

"Thanks for the tea," said Mattie.

Allison smiled back at her and closed her door, went back to her room, and dropped off into a deep sleep, then woke with a jolt. She got up, had a shower, and coming out of the bathroom she could hear music coming from Chris's room. He was up and he passed her in the hallway, singing one of his favorite Kenny Roger songs. He stopped when he got to the kitchen.

"Did anyone remember the money for my Cricket jersey?"

"I haven't any cash on me," said Allison, passing the kitchen.

"I have a team photo this morning… you know for the First Eleven."

"I'll go around to the bank. It won't take me long," said Mattie, coming out in her robe.

"But I'll be late," said Chris, skipping down to his room.

"You'll have your money, said Mattie."

Mattie went into the bathroom, then back into her room. Allison hardly heard her close the front door and, before she could stop her, Mattie had backed out in Allison's car. Allison stood at the kitchen window, boiling the jug for their coffee and looking at the time. She shook her head, as she watched the yellow car slowly take off. She knew Mattie was a safe driver.

"How long do you think it takes to go to the bank?" said Chris staring out the kitchen window.

"Nana does things in her way. I should have gone myself," said Allison.

"Hmmm, I'm going to bike around the corner and see." muttered Chris.

Chris rode off on his bicycle, leaving Allison watching him through the window, listening to more Kenny Rogers' voice crying out to her. All her heart-filled aches stuck in her chest. It fitted her mood, as did the gentle rainfall outside. Her mind drifted to the precious moments she had spent with Chuck. How she loved his soul, his gentle touch. She closed her eyes and hugged her body, rocking to the sounds drifting from Chris's room. She missed the sound of Chuck's voice. His calls were less frequent now. The loneliness set in. She sat down on her lounge seat, when suddenly Chris appeared and sat down beside her. His face was ashen.

"Something's wrong," she touched his forehead. "Are you ill?"

He didn't answer her. He just stared out the window.

"Something's wrong, Chris. Tell me what's wrong." Allison put a hand up to her mouth and gasped.

"Oh my God, you don't think anything's wrong with Nana?" Allison pulled at Chris, trying to search into his blank eyes.

"Go see for yourself."

"But can't you tell me anything?'

Chris kept staring at the carpet and turned to face Allison. "I don't know. I just saw a car being towed away, that's all."

"Would you come with me?"

"No. You go. Don't ask me."

Allison staggered out the front door, and towards the gate, clinging to the rhododendron bush for support as she pulled herself around the corner. She grabbed the fence and stumbled towards the main road, crossing in a daze. Around the corner, a group of people assembled outside the Shopping Mall. On the road she could see heavy tire skid marks, and an ambulance pulled over, under a tree on the other side of the road. She took in a breath, and for a moment ran with confidence to the people and police, waving her arms and crying out.

"What happened, what happened?" She stopped still when she saw Lloyd James' father, Jim, coming towards her. His face was ashen. He shook his head.

"No, No, No! Not my Mother. No. Not my Mother. Where is she?" cried Allison, tears now uncontrollably gushing out. Screaming, she fell into the gutter, clawing at the debris and mumbling, "Someone tell me, No!"

"Allison," said Jim, bending down to try to pick her up. "You have to go the hospital."

Allison kept her face hidden, and stopped screaming for a moment.

Jim repeated, "You have to go to the hospital. Are you able? Otherwise I'll go."

"No, please. I want Chuck to come with me... only him," she mumbled out the words, her saliva and tears falling out onto the pavement.

"Chuck, the American?" asked Jim.

"Yes," screamed Allison. "Please, someone help me!"

One of the policemen and Jim helped her into the back seat of the Police car, and Jim, leaning into the car, spoke to the second policeman sitting in the passenger's seat, "If you go up to the United States Base Headquarters, someone will get a message to Chuck. His second name is Bronski. This poor woman is in shock. You won't make any sense out of her."

"Thank you, we will take care of it," said the Police officer.

Allison lay face down in the back seat of the vehicle and didn't stop crying. The car began to move, jostling her around, and then finally stopped. She lay, listening to her heartbeat and the sounds of the Interpol radio system. The car door opened and Allison sensed a warm body sitting next to her.

"What happened?" asked Chuck, putting his arms around Allison's shoulders.

"There was an accident around 9:30 this morning. A collision with an ambulance. The other vehicle was obstructing the road. Both vehicles ended up on the other side of the road," the Police officer in the passenger seat explained as he turned to Chuck.

Chuck wrapped his arms around Allison. Allison ignored the words, drew in a breath, and continued to lie face down in Chuck's lap. The ride was bumpy and endless. The daylight stung Allison's eyes. Finally, they came to a stop outside the hospital.

The Police officer turned to Chuck. "We will wait here." He got out and opened the back door, and continued to speak to Chuck, "You have to walk up that driveway and someone will direct you." He pointed to a pathway. It led to the little Chapel, perched on the roadside, alongside the hospital. The old building sat amongst rows of roses, blooming, dripping in the light morning rain. Allison took a step forward and stopped.

"Why are we going here? This isn't the hospital. Where's my Mother?"

The Police officer steadied her balance, "I know Ma'am. You have to go and see her. Your friend will help you."

"Go and see her how? Chuck, what are they saying?"

"Shhhh... baby... shhhhh. Remember, your Mother loves you. She's here with you. Come on, you can do it. Do it for her." He took hold of her arm and they walked down the path.

The smell of the roses forced more tears to flow. Somehow Allison knew she was in danger. She hung onto Chuck and together they stepped up the concrete blocks of stairs, and walked into the cold of the Chapel. It was a brightly lit room, although it was built of stone. A single room with a slab, set up like a shrine. On the shrine, lay her Mother. Allison took a step back, and shrieked, and clung to Chuck. She hid in the folds of Chuck's arms.

"Oh my God, promise me this is not real," she looked at Chuck, who was staring across at Mattie and shaking his head.

"Allison, say a prayer. Say it to yourself and step closer." He gently clutched her shoulders, bowed his head, and whispered the Lord's Prayer. He repeated it for Allison, and took hold of her as they stepped up onto the platform to stand by Mattie.

Allison thought of her fairy stories, when Snow White lay in a glass casket. But it was her mother lying there instead. How could this be? Lying still, her eyelids closed, with traces of blue shadow, her lips closed. Allison bent down to loosen the white cloth draped around Mattie. The folds of her pink trouser suit became visible but strangely still. She bent closer to touch her. The coldness of Mattie's face alarmed Allison. Allison threw her hands up to her face.

"My mother's gone." Tears falling freely now, she looked at Chuck, "She's gone. She never said goodbye. It's over. What have I done?"

"Shhhh. You haven't done anything. It was an accident."

"No it wasn't. She shouldn't have gone."

Allison threw herself on her Mother and wept. Touching her face and pulling at her clothes. "Where's your belt, Mother? Here it is, you should be going out with me."

"Come on Allison, you can't stay here."

"But I can. Please don't leave me, Mother," she broke down, still crying and slid down beside the draped cloth and sat on the platform, leaning against the draped cloth. Someone appeared and spoke to Chuck.

"Come... Allison," Chuck bent down, still whispering, "Your mother's not here... she's with the angels."

Allison stopped crying for a moment and looked into Chuck's eyes. "But it's too soon for her to go. She didn't tell me." She went on weeping, pressing herself against the folds of cloth.

"Mattie did say goodbye. You must believe that. Now come on, she wants you to be strong."

Allison allowed Chuck to help her up. With wobbling resistance, she stumbled back out into the light of day. A small crowd had gathered by the police car, as they walked towards the car. The Police officer in the passenger's seat got out and opened the door, asking Chuck where Allison lived. The car drew away from the curb, when Chuck caught sight of Jack staring at them in the distance.

Chapter 27

Allison was too afraid to come out from underneath her bed, whimpering with her door closed, not remembering how she got there. She only knew it was the safest place to be. Crying in the dark alone, she could hear muffled voices. The carpet beneath her was damp with mucous and saliva dripping from her nose, mouth and eyes. Rotten air seeped up her nostrils and stifled her breath. The voices outside her room got louder and louder. The door banged.

"Not you again – I thought I told you not to come back."

Allison could hear Jack's booming voice, but she could not hear the response. She squeezed her eyes shut, and crawled further under the bed. She heard footsteps right outside the glass doors. She knew it was Chuck... he was leaving. *How could they treat me like this... how could they?* Nothing was making sense. She heard Sarah's voice above the commotion, discussing Chuck with Jack... muttering. Sarah said Chuck's name, over and over again. She put her hands up to cover her ears.

"How could they, at a time like this?" sobbed Allison, unable to move. Allison was past rescuing as the sorrow worsened...

"Allison. It's your doctor... Doctor Taylor. Allison can you hear me?"

Allison looked up and she could see the doctor's face staring at her from under the bed.

"What?" Allison began to claw her way out, mumbling, "I don't know where I am."

"Come on. Here let me help you." He spoke firmly.

She squinted at him as he helped her up.

"I'm only going to give you a few pills to calm you down, and then, I know you'll have the strength to pull through. You will do it." He put a couple of pills in her hand, and handed her a glass of water to drink.

Allison swallowed the pills, still looking extremely pale and shaking. "I... I... don't want to... have to... talk to anyone," sobbing and pleading, as she looked at him.

"That's fine, I will see that they all leave. Your girls are being picked up from school."

He had been her doctor for all the time they had been in Christchurch, and he was great at taking the situation in hand.

Allison settled down, hearing doors closing and people's voices slowly fading into the background. She blacked out for a while, but as she stirred, she heard the little voices and called out. The girls came running into the room.

"Mummy, Mummy what's happened to Nana? Oh, Mummy. It's so horrible, we don't understand." Their little faces, tears streaming down their plump cheeks with hot, dirty hands gripping at Allison's cold fingers as they tried to comfort her. She was instantly aware again of her own mortality. She was now the next generation, comforting the new generation. *How momentary life is*, she thought.

The night before the funeral, the small family drove down the familiar road around the park to the funeral parlor.

Allison gripped the two girls' hands as they entered the building. Chris had said he couldn't go. He'd gone off into the park, to find his peace in a familiar place. One of Allison's cousins had come for support. Lucy stood beside the open casket and looked in to see a lady dressed in a pink gown.

"That's not my Nana," Isabel said, looking up at Allison. "My Nana is prettier than that... there is no one here." Isabel just stared and began to cry, saying, "Why Mummy? Where is our Nana?"

Allison gulped and clung to her cousin, and buried her face against her.

"Isabel, I know this is hard, but she's gone to heaven where Grandad went. She just didn't stop to tell us."

"But I'll have no one to take me town anymore," whimpered Isabel.

"Yes… you will darling. Yes you will," Allison hugged her, and nodded with steady, small tears trickling freely down her cheeks.

Allison then said to the funeral director, "Thank you." That's all she could say. The words just didn't come out. They walked back to the car and drove home in silence. Jack stood watching them as they drove past. He had such a look of sadness in his face.

Mattie had passed away that Monday. She kept this verse. They bowed in silence, drinking in the moment. They said Psalm 23, "The Lord is my Shepherd…," her favorite psalm, and the words could not stop the tears. No matter how strong the message was, the ones left behind must go on and face the Valley of Death too, and journey on to be brave for tomorrow.

The drive to the Crematorium was a bad dream and the fragrance of the flowers and the music wafted by Allison. For now, it was the end of the world for her. She was empty, playing a part, as Shakespeare told of life… a play full of acts, and this was the stage. The flowers contributed to set the scene for departure and leaving behind a lifetime of memories.

Chapter 28

Jack drove towards the United States Military Base. Confident in his mission, he walked into the main headquarters and stood at the reception.

A woman in uniform looked up, "Can I help you, sir?"

"Yes you can. I'd like to see the person in charge of one of your military men, a Chuck Bronski."

"May I ask what this is about?"

"A personal matter."

"Your name please, sir."

"Oh, I apologize, Mr Brownley."

The woman got up and went out through a glass division. After a while, a man wearing full military uniform appeared. Jack was quick to introduce himself, and the man showed Jack into a small cubicle.

"Allow me, I'm Lieutenant Commander Hoskings. I am only permitted to hear your problem, but not reveal any personal details about my men, if you understand, so please do go on."

"I'll get straight to the point. Chuck Bronski has been screwing my wife and I believe he's married."

"What evidence do you have?"

"Plenty. My wife's mother has just been killed in a car accident. Your man, somehow got permission to get time off to go to the accident. It was *my* wife's mother in that crash... not his wife... *mine*." Jack stood up pointing to himself. "I reported this man seeing my wife a few days ago and nothing's been done about it. Now look what's happened."

"I'm sorry to hear that." Hoskings beckoned him to sit back down. "We can't get into domestic arguments, but I will make a record of this, and look into Lieutenant Bronski's activities during leave."

"It's more than domestic. It's bloody murder."

"Excuse me..., but you're not making sense. As I said, I will make a record of this and look into Lieutenant Bronski's activities during leave."

"You better, he was the one driving my wife's car. Are you in a habit of servicing civilian's cars up here?"

"It depends on the situation. Our men do go on leave."

"What's that supposed to mean?"

"We will look into it... and his marital status certainly puts pressure on the matter. He will be dealt with under the Code of Conduct while here in New Zealand. We don't tolerate any misconduct. I appreciate your concern and I will get in contact with you. I am sorry about your wife's mother. My deepest condolences."

"Thank you. I have notified my lawyer about this. It has been extremely stressful and I am relieved that I can get my family back and everything returned to normal. I will look forward to hearing from you."

"Would you like us to contact your lawyer?"

"No."

"We don't as a rule correspond with New Zealand civilians. If there is a problem, we will look into this and take appropriate action as we deem necessary."

Jack rose up out of his chair and strode out past the woman in uniform. He took a sniff of the polluted kerosene air and listened to the Hercules' huge propellers.

"Last plane that bastard will fly down here," he smiled as he drove away from the United States Air Base.

•   •   •   •   •

Nothing could stop Allison from gazing out the window of her little room in a fixed stare. Her Aunt Elsa stayed with her until the end of the week.

"You're going to go for a walk today, get some fresh air, Allison," said Aunt Elsa, watering the plants with Mattie's watering can. Her hanging bangles rattled as she wiped the splashes of water off the edge of the window. "You'll have to get some help. Go see that counselor. Do you want me to make the appointment?"

"No, I can manage.'

"I don't believe you. Where's his number? I'll get this done and then I have to leave." She reached for the phone and dialed George Geoffrey's number.

"Ten o'clock tomorrow," poking her head around the corner at Allison.

"Your mother's with you. God Bless." Aunt Elsa kissed her cheek.

Allison hugged her and they walked down the steps. Aunt Elsa waved goodbye, out of the taxi window.

The house felt deafeningly quiet with Aunt Elsa gone, and Chris away playing sport. All her mother's treasures left around to haunt her - just as she left them that Monday morning. Allison sat down on her couch, put her head in her hands and began to cry. Tears flowed until she lay back in the warm sunlight, and closed her eyes. Just as she felt the warmth starting to sooth her, the phone jolted her back to reality. Allison sat forward, got up and staggered to the phone. It must be Tom again, she thought.

"Allison, is that you?" said Chuck.

"Yes," she gulped.

"Listen, something's come up. I can't explain."

"Are you going somewhere?"

"I've got to make an urgent run to the ice."

"Will I see you again?"

"No."

"But..."

"You'll make it. The ones you care about... love you."

"I don't understand."

"Just remember what I've said. Promise me you'll be strong." And then loud male voices called him - then silence.

Allison put down the phone, and pulled her robe tighter. She walked across to the little window and looked over at the park. This was where it all began. She drew in a breath and walked down the passageway, dropped her robe, and stepped into the shower. The gush of the warm water soothed her and finally she stepped out, dried herself and pulled on a turquoise-colored tee shirt. She heard a knock coming from the front door. Her heart missed a beat. She hopped into a matching colored skirt, flew around the corner of the hallway, and ran to the door. Tom was bending down, staring in to see if he could catch sight of her. Allison opened the door.

Tom put his arms around her, "Come on... you're getting some fresh air."

"But... I thought it was...,"Allison began to cry. "I've just had a shower. Can you wait while I tidy up?"

"You look great as you are."

Allison left him and put on a string of pearls. She took a look at herself in the mirror. The pearls reminded her of Chuck and their nights of dancing. She joined Tom. He didn't say anything, but took her hand. They walked in silence, until they turned out of her street, and she took a breath and stopped.

"This is where it all happened. So quickly, I can't believe it... and I never will," pointing to the corner.

"So what do you think caused your mother to go out into the road?"

"I don't know. All I know is, I've lost my mother and I have no one except...,"she stopped.

"Is there someone who you think might want to harm you?"

Allison shook her head and they walked on around the corner. "Only Jack, but he wouldn't dare do anything to harm me or my mother."

"And you've never let anyone else drive the car."

"Only Chuck."

"Who's Chuck?" Tom didn't wait for her answer, but opened the door to the little lunch bar.

"I've been seeing someone, but I know it's not right." Allison took a seat and looked at Tom with tears in her eyes. "Why is it that I feel vulnerable with you? The first time we met, I had this feeling. I'm telling you things I don't mean to tell you. Remember in the library? I told you too much."

Tom pulled up a seat next to her, "I'm only here to help you. If you don't want to tell me about this man, and why it's not right... you don't have to." He lit a cigarette and blew the smoke out into the room.

"He's an American. He's a pilot. He's only here for a short while. I shouldn't have... let him drive my mother's car."

"What makes you say that?"

"Well, we did go out driving... maybe I should report this."

"It might harm Jack if you don't, and that would not be the right thing to do, no matter what's between you and Jack."

"But Chuck had nothing to do with my mother's accident. He only drove it with me," Allison's voice rose in defense.

"No one's saying that, Allison," Tom looked up at her.

"I... I fell in love."

"It happens to us all." Tom wanted to take her into his arms, but picked up the menu instead.

"I'm going to see my counselor again, and I'll talk it over with him. I'm so confused. I met Chuck, quite by chance... when I went back to work."

Tom could see she was hesitant, and took her hand to relax her and help her explain. He understood this man must have meant a lot to her.

"Chuck was so kind. Jack said he'd found out he was married. Chuck said that was a lie. What does it matter anyway? He's gone. Tom, I don't know if anyone tampered with my car."

"Did Chuck ever take your car?' Tom could tell there was something wrong. "Allison, I hate to say this, but this man, Chuck... if he didn't tell you he was married, how can you trust him on other matters?"

"Oh my God! It's the same story, over and over again." Allison pushed her chair away and went to stand up. "You don't believe me. What if he is for real? What if Jack took my car?"

"Look, Allison... I'm sorry." Tom stood up. "They examine everything, and the car will be checked thoroughly."

Allison continued to move away from the table. "You're just like my aunt who was here, helping me, but all the time telling me, I have to face up to life. Now you…"

"Hey, I didn't mean to threaten you. Your aunt's right. I'm just warning you. Facts are facts and they will find out if the car has been tampered with. That's all. You should know that." Tom admired her even though he was hard on her. She was so beautiful standing there.

"Here… sit down. Come on," pleaded Tom.

Allison sat down again. Tears welled up as she looked down at her clothes.

"You are such an amazing lady, you know that, don't you?" Tom reassured Allison.

"No. Only Chuck would tell me, but he's gone. And now he's a liar. That's what you say."

Tom realized it was useless. It was as if she were in a dream. A dream that he could never penetrate.

They left the lunch bar, walking in silence past the corner, around to her house. Tom walked her to the door.

"Thanks for always being here, you seem to know the right time." Allison lamented.

"I'm not a cop for nothing, it's my job." He walked away.

．　　　．　　　．　　　．　　　．

Jack moved fast over the next week. With the accident, everything had changed.

Josh had moved from his apartment and was living in town, close to Bellamy Labs. He was poised in a sundeck chair on his balcony. The apartment faced Hagley Park, with a view over a sea of giant oak trees. He could see the playing fields with teams of cricketers, and watching them was his favourite pastime. He leaned back and smiled at Mark as they sat together, admiring the view. He loved his privacy, and he could see everyone who came to visit him. *No more snooping neighbors*, he thought to himself. Life was good.

"It's all going to work out nicely, old boy," said Josh nodding.

"Yes," said Mark, enjoying a puff of his pipe. "You'll beat Jack." He smiled out towards the park. "Once he got those papers, he was off the scent."

Josh took in a deep breath, enjoying the feeling of self-worth.

"He handed out that business card to your receptionist." Josh pushed his chair and put his feet up on the railing of the balcony. "Why do you think he never came in to see you?"

Mark wasn't in a hurry to reply. He liked to think and stare into the day's sights. "Jack's got more shit coming down on him than he can pray over."

"Yes, you're right... the accident. He didn't see that coming. He's blaming the Yank," Josh smirked. "They'll never think to look in the tank."

"Yes, but there's still that chance. There's a full report to come in," warned Mark.

"It's worth having your help."

"We'll keep it this way. Just lie low. Don't get too cocky."

"But he brags," cautioned Josh.

"Let him brag. It's his style. Stay on task. You must get that formula done. It's all about focusing, boy." Mark's presence always gave Josh confidence. Enough to keep working the weekends out at the plant... the deal was almost over.

"I hear ya. The formulas coming on. It's got a real kick. Plenty of dickheads to test it on, eh?" answered Josh.

"I know..., but be careful and keep an eye on that plant out there," said Mark.

"Yeah, well I have to work in with Jack."

"When the time comes, we'll outsmart him. He'll wonder what's hit him. He brags. Look at the tank in the car. What does that tell you?" answered Mark.

"I know."

Mark didn't answer any further, and they sat for the rest of the day until the sun went down behind Josh's building. Mark always left in the dim of the night.

Chapter 29

George Geoffrey opened the door and put his hand out to greet her. "I'm deeply sorry, Allison." He gestured for her to take a seat and sat down opposite her.

"I don't know where to start," responded Allison.

"Why don't you start with yourself?"

"It's everything that reminds me of my Mother... my memories are so vivid. The shock is too hard to bear. Jack and the guilt I have of leaving him... and I have met a man."

"You have said too much. You can't change the past. It's the *now* that matters," cautioned George.

"Yes, but this man may be the cause of my mother's accident."

"Why would you say that?"

"Well, I have an agent, who I trust, and he tried to warn me. It's all too much."

"Where's the man now?" asked George.

"He's gone."

"Gone where, Allison?"

"Gone back to America and he didn't even say goodbye. He..." she reached for her handkerchief and George handed her a tissue box. "He was too kind to have caused the accident."

"Why would you even think he would have, Allison?"

"Well he offered to change the oil and tune-up my car. He worked on it up at the base. He's a pilot up at the American Base."

George sat there, thinking. "Hmmm, I wouldn't worry. This will all come out sooner or later." He reached over to his shelves, and pulled out a book and flicked through it. "I'd like you to do some reading."

Allison stared at him.

"You can get this book out of the library, but I'll loan it to you for a while." He turned the pages, and went on, "These building blocks are like your life. Your life comes in stages... the things that you learn when events happen, interweave to change your destiny. It is how you tackle your obstacles that builds and continually molds your character." He opened the book and read out some of the stages.

"In the beginning it's denial that drives you, then guilt... which seems to be your current stage. This man, Chuck, is gone, and there's nothing that can bring your mother back. Trying to pin blame on someone who's gone is part of your denial process. When you've had some time, you'll slowly see how things can change." He closed the book. "I know it's early days, but have you thought about what you're good at doing?"

"Well, I paint," Allison looked up from her lap.

"You paint. What sort of painting do you do?"

"Oils, on canvas. Scenes. I can take a card with a picture, any picture. It might be a painting, a photo, and I paint it." Her face brightened as she spoke, "I see what you mean... I forget who I am."

"What a fantastic talent. You are who you are, Allison, a very gifted artist. Don't forget that." He smiled at her. "You will excel. I know you will. You've suffered enough pain, you're strong underneath." He smiled again, nodding. He handed her the book and opened up his file. "Here... take this." He handed her a pamphlet. "This is for the Women's Outlook Course which gives you all the career opportunities." George stood up. "I'd like to see you again in a couple of weeks."

Allison left and sat in her car, turning the pages of the book, until she came to the last section – "Freedom".

"Freedom," she said to herself. That was her wish long ago. How could it be so far away? She threw the book down on the passenger's seat, and drove home.

Allison missed the sounds of Chris's music playing in the background. He'd been chosen for the First Eleven cricket team and was at cricket practice. The girls' chatter helped her mind heal little by little, and George's comments inspired her to pick up her paints, squeezing out ultramarine blue, titanium white, and viridian green. She thought about the papers for the creative courses she could do. She pushed her chair away and picked up the pamphlet that George had given her, went into the kitchen and rang for a booking to join the Woman's Outlook course. She picked up her paints again and sat down at her easel.

Just then, a car's engine sounded outside her room. It was Julie. She smiled at Allison through the window of her car and then came up the steps.

She threw her arms around Allison and they went into Allison's room and sat on the couch.

Julie looked at Allison's painting. "I see you've started painting again."

"Yes. It helps my mind."

"You come back to work when you feel like it."

"Thanks, but I need to do some thinking. I've booked into a course to help prepare for the work force."

I have to do something with my life I miss… I miss Chuck."

Julie reached out and hugged her, "I'm sorry. He probably made it back."

"Made it back?" Allison stared at Julie.

"I thought you knew. There was a crash down on the ice and he was the pilot. There's been an inquiry into his performances and last I heard he was shipped back to America. God knows what damage was done to the plane."

Allison went cold.

Julie went on, "Oh, that's what I meant to tell you. That night, at New Year." She set her car keys down and leaned forward, "Yes, it was on my mind to come and see you, then your mother. I never knew you were seeing him."

"It all happened so fast… and he liked coming here," replied Allison.

"Yes… that's why he never brought you up to the Base, because he didn't want to be seen with you."

"But he was so genuine."

"Allison, you've got a lot to learn about men. Anyway, I heard he had some engine trouble down on the ice."

"He probably can't call me."

"If you meant anything to him, he'd have sent word to you." Julie had a coldness about her. "I know he was charming, but there's more to it than that. Hey! I've just met this guy in this club. It's the Non Ski group and he's a nudist. Great guy. He hasn't much money, but he knows how to make love with his big equipment and chill out." Julie looked at her watch and got up to leave.

"Big equipment seems like a good idea at the time, but come the orange juice in the morning... you have a giant one-eyed snake connected to a fucked brain... looking for his next horizontal Mambo."

"Non-Ski... what a name for a club, sounds weird," commented Allison.

"Don't be so negative, dummy. Not all of us ski round here. I'll get you organized for the next meeting. There's an end-of-summer bash in the gardens down here in Mona Vale. It would do you good. You love the gardens and you'll meet women as well as men. Men that aren't out for a quick screw."

"But Chuck wasn't like that," countered Allison.

Julie didn't answer her and walked towards the door, "I'll call you about it."

Allison opened the door for Julie and said goodbye.

Allison drove like a mad woman, clutching at hope, as she raced towards the Base. She introduced herself at the entry desk of the United States Base.

"My name's Allison Brownley, and I have a friend, a Charles Bronski. He may have left a message for me."

"Just a moment," the officer came back. "No. If you write a letter, we'll forward it to the appropriate address. Sorry, these are military premises and we are not obliged to give out addresses or any other personal information about our men." Allison turned and drove home.

Sarah drove into Allison's driveway, got out of her car holding a newspaper, and hugged her.

"I know it's hard."

"Julie was over here, and I mentioned Chuck. She said he was married."

"I never knew that. I think she's making it up."

"I do too. She told me he'd had some sort of trouble down on the ice."

"Trouble! Where?" exclaimed Allison.

"I don't know. It was an accident. I've just been up to the Base to find out more, and they told me to write a letter and they would pass it on to him." Allison opened the front door and flopped down on her couch. "I'm so upset, why didn't he tell me?"

"He must be alright, otherwise why would they say to write?"

"I hadn't thought of that."

"Listen, I've got something else that'll cheer you up. You know that pen friend you had?"

"You mean Randy?" Allison reached for a tissue and blew her nose.

"Yes, well read... American men want New Zealand women to write to. There's your chance for another Chuck." Sarah patted Allison's knee.

"You're right in a way. But Jack will find out and stop it, like he did Randy."

"Jack's a lot better now. He won't bother you."

"How do you know?"

Sarah turned away and walked towards the door. Allison's painting was on the easel in the lounge. "Glad to see you're painting again. I'll commission you for one for myself next time." Sarah left Allison standing at the door, holding the newspaper and staring at the advertisement.

It felt so familiar, sitting, talking to Chuck in written words. How easy it was to pretend. She drove with the letter to the Base, and gave it to the same officer. She put the pen friend application in the mail.

Chapter 30

Allison went back one more time to visit George and take the book back. She'd read it and told him she now had hope. That's why she started to decorate and paint her house with money from her mother's estate. Allison added a conservatory that opened the lounge out into the garden. It was so much fun designing the whole project, and she was confident the Interior Decorator's course was for her. But, having children to care for, unfortunately she was not accepted.

"Are you ready, girls? Come with me... we're going to have some fun," said Jack, knocking at the door.

"Look, Daddy. We have lots of windows," said Isabel, pulling him into the lounge and the new conservatory.

"Hello," he nodded to Allison. "Can't see this will not do you any good? It should have been bulldozed. Why are you here now anyway? Your mother's gone. You need to come back."

Allison was shocked at his direct stare. "I need to come back? Why? Because I can't manage without my mother?" She stared back at him.

"Oh," he shrugged. "All this bullshit talk. You've been seeing too much of that stupid counselor. They put all this crap into your head." He moved forward, talking louder, "Listen, we're almost there with the money. A few more house sales, and we can retire for good."

"Is that all you care about... money?" asked Alliston.

"Fuck, here you go again. Fuck your Yanks. That Yank of yours was married and he's been disqualified."

Allison stared hard at him, "What do you mean?"

Jack continued ranting, "Trouble with you is you don't know the half of it. You live in such a dream world. Your Yank got charged with interfering with personal property... our car. I found out. Stupid little fool... I saw you up there at the Base. You're so obvious. Writing letters for Christ sake."

"How do you know I write letters?" asked Allison.

"How do I know? I read them."

"Rubbish... you're making this up," countered Allison.

"Alright, I'm making it up. Go write your stupid letters. See how far they get you. Live in this hole... I'm out of here," Jack turned, shrugged his shoulders and walked away towards the door. "Come on, girls."

Allison was stunned, but she led the girls towards Jack to smooth their departure. Jack's words made her all the more determined. She waved goodbye to the girls, and went into her mother's room. She had come across a photo of her mother, hairdressing her client back in the 1940's, reminding her of Snow White with the red bow in her hair. She stared lovingly at the photo. *Mother, they're all against me. Help me survive. Chuck wasn't horrible, nor was your Charlie. You looked into Charlie's eyes and instantly believed it was your destiny. Damn it*, she thought. She grabbed up the newspaper Sarah had brought. An advertisement for a nail technician jumped out at her. She would call them.

The receptionist said she'd need a Certificate, and to apply to the Southern School of Aesthetics. Allison kept her brave thoughts, dialed the number for the school, and cycled into town.

At the top of the richly carpeted staircase, in the school's elaborate foyer, were two charming men. One of them spoke precisely, "Good morning... and you must be Allison."

"Yes. Thank you for seeing me at such short notice."

"Oh, that's what we're here for. Our school is taking a new set of students right now, so you may want to consider a beauty therapy course." He smiled at her. "You're lucky, you just came at the right time. I'm Matt, by the way, and my partner is Ivan. Matt beamed at Ivan, an older man with bushy eyebrows that were obviously dyed, and brown eyes that sparkled as he spoke.

"Hello Allison. I look forward to training you," he kept smiling at her as he went on. "You feel it in your heart, this work. Both Ivan and I are very passionate, and we like to tell our students it's a lifetime commitment. We're lucky we live at Ivan's Mum's house. She helps us and supports us," he smiled over at Ivan and Allison realized they were gay. They had a look of contentment, and were open about it.

"I can show you around," said Matt, opening the door of the foyer. "This is our lounge for the students." Allison's gaze took in a burst of flowers, arranged in huge vases on the side tables of lavishly upholstered couches. "Nice, isn't it?"

"It's all so inviting up here, and you have a great view of the street out here," said Allison, walking over to the windows that ran the whole width of the room.

"Remember, ascetics my dear, always your first appearance that counts," Matt replied. He opened the side door that led into the lecture room. Allison gasped in amazement at a life-size skeleton suspended to face the rows of chairs. Enormous charts of muscles, bones, and systems of the body were pinned to the walls.

"This reminds me of my nursing days. I loved anatomy."

"Did you like nursing, Allison?"

"Yes, but I'd like this better."

"I'm sure you will. Come... I'll show you the rest of the facilities for our students." They walked back the way they came and past the reception to another door.

"This is where our practical rooms are," Matt continued.

Allison looked in at the six massage beds in a row. "But I thought you were training nail technicians?"

"Yes, we do, but that is only a night part-time short course. Sorry, I didn't realize you weren't interested in the Beauty Therapist course."

"Well now that I'm here... how long is the Beauty Therapist course, and what do you achieve?"

"The practical classes and lectures run from February to November..." Matt paused. "And as I said, it starts next week. You saw the classroom; well the study can be as much as Third Year Medical training. It's

a huge commitment, but at the end, you are a fully qualified Aesthetician."
He looked at her and said, "It's the gateway to a reputable profession. You
can open your own business."

"What time and days are the classes?" asked Allison

"They run in the morning, and you go home and study in the
afternoon." He walked into the small room for the nail technician training.
"If you're looking for something more achievable, my advice is the Beauty
Therapy course. The Nail course is only for three months part time. But at
the end of the day, it's up to you; I know it doesn't give you much time."

Allison followed him back out to the reception area. "I'm not saying I
disagree with you. It's a lot to take in... and I have children to think of."

"We'll need some school certificates, something to show us your
qualifications. The rest is up you."

"I'll be right back with my papers."

"Great, then we'll see you back this afternoon." They both smiled at
her as she left them standing, watching her leave.

Allison was excited at her instant decision. She sat in her kitchen. Six
thousand dollars, Matt had said. She grabbed the phone and dialed the
number for information about a Government grant. It was possible, and she
could pay it back when she started work.

It would be a struggle, already being on a government benefit. Allison
jumped on her bicycle and cycled over to Jack's. She still had a key, and hoped
it would fit. She opened the door and walked into their bedroom to get the
papers out of the cupboard. Facing her, a woman's cosmetics tray lay on her
dressing table, all neatly placed into a beautiful display of drawers. A mirror
sat by the bedside. A pair of stilettos were on the floor by the far side of the
bed. The side Allison had once slept in. Allison stood there staring, aghast.
She didn't want to pick them up. *Who did they belong to?* The size puzzled her.
Without trying them on... they seemed larger than her shoe size. Over at the
wardrobe, she looked inside where her clothes once hung. There were a
couple of coats and a dressing gown, unfamiliar to her. She fingered them
and looked in the labels. They had numbers, a size ten, and yet it was big for
a ten. She stooped down to get her box of papers, when a piece of jewelry
caught her eye - a bracelet with paua and silver leaf design. She'd seen that

bracelet somewhere before. It was not hers. She left it lying there, and took her papers out of the box, left the house, and cycled back into town to the Southern School of Aesthetics.

Chapter 31

The first morning for her classes were like being back at nursing school.

"Mummy, you're dressed like a nurse," said Lucy, giggling to Isabel.

"Yes, and you're not biking with us," said Isabel.

"No, I'm not, but you be careful crossing that road with Lucy."

"Yes Mummy, we'll be fine… but you're going to look silly. You'll get your white clothes dirty riding your bike."

"No, I won't," and she waved goodbye to them as they set off safely through the Park to school.

Allison rode out her gate, her feet firmly on the pedals, her new white uniform tucked up between her legs, out of the way of the bicycle chain, but she still worried about Sarah's activities. She arrived to find easy bicycle parking right outside the school. Groups of girls in white uniforms with red cardigans were making their way across the road and up the stairs. Allison merged into the throng of unfamiliar, but friendly faces.

The plush red and yellow carpet splashed its way up the stairs and across the student's recreational room. Allison quietly lowered herself into one of the richly upholstered red velvet couches, and glanced around the room at the other students chatting to each other. She wondered what her class was going to be like. There were age groups ranging from twenty-year-olds to some in their thirties.

A buzzer went and a woman with blonde ponytail came in, dressed similarly to Allison, but with a large black and gold badge on her uniform. She called out ten names, "Allison Brownley" one of them. Allison stepped forward and followed the other nine students into a side room. The tutor wasn't much older than the youngest student in the class, but very professional.

"Good morning girls. My name is Robin and I'm going to be taking you for your practical studies and duties. Today I'm going to be handing out papers on hygiene. I'll hand out notes and we'll be having a questionnaire tomorrow." She looked across at the group. "I'd like everyone to introduce themselves. We will be spending the rest of the year together, so let's start with you," she pointed to the woman standing next to Allison at the end of the row.

"Hello, my name is Gwen Thomas. I'm here to be a therapist. I'm not a beauty, but by the time all the crèmes go on I might be, except for these...," and she pointed to her thighs.

Everyone laughed.

Allison's turn gave her a chance to speak about herself. She took in a long breath, "Hello everyone, my name is Allison Brownley," she hesitated for a split second. All eyes were on her, and suddenly tears came to her eyes. She swallowed hard and continued, "I'm here because I want to support myself and my family." She looked around, "I went nursing a long time ago and this is even better. I even want to open my own business one day."

"Well, there you are girls. That's a good start. Allison has visions of success already."

The rest of the students had a mixture of reasons; another one had similar views of working for herself, and had already started her business.

The morning flew by with a morning tea break at eleven, and class finished at one o'clock.

Allison left the building with the other students, splitting off in all directions. She rode home a different way, past the duck ponds, leading to the tearooms and the greenhouses of Hagley Park. She felt the warm sun on her back and the breeze on her face, as she made her way up Fendalton Road, and through the Park until arriving home. She knew now she would have many wonderful experiences, and meet new friends, and hoped Gwen would be one of them. Throwing her backpack down, she wiggled the faucet for a glass of water, fell back onto her chair in her old room, and sighed in satisfaction.

Chris appeared out of nowhere through the doorway with his ball cap jammed on his head.

"Been riding in the park?' he asked her with a cheeky grin.

Allison didn't answer him.

Chris walked off back to his room. He had become a recluse and this worried her. His actions were hard to predict, and she had caught him smoking outside with his friends. Later that afternoon, the girls came running in.

"Mummy... did you get to play nurses?"

"Not really, dear, but I met my classmates and they have uniforms like me, and I have homework like you."

"I've got a book to read out loud," said Lucy. "The teacher said I can't read."

"We'll take a look at that, but we'll get a drink and something to eat first, eh Lucy?"

Lucy ran back down the passageway, and came back out tucking her top into one of the gathered skirts Mattie had made her.

"Look, I have one of Nana's skirts on."

"Nana would love that, Lucy."

After the evening meal, Allison helped Lucy read and then finally sat down in the kitchen, and began the new routine of studying until late.

Next day, in the lecture room, Gladys, the retired nurse, gave them their first assignment. She pointed at the muscle chart Allison had noted when she first saw the lecture room with Matt.

"Your first assignment is on muscles," she looked out at the classroom of students. "Now... if you recite all these Latin anatomical names out loud, eventually they will stick in your minds. Write them out; say them out loud often. Her wrinkled face was stern, as she leaned on her lecture stand. Her notes were precise and Allison knew she had to concentrate.

Allison rode home from class, into the wind, across the Park, and almost ran into the open letterbox. Throwing her bike down, she snatched up the letters that had slipped out of the box. She gasped at the American stamps and carried the letters inside, threw off her backpack, grabbed a drink of water, and sat down to find Chuck's handwriting. A photo slipped out onto her lap - a small square instant photo, thick in texture, of a stranger, a man in his twenties. Skimming over the introductions, she opened another letter, ripping at the envelope, and another, and another.

The letters started with simple messages like

"Dear Allison,

I've never been to New Zealand, but I'd like to come someday."

One envelope had a comic picture on the front. Inside was a brochure of a cycling tour and read,

Hello to you, Downunder,

My name is Paul, I have two sons, Dave and Larry. I am hoping to visit your part of the world in April 1991.

She looked at the date. Why two years ago? She skimmed over the rest and put them to one side. Another, bigger envelope drew her attention. She opened it to find a brochure of a company, with a picture of trucks and something blasting out of a pipe. A business card fell out. A company owner. Looking again in the envelope, she found a photo, and some postage reply coupons! Allison stared at the happy face of a man standing underneath a tree, in a striped shirt with his hands in his trouser pockets. He had good skin, something Allison found important now. She found herself automatically studying everyone's skin. He sported a moustache, and brown hair with a tinge of grey appearing at the sides of his temples.

Dear Allison,

"My name is Buster Turner. I am a white male, born in 1942, divorced, five foot nine inches and 157lbs."

Allison smiled at this fresh approach and read on. She had almost reached to the bottom of the pile when she opened a small envelope, lined yellow paper. It read,

"Hello Allison, my name is Terry Ross, and I am in the United States Navy. I want to explain my circumstances before you decide to write to me. I got involved in the "Iran Contra Affair" with Oliver North. I was trying to free hostages in another country. Now because of the scandal, the whole thing has escalated, and for the men involved, we have no rights and remain guilty of the crime attributed to us.'

I am a writer and I am temporarily discharged, until this mess gets cleared. Should you read this and want to know more, I'd love to hear from you.

Yours truly,

Terry Ross.

Allison could hear the girls coming up the drive, and quickly ran to her room, stuffing the letters away in her cedar trunk box.

In the calm of the evening, Allison sat down on her bed and re-read the letters. It was hard deciding which one to write to. She had picked out postcards to write short messages of thanks to those she thought she would not keep writing to.

The military man appealed to her. His message was honest. Perhaps not like Chuck. She was beginning to think he had deceived her. It made her sad as she picked up the pen to write to Terry Ross.

CHAPTER 32

Julie called about the Non Ski group. It was a nice diversion from all the study. She parked her car and, as she stepped out, a bird flew over and crapped all over her jacket.

"Shit happens," she laughed, brushing at her jacket with a moist napkin. She hurried to join the meeting.

Men and women stood under a huge oak tree, past the circular driveway, in front of the Victorian homestead, part of the Dean's estate back in 1899. The building, a picture-book story of England, with its peaked roof and gable, Tudor half-timbering and white walls, nestled amongst huge conifers and maples. Part of the ground floor had been converted into a café, opening out onto the porch overlooking the garden outdoor café. Allison saw Julie waving at her.

"Glad you could make it. What happened to your jacket?" asked Julie with an obligatory smile.

"Oh it's bird-shit... I have been anointed," Allison rubbed at it again, this time with another moist napkin.

"This is Allison, everyone."

"Hello," said Allison with a smile. "Sorry about my jacket. I don't always come out with a dirty jacket. A bird dive-bombed me."

"Oh no, we can't have that. Go home and change," laughed a tall man, standing at the back of the group.

"Okay, now that everyone is here," Julie said, ignoring the heckler, "we'll go over by the Avon. There's a nice place to sit and chat."

The group followed Julie along the twisting pathway to the water. Beneath the huge trees, gardens were ablaze with rhododendrons and azaleas, reminding Allison of her father and the garden he loved.

"Which way did you come from?" one of the women in the group asked, interrupting her thoughts. "By the way, my name's Betsy."

"Just up the road, across through the Park," said Allison, turning around to smile at her. "Oh, and I'm Allison... What about you?"

"I live across the road," pointing beyond the tennis courts to a street that ran beside the rail tracks. A group of tourists arrived in a bus, and all got out to stand and admire the flowered bank. Some of them had brought food and threw crumbs at the ducks, which had come out of nowhere, deafening everyone with their quacking.

"I'm Gary, anyway, ladies," he shouted over the ducks. "It's my first time with the Non Ski Group," he laughed, "Yerrr and I don't ski, I'm a builder." He bent down to pass under the hanging branches, as he caught up with them. "Today is my day off. What do you ladies do?"

"I am a publisher for a magazine, and I'm new, too. I've recently moved back here from Australia," Betsy quickly replied.

"So you're an Aussie, eh?"

"No... I'm from New Zealand. Can't you tell?"

"Sorry, you're right. You don't have that twang." He turned to Allison, "And, what about you, young lady?"

"I'm studying to be a Beauty Therapist."

"Sounds glamorous. Anything you can do for a sun-scorched builder?"

Allison giggled, looking at Betsy. He was tall and muscular, and she liked his sense of humor.

The afternoon was relaxing, sitting on the soft grass. The time passed quickly, and when it came time to leave, Allison walked back to the car with Julie.

"So how did you like our group?" asked Julie.

"Yes, I enjoyed it, thank you. I have Betsy's number. She lives over there," Allison pointed to the tennis court.

"See! I told you you'd meet nice people and they don't always have to be men."

Allison opened the car door, winding the window down.

"The builder was friendly, Gary, but I'm not sure about a man-friend right now."

"He'll have your number, but women friends won't let you down, remember that," said Julie leaning against the car. "How's everything going?"

"Sarah's put me on to a pen friend column. It's quite exciting and should be pretty harmless… just writing letters."

"She'd like that."

"Why?"

Oh, nothing. I see Jack up at work quite a bit, and Sarah sometimes dines with him."

"Sarah was with him when the accident happened. I don't think anything else is going on. She's married, but that doesn't seem to slow Jack down."

"So was Chuck," replied Allison.

Julie walked away towards the group.

Allison started up the engine, and waved at Julie.

Soon after the meeting at Mona Vale, Gary had called to invite Allison over for a meal. He was a basic cook, and Allison couldn't help but feel relaxed in his company. It was the first time Allison could feel comfortable in a man's company in a while.

Betsy's location was only a walk away, and the two women quickly became friends. Betsy sounded excited when she told Allison about the new bar that had opened in town, and they talked about going one evening.

But Allison's classes took up most of her time and making new friends was not always a priority. The first part of the practical sessions had concentrated on nail applications. Allison found it hard to focus with the acrid chemical smell of the nail polish remover, making her feel sick. She was glad she hadn't become a nail technician after practicing nail applications over and over again.

Robin had moved them to the room with the six beds where they began their next phase of training.

"Good morning ladies," Ivan said, swishing in, wearing a short white coat. "I'm Ivan. I'm going to be demonstrating the art of facial massage." He spoke with commitment, looking around the room. "Now who is going to be the lucky one? How about you, Allison?"

"Well, yes, of course."

"Then I'll have someone get her ready."

Allison lay on the massage bed, wearing a slip-on gown with her shoulders bare, ready for the first part of the procedure. She closed her eyes at the touch of his hands. Ivan's hands moved slowly but deftly, touching the pressure points and molding her face. It felt like a dream. This was an art that could not be learned easily.

Allison was full of enthusiasm when she moved her old treatment bed in the sunroom back into the side room by the garage, where she planned to have her clinic.

Allison moved the old sundeck lounger into the sunroom. It was going to be her first massage table, only she had to kneel to practice. Isabel was going to be Allison's first client. She lay patiently, with her little face up, in anticipation for what was to come.

"This is fun, Mummy. What are you going to do to me?" Allison placed a head band around Isabel's auburn curls to pull her hair away from her face.

"Close your eyes. I have to cleanse your skin and start by placing my hands on your forehead. Ivan says to connect with your client."

"Who's Ivan?" said Isabelle, opening her eyes again.

"Our director. Now close your eyes... and feel our new connection."

Isabel wriggled back down the lounger. Allison went through the motions, teaching her hands to become the hands of a potter, to mold, to shape, just like Ivan.

Robin had also prepared them for their first class in electrolysis.

"Today I'm going to demonstrate just how careful you have to be to insert this tiny needle into the skin," said Robin, holding up the packet of needles. It was passed around the class. When it was Allison's turn to study the needle, she stared at its tip. She could hardly see it.

"You girls practice on each other's legs. We won't be working on the face until you are proficient at careful and exacting needle insertion."

Everyone looked at each other in great expectation. Needles into their legs and their faces showed horror.

"I'll have one of you up on the bed please."

At first there was a pause, but Allison moved across and spoke, "I don't mind."

The rest of the students crowded around and Robin sat down, put on some disposable gloves and spread an area of Allison's leg with white meth's to sterilize. "Now see how I angle the needle. Why do you think that is?"

"Because that's the angle of the hair follicle," said one of the brighter students, who was always answering the questions.

"Yes, and that's why you have to know that skin diagram off by heart. The follicle doesn't just come up like grass seed. You'll burst through the wall of the follicle if you don't follow it."

Allison felt nothing but the sharp stab of the needle, and a sudden jolt of electricity and heat. Then Robin slid out the dead hair. She took off her gloves and pointed to Gwen, the student that sat opposite her in class. Gwen repeated the procedure, and poised the needle ready to insert. Allison waited, gripping the side of the bed. It was a sharp pain. "Now girls, I want you to study that part in your text books over the next few days, and we'll begin needle insertions on Monday."

Allison rode home, picking up speed as she rode through the Park; she skidded her bike to a halt and bent down to open the letterbox. She recognized his large scrawl, spread across the envelope. A parcel from Terry. She threw her bike down and rushed to unlock the door. It was already open.

"Chris, are you home?" She walked inside and put her things down in her room. She heard a crash from the back room. She ran to see what had fallen, and flung open the door to Chris's room. Chris was lying half dazed on the floor.

"What the heck…"

"Shut the fuck up," said Chris, rubbing his head. He looked up at Allison. She could see his pale face and blood-shot eyes. He glared at her, and got up and slammed his bedroom door in front of her.

L M HEDRICK 201

Allison stood there. She had never seen this behavior before in him. She left the hallway and closed her bedroom door. She sat there for a while, staring out her window. She could hear squeaking noises coming from the trees outside her window. She recognized the sound. She peered out. There they were two fantails, flitting amongst the branches, showing off their fans. She felt like it was her mother calling her - whistling to her. She always said they were the first sign of winter.

Later that evening, Chris had music playing in his room.

"Chris are you okay?" said Allison, poking her head around the door.

"Yes, why?"

"You startled me today. You were still in bed when I came back from school."

"Oh, you're out too much in that Park," Chris laughed.

Allison shook her head and closed his door. She said goodnight to the girls and went into her bedroom. She reached inside her cedar trunk box. Terry's handwriting was scribbled on a large envelope, and Allison found her fingers trembling to tear open the paper. Out tumbled a book and photo. It was a photo of Terry, standing, smiling at her. He was leaning up against a wall, wearing blue jeans, with a white shirt tucked in at the waist and one leg crossed in front, to display a very smart pair of cowboy boots. She picked up the book. A younger version of Terry, among the six men in the picture on the front cover. A chill ran over her as she held the book and looked at the weapons. All this had to be true. She looked inside at the publishing rights - a well-known publishing house in New York. She had a celebrity on her hands, and he had picked her to be his friend and confidant. She opened the letter.

"Hello again.

I know you won't be disappointed with your decision to keep writing to me. Let me tell you more of my career. I was drafted to Vietnam. The survival was very difficult and hard to relay to the American citizens when we returned home. Some of us got spat on and lost our identity. This is mainly my story. I got involved with Oliver North, while he was in Vietnam, and then later went on to get involved with the Iran Contra Affair. A scandal the United States wish they never had. The President could turn a blind eye, but had to have a scapegoat to run the course. You see we had to free American hostages, and to do this... weapons were what the kidnappers wanted. But that was an extremely embarrassing thing for the people in command to admit. I was part of the U.S. Green Beret in North Vietnam - seven crack special operatives. I wrote this book under a pseudonym along with another partner. It was a suicide mission. We were sent to kill Chinese political leaders. Once in our assigned mission, we had no outside support. We relied on each other. We had individual skills that enabled us to survive the treacherous jungle. I was the medic in the team. Leeches were sucking our blood, sores arose from wet clothes, and a lack of sleep were daily dramas. We were constantly on maximum alert. Nobody will ever appreciate what we went through. You'll see my photo is on the front cover with my teammates. This is not a figment of my imagination. I'm sorry to sound sarcastic but when you've been detained for acts of bravery so that others can benefit from a free democracy, I get a bit annoyed.

I will elaborate more as we go along, as I think about how this is going to unravel.

Your Pen pal, Terry"

Who was more dangerous, Terry or Jack? thought Allison.

Chapter 33

The silence of the house brought anxious thoughts to Allison, and Chris was beginning to worry her. She had text books and study, which soon occupied her doubting mind. That evening she put her study down, and crashed on her bed. She picked up Terry's book by her bed, and started to read. As she skimmed the story, she found the descriptions frightening and intense. The reader learns of the brave men, shooting as many of the Viet Cong as possible as they charged in for the kill. They constantly faced ambushes when they were so close to being captured. The main character in the story shot the first "Charlie" straight through the neck, and he somersaulted backward down the steep hillside. Allison kept reading the gory details when suddenly the phone went and startled her...

"Don't let the bed bugs bite."

"Is that you, Terry?"

"Course it's me who else would it be?"... There was silence.

She couldn't remember what happened. The phone must have gone dead. She was sure someone was in the room.

She was wakened when lights shined on her. For a moment, she was captured in a Viet Cong tunnel. The lights became brighter, and there was a loud sound of an engine running, like gun shells. She fell out of bed, peering into the lit stained glass window. Was she being ambushed herself? Her heart raced. The engine kept running.

She scrambled across the living area, trying to dodge the gleaming lights. She could hear loud voices, over the sound of the engine. Then the engine became quieter as Allison reached the front door. She could see a crumpled form lying on the driveway in the light of the reversing car.

"You can have him," shouted the voices, as they backed out the driveway. She opened the door to this battlefield jungle. But this was not a dream. She ran towards the form and bent over it. It was Chris. She tried to move him. She rushed inside. She thought he must be sick, filled a pot with cold water, and went back out. It was dark and nobody was around. He moaned as she poured the water on to his face. His eyes suddenly opened, he looked up at her, and sat up.

"Who the fuck…," he yelled, wiping the water out of his eyes. He pulled himself up, and lunged forward at her with new vitality and staggered to the front door.

"Chris, you're hurt, let me help you."

"Get out of my way… get out! Who are you?" He had a glazed look in his eye.

"It's your mother," answered Allison.

He pushed past her and slammed the door shut. Allison found herself staring at him through the front glass. She was outside in the dark pounding the door. Chris swayed, and went for the glass door.

"Get out, Go away."

Allison took a step backwards, and landed down on the concrete. Thick blood fell out from her head onto the concrete. Thick and fast. *The shock must have brought on an attack*, she thought to herself. She lay there wondering what to do. She began to cry, but nothing was going to help her. The house was in darkness and there was no sign of Chris. She stood up and more blood flowed. She stumbled past that same corner of the rhododendron bush, rounded the rear corner and slid open the old door at the back of the house. Allison entered and stood for a moment watching Chris breathe. He was so silent, so still.

The next morning, Allison ran the shower as she waited for Chris to wake. Finally, late morning he stumbled out of the sunroom, rubbing his eyes.

"What was I doing in there?"

"You were dumped in the driveway about three in the morning."

Chris stopped and looked at her.

"You wouldn't drink like that, would you?" asked Allison.

"I sure as hell would. Okay... Okay. I've been drinking. So what's new?"

"Drinking, drugs, or both? You abused me," shouted Allison, following him down to his bedroom. "You're not responsible? You're missing school. You're not studying. You're out drinking, damn you... acting like a bum."

"Look, forget it. Last time you went riding off, over to those stupid counselors, what did they do? They said it was nothing. Don't go on. I can't remember what happened last night. I just can't." He slammed his door.

Allison ran out to the conservatory, holding her head.

Later, Chris came out and sat down. He was silent like the day of the tragedy. He got up to leave.

"You can't touch Nana's money. That's mine." Chris picked up his cricket gear and went towards the door. He left, and Allison sat watching him cycle off towards the park.

•   •   •   •   •

Allison sat in Doctor Taylor's room. She was having trouble again with her menstrual flow. He was quiet and looked up at her with just a curious smile.

He looked at his computer for her notes. "When did you last have a smear test?"

"Back in Chicago... they were to send the results to the hotel, but I left."

Dr Taylor made a face and went on typing. He got up and showed Allison into his side room, and once more she had to endure the same procedure and wait for the tests.

"We can request those results urgently, but we'll have to wait and see," advised Dr Taylor.

Allison left and hoped it would be nothing.

The next day Allison was late finishing school. She had a lot on her mind. She biked into the driveway, and noticed Chris playing with the girls in the conservatory. She could see they were all on the floor, scrambling around with the girls screaming. Allison threw her bike down and rushed to join them.

"Mummy, look what Chris has brought home."

"Well for goodness sake, where did you get it?" Allison bent down to touch and pat the tiny kitten. It let out a small cry and its little teeth munched into the straw matt.

"Jenny's parents," said Chris moving forward to catch it.

"Chris's got a girlfriend." said Lucy looking up at Allison, half squeezing the kitten. "Look Mummy, it's hungry. Mummy, can we keep it?"

"Don't do that," said Isabel, pushing Lucy over. "Mummy, Lucy's mean."

"No, we won't be keeping it. Look you're frightening it already."

"Can we take it to Dad's?" asked Isabel.

"We'll see," Allison got up. The kitten ran after her. "Do you want something to eat?" she said bending down to pick it up. She looked at its little face. "You've got lots of whiskers, haven't you? What is it, a boy or a girl?" she called back to the three faces following her.

"It's a boy, and his name is Monty," said Chris. "That's the first decent thing that's come here. You sure as heck don't have any decent friends."

"I beg your pardon. You apologize for that, after all I've done for you," scolded Allison.

Chris had gone back to school. Having the kitten seemed to give him a sense of belonging.

•　　•　　•　　•　　•

Jack's car arrived early and he beckoned Allison to come outside. He never came to the door anymore, but usually perched like a King with the engine running.

"What's this bullshit about my giving Chris drink. Eh? You're always thinking of something."

"I am?... and what the heck were you doing over here when I'm at school?"

"School's for kids you dumb shit. Get a life and leave mine alone."

"Daddy, Daddy. Look what we've got," Isabelle held up the basket with Monty, swinging from the basket with his white paws poking out, and his tiny face mewing at him.

Jack's face froze. "You're not bringing that fleabag into my house."

"But Daddy... Mummy says it's okay."

"Get in then," said Jack, staring at Allison. "Where'd you get this stray, eh? Same place as your other strays?" He shook his head at her, "Trouble with you is you're fucked in the head. I warned you, don't make any more trouble." He backed down the driveway with the girls and Monty.

•　　•　　•　　•　　•

The results came back from the tests Allison had done, and she had to go into hospital for a short stay. It was a repair and a cone biopsy. Doctor Taylor was more concerned about getting Allison into hospital than worrying about the last smear test in Chicago.

It was the end of the term and Jack had taken the girls. Allison was able to recover and Jack had seemed to be very nice when he called for the girls.

Chris was doing well at school and Monty had several trips over to Jack's. The car rolled slowly up the driveway at the end of the weekend. Allison felt better, and could see the happy faces on the girls as they opened their car doors.

Isabel held the kitten in the basket, and raced in the door, "Mummy, we're back!"

"Hello, how's Monty doing?" said Allison, going out to Jack's car.

"Bloody cat. Pissed and shit in my shoes! It's not coming back over, that's for sure!"

"It's only a kitten. It has to be trained, Jack."

"Well, I'm not ruining all my shoes. You can buy me some more. It was your stupid idea in the first place."

"Anyway hope you got yourself fixed up. I can't be a nursemaid."

"No one's saying you can. I'm better now. Did you ever see a letter come from the hospital in Chicago?"

"No, why would I? It's your bloody problem, not mine."

Allison shrugged, and left him staring at her as she went inside and closed the door. The girls were giggling.

"Mummy it was so funny. Dad's shoes were the potty for Monty." Isabel kept laughing.

"Did you help Dad clean up?"

"Of course we did. We took all Dad's shoes out of the closet."

"Yes, and I helped," said Lucy, grabbing at Monty as he ran outside.

"I didn't leave anything of mine back there did I?"

"No, only a bracelet, and Dad said I could have it. He said he found it."

"Can I see it?'

Isabel pulled out her arm. Allison felt a rush of guilt run over her. It was the bracelet she'd seen on the floor.

Chapter 34

Winter had come quickly, and Allison had hardly noticed the barren scene out her windows. A sharp pang of anxiety flashed by Allison, as she took a brown envelope postmarked District Court out of the letterbox. She walked back inside and sat down, fumbling to open the envelope. "Coroner's Report" was the heading.

She began to read quickly. Her vision blurred, but the strong black typing wouldn't go away. It was the report from the driver of the ambulance stating that he received an emergency call and it was given code blue 50. That indicates a siren and lights. Approaching the intersection, he stated he would normally slow down, but he had the green light at the intersection. Then he saw another vehicle come around the corner without stopping. He tried to brake, but it was too late. His foot was heavy on the brake when he hit the car.

Allison put her hand up to her mouth and sucked in a gush of air, as if to synchronize with her mother's last breath. Oh my God! Mattie was taken to the emergency department was found to be dead on arrival.

Why are these words so cold... so cruel... "dead on arrival". She couldn't finish; tears streamed down her face. It was too soon, too raw. She peeked once more at the answer. Dead on arrival - *her own dear mother, just a statistic*. The report went on to say she had suffered head injuries, and the cause of death was a fracture and dislocation of the cervical spine. She closed the report and wept.

She sat there awhile and put the report back in its envelope when she noticed the Police report on the car. Further Inquiry Stating the Condition of the Vehicle. It stated that the ambulance was a Bedford make and all connections proved to be satisfactory but the yellow car owned by Allison Brownley - she stared at the statement – *had undergone extensive tests, and the conclusion was classified.*

Later that evening, there was a knock at the door. Tom stood there.

"Tom... You surprise me," exclaimed Allison.

"I was in the area. Can I come in?" Tom bent down as he always did, as he came inside. His hair was longer than usual, and he had a haunted look about him, but his eyes were still kind and intense. "You got a letter from the Court?"

"How did you know?" said Allison, catching his gaze, and showing him into the conservatory.

"Well... the car; I knew you would want to know. They did question that friend of yours, and because of the military, they were not at liberty to say."

"So what does that mean?"

"I looked into it, and there's nothing. Your friend didn't do anything."

"Well thank goodness." Allison leaned back on her chair. "Thank goodness."

"I knew you'd be pleased. It's a mystery how it stalled... your mother must have had a bad moment." He sighed and shared Allison's moment of doubt and turned around.

"Wow. You've done this place up nicely."

"I wanted to make it like a home. I love light and the open spaces. It seemed a waste... and dreary... all those little windows. Jack hates the idea of my staying here."

"Still going on with it?"

"Of course... the accident." She turned back to face him. "What did you really think?"

"Yes, it was a set up."

"In what way?"

"I almost got framed. Mark Fenton would wish me dead. I thought I'd warn you to watch your back."

"You know... I never know who to trust."

"Yes, well you aren't playing a simple game Allison. Things leak out."

Allison frowned and looked over at him.

Tom continued, "Christchurch is a small place, and whatever you do around here, if it's something different... people talk." Tom walked over past the conservatory, towards her room.

"Yes I know they do. Everyone thinks I'm crazy doing this Beauty Therapy Course. One of my friends thinks I'll never make it. It's a luxury people can't afford... so they say."

"I wouldn't say that. I admire you. Look at everything you've done so far." Tom stood by her room and looked around the corner. "This stained glass window. Did you design that?" he moved about to admire it from her room.

"Yes I did."

"You're so artistic. The peacock on the branch with the sun behind it, the colors, and it shines into your room. Well done, Allison." He put a hand on her shoulder.

"Thanks, I love it, and I get to wake up to it every day."

Tom gave her a quick hug, and moved away towards the photo frame, sitting on the corner of her dressing table.

"It's my pen friend." said Allison, picking it up to show him.

He took it and stared into it. "What? This is the man you were seeing?"

"No. It's really my pen friend... we have never met."

Tom handed her the photo back.

"I've lots of passions, and writing letters is one of them. It's fun... and harmless."

"Do you know much about his background? May I?" Tom studied his face, and put it down again with a frown.

"I know enough to trust him. Look at this," and she showed him the book.

"You're a gutsy lady," said Tom, taking the book and flicking through it. "So he wrote this?"

"Yes, under a pen name. That's him in the back row." Allison pointed, and leaned in against him.

Tom stood still staring at the cover.

Allison could sense his breath on her.

Tom put the book down, and turned to leave.

She had a great respect for him and his opinion, and followed him out of the room.

"So what do you think?"

"If you need me for anything, I'm only a phone call away."

Tom left her watching him walk down the drive.

Allison was glad to lock the door and go to bed. It wasn't too late to call Betsy. She answered the phone almost at once.

"Hello, I thought I'd give you a nighttime call. I'm not too late, am I?"

"No, I was just off to bed."

"I'm in bed. I got this book in the mail from Terry, my pen friend. It looks gruesome."

"You be careful."

"I had the same pep talk from Tom, who just left."

"Who's Tom? I can't keep up with all your men friends... how did you get on with Gary?" asked Betsy.

"He's going to look at moving over here to a place I told him about behind mine... and he's going to give me a quote on building onto the room out the back of my garage. And Tom, he's the private investigator. I told you about him. He doesn't contact me very often, but when he does, it's at a funny time. Like tonight...late. He's done that before. Kind of spooks me out," responded Allison.

"I bet it does."

"Anyway, about this book. I'm a bit of a sadist. I love horror movies. I can't help myself... I can't wait to read it."

"Well, I better let you get on with it," said Betsy laughing. "I'll pick you up tomorrow night for the country bar, if you're still alive."

They both laughed, and Allison hung up the phone and settled down to read the book.

The next night Betsy called by in her new sports car. She hopped onto the driveway, "I see you've got your cowboy boots on."

"Well, if you can call them that," said Allison, getting into the passenger's seat. "Wow, who needs flash cowboy boots, when you've got this little beauty," Allison turned and smiled to Betsy.

Betsy nodded, half listening to the music. "Bourbon Street Bar is not too far," she yelled out over the music. They rounded the corner, past Bellamy Labs, and Allison smiled to herself as they parked the car. "Come on, we might get a lesson if we hurry."

They ran up the stairs to the sound of country music and boots stomping all together on the wooden floor. At the top of the stairs they could see cowboy hats moving to the music. Betsy and Allison went straight for the bar and ordered a beer each. Betsy had a twinkle in her eye, as she stood next to a tall man sporting a huge brass belt buckle, and she nodded to him. Allison smiled as she recalled the old adage "The bigger the belt buckle... the smaller the penis."

"Are we in time for the line dancing?" Betsy asked the man. She was petite like Allison, only her hair was dark and her eyes were brown. She had become fascinated with Allison's story of how she met Chuck, and his American charm. The man smiled at her and offered to pay for their drinks.

"Why I wouldn't hear of ladies buying their own drinks," he said in his Southern drawl, tipping his cowboy hat. Sitting next to him was a face Allison was sure she'd seen before. The man looked across, and smiled instantly at her. He got up from his seat and came over.

"Howdy, didn't we meet up the road?"

"Yes, you're Bill. Oh my God. Why are you here?"

"It's our midwinter drop. We're down to help with the loads, but too cold to shut the engines down – so it is in and out as quick as we can. It's so nice to see y'all again."

"Betsy, this is Bill. He talks rreeeaaallll slow," Allison turned to Betsy.

"Oh, come now," Betsy moved over to Bill's table, lifted her glass at Bill. "Let's make a toast to these wonderful American men," she laughed.

"Bill, can you tell me anything about the plane crash, the one that happened at the end of the season?"

"Weeeeell," said Bill scratching his head. "If I can recall, there was a plane had some runway trouble. It was the pilot had more trouble than the plane."

Allison's voice trembled, "Who was that?"

"I don't know his name offhand, sorry." He took a drink of his beer and seemed to sink into his chair and gaze at the bar.

"None of this conversation is going anywhere, if you ask me," said Betsy.

"I'll drink to that," said the man next to her. "My name's Al, by the way," and he put his hand out to shake hands. He wore a cowboy hat, and appeared very friendly.

The music started, and one of the men was up on the stage calling out steps.

"Come on ladies, it's time to dance," Al leaped onto the dance floor.

Allison and Betsy put down their drinks and joined him, but Bill sat and watched. Allison stood in line next to Betsy, away from Al who seemed to want to take over the floor.

"A grape vine, kick ball change, now turn," called out the man on the stage, to the tune of Boot Scootin' Boogie. Everyone moved in synchrony, some bumping into each other, with the beat carrying them through, until they repeated the movements, laughing at each other.

Allison couldn't help staring at the tight jeans and cowboy boots on the men in front of her, and wondered what Terry was really like. Chuck hadn't danced this way. How much she wished she could dance with Chuck. The subtle whine of the songs, and the country lyrics soothed her soul. She danced until the heat of the night ran through her cotton tee shirt. Betsy was such a good companion as she laughed, and seemed to focus on the same men. The music stopped, and they went back to join Bill who was now standing by the bar.

"Why don't you dance with us?" asked Allison taking a huge gulp of her beer.

"No ma'am. I have two left feet, when it comes to dancin'. I just wanted to say goodnight, and it was a pleasure meeting y'all again. I'll stay in touch if you like?"

"That would be nice." Allison wrote down her address and handed it to him.

He didn't say anything but nodded and left. Betsy called out, "Don't forget to tell us when you're coming back."

They arrived back at Allison's, and sat with glasses of orange juice to finish off the night.

"It's thirsty work alright," said Betsy taking a mouthful of orange. "Where did you meet that hunk?"

"Bill?... up at the base. He's a good friend of Julie's. Very quiet. I get the feeling he's happy to have the world pass him by."

"Yes, but he's not stupid... not when it comes to planes. Only the very, very best pilots come here for the mid-winter drop."

"No, you're right. I've got something to show you."

Allison got up and brought Terry's book out. Betsy put her orange juice down, opened the cover, and then looked back at the front cover.

"Which one's him?"

"The one with glasses."

"How do you know it's him?"

"Everyone's saying that. But take a look at this." Allison went and got the photo. "See the eyes, rather large ears, and the dimple on the chin and his hands."

"Yes, but he still could have a double." Betsy put the photo down, and brought out Buster's photo.

"Now, he's nice. Where's he?" Betsy moved the photo closer and smiled at Buster.

"He lives in Los Angeles. He has four kids and a huge court case going on. I didn't write back to him. He's not a potential lover."

"Oh, come on, Allison. That has to be built slowly, you should know that." She put the photo down.

They finished their orange juice, and Allison said goodnight to Betsy. She closed the curtains and got ready for bed. Down the passageway, she heard something. Her heart raced and she peered around the corner. A figure was standing at the door.

She knew it would be Tom, and opened the door. "Ohhh...Bill, what a surprise?"

"I'm sorry to bother you so late."

Bill was fumbling with his pockets, and had this strange way about him that Allison noticed at the bar. He took a crumpled letter out of his pocket and handed it to her.

"I got a surprise to see you tonight. Are you not living with your husband?"

"Why... who would ever tell you that?"

"Chuck. That's why he gave me this letter. He wanted to make sure you received it. You asked me about the plane. It's confidential who the pilot was, but I think you know."

"I'm sorry, I understand," said Allison clutching the letter. "Don't leave. I want to see what he says."

They sat in the lounge and Allison, with trembling fingers, opened the letter:

"Dearest darling,

I knew you'd make the right decision. I am down here on the ice. Sorry my phone call was rushed, but I had a bad time back there. They almost threw me in jail. They had me for your mother's car accident. I nearly lost my license. Then I got a letter from your husband telling me you were back together again. I am so happy for you. I know you always wanted a home, and someone to care for you. Remember I told you, I have a wife back home and sometimes you have to make the most of what you have. I am getting over the crash. I know we had something you cannot find."

Allison's face froze, and stared across at Bill. "Bill I'm not married to that bastard. How did this happen?"

Bill shrugged. "Hey, don't shoot the messenger. Is that all... can I go now?"

Allison glanced down the page with blurry eyes at the last few words of goodbye.

Bill was as tall as Tom and he looked kind of familiar with his dark wavy hair, as he stood out on the porch to say goodnight to her. She watched him leave, and closed the door and leaned against it, and read the letter again.

"My Darling, I am giving this to a friend, he's coming down for the mid-winter drop, so I know you'll receive it, all my love, God Bless, Chuck."

All she could think of was the time she flew up the road, burst into the base, and handed a letter to post to Chuck. *My God... he was married.*

CHAPTER 35

The long flight down from Travis Air Force Base in California, gave Chuck time to think. How many times had he made this flight? He was relieved he'd managed to keep his pilot's license, after all the upset. Sitting on autopilot through the dead of the night, felt like he was chasing the lost horizon. A dead zone, where thoughts became dreams. It gave him time to reflect. There was nothing he wanted to change. He would never forget those moments; he'd cherish them. He was glad he gave Bill the letter for Allison. It brought closure to the bitter issue, and he could go on with his life. Closure was so important. *Poor Mattie*, he thought, *she never had closure.*

After a refueling and rest stop in Hawaii, the engines groaned on into the night for the 10-hour flight from the Aloha State to New Zealand.

Biting southerly winds reminded him of his mission, as he stepped off the mighty Starlifter in Christchurch, and headed for the White Heron, now with an ache in his heart. Setting his bags down, he sank onto his bed, and stretched out. The memories of Christchurch overpowered him, and he fell into a deep sleep.

The wake-up call startled Chuck, and he jumped into a shower, grabbed a bite to eat, and put on his hooded fur-lined jacket. He was on the team for the winter season, and he wouldn't get time to catch up with Bill. Chuck knew Bill would have seen Allison, and given her the letter. Bill and his team had been part of the preparation team, and they were heading home, back to North Carolina, and not due back till October. Chuck's plane was stalled down on the Ice from last season, and it was Bill and his team's mission to restart it, when they returned in October.

The big Starlifter was loaded with supplies on the Christchurch taxiway, ready for the mid-winter drop to the Antarctic base. The timing had to be perfect. No fuckups. The engines roared to their full capacity and the runway came alive, disappearing under the giant wings.

It was an aircrew of sixteen officers and airmen, three pilots, two navigators, eight loadmasters, two flight engineers and one flight surgeon. The pressure was on; all hand-picked men, ready for their most dangerous flight ever.

"The mid-winter airdrop."

The C-141Starlifter in all its glory, set off to the southern skies once more, and Chuck's heart skipped a beat as he caught a quick glimpse of Canterbury, the land of the long white cloud. He blinked away a tear, and drew back the throttle a little as they neared cruising altitude.

Hypothermia was the greatest peril when the doors opened for the drop, and the pallets of supplies hurdled out the side door with their parachutes poised to open. It was a moment of truth and high risk. As risky as the refueling mid-air, at 450 miles from the South Pole, the Travis KC-10 proceeded to refuel the Starlifter.

To help the crew find the drop zone in constant darkness, the people at the South Pole Station had gathered drums filled with wood and diesel set ablaze to outline the drop zone. Driving snow reduced visibility to less than five miles. The crew members grabbed their night vision goggles to see into the dense fog and thick Antarctic total blackness.

Chuck barked, "Loadmaster, prepare the bay, and rig the troop doors to open. We are five minutes to the drop zone."

"Roger, troop doors ready to open. Loads ready for drop."

"We are one minute to drop, open doors and make ready. We're at 700 feet."

"Roger that, doors open, fuckin' freezing here."

Chuck yelled, "Holy shit, where'd these ice crystals come from? We have lost visibility in the cockpit. We're in an ice storm."

Co-pilot calls out, "Snow has changed to ice crystals. Outside temp now sixty below. Losing power in one and two. Fuel is freezing. Applying heat."

Chuck screamed, "Loadmaster, drop cargo now, we are there."

The massive Starlifter banked sharply to the left as the two engines failed. The cargo bundles broke loose and swept out the door with the Loadmaster, hanging outside the plane by the static line.

Chuck yelled, "We're tip stalling, max power on three and four. Secure the troop doors, forget the fuckin' drop."

Another Loadmaster blared, "Sam's out the door with some of the cargo... the rest is bashing the shit out of the tail."

"We're going to level off and land. Standby for a hard one."

But it was too late. The C-141 just quit flying and fell valiantly sideways, like a knife from the sky, erupting in a giant fireball on the ice.

CHAPTER 36

Terry Ross was confident in his mission, and even more so now that he knew about the crash. News had leaked about the mid-winter fuckup. He sat opposite the one man he knew he would have to convince. In the darkness of a Chicago shipyard, the meeting took place.

"I'll stack out Jacko's deal. He's a bully. I ruffled him up, real good," Terry smirked. He had a twisted smile, thinking of Jack's look of terror and Chuck's final hours.

"We need that layout. Quit terrorizing the bastard," the man glared at Terry, "...and stay off the women. Keep your hands clean. We can track you."

Terry stubbed his Camel out on the desk ashtray, and leaned over, "Track me? I'm the CIA, motherfucker." He got up with an air of confidence, and leered at the man sitting down. The man was not as agile as Terry. He splayed back in a seat that swung around. He wore a turban, but didn't have an Indian accent. The two thugs behind him, their arms folded over their huge bellies, wore turbans and were Indians. They moved towards Terry.

"Tell your rats to lay off."

Terry left, disappearing into the streets of Chicago.

· · · · ·

Arriving in North Carolina, Terry Ross signed up with the National Science Foundation. He carried a New Zealand passport, and applied under the name of Terrence Riley. He had skills that matched the requirements of salvaging the aircraft that had crashed last season. He smiled to himself about Navy Squadron VXE-6. Next time his plan would be better.

He sat in the Hercules C130. He was just one of the maintenance hands, and nobody spoke to him. With thick spectacles and greasy hair hanging over bulbous, waxy ears, an overweight belly, he slumped down with his head bent reading… he didn't eye contact anyone. The flight was thirteen hours to Christchurch and most of the crew slept until touchdown. When they disembarked, the southerly winds snapped at Terry's chest, reminding him that the icy frontier was close. The Customs man wasn't concerned much with the team. They were used to Americans coming through for Operation Deepfreeze. Terry looked at his watch. Time to call Allison. Then he'd go looking for this Julie woman. He liked the sound of her. This Julie knew Chuck, and he'd have to be careful. He'd have to watch himself.

He checked into the hotel with the rest of the crew, and went to the phone in the downstairs lobby. Sitting in one of the chairs across from the bar against the wall, he could see the restaurant and knew that Julie worked here, so he could watch for a likely woman employee. The rest of the men had gone into town, and he could sit unnoticed by the crowd. It was perfect timing. Terry lifted the phone, called Allison, and heard her voice. "Whatcha doin'?" he asked.

"Terry, I wondered when I was going to hear from you," replied Allison.

"It's all very hectic. I've got orders to go to the Gulf," said Terry.

"Oh…"

"Is that all you can say?"

"No, I hope you can come down here one day, that's all," said Allison.

Terry smiled, looking around. It seemed ironic. He was slow to answer. "Listen, they're calling me," he paused again, and said, "Okay, I'll be there as soon as I can. Sorry, I'll call you when I get back… just wanted to hear your sweet voice." He hung up, and just as he did, he caught sight of a woman that might be Julie strutting across the floor. Looks like she's going for a pee and he liked the taste of pee. Yes her fanny, was it tasty Downunder? He watched the women sitting over near the bar, searching for the new arrivals. He could get amongst that pussy... but he had his hands full.

Next day the team met at the International Antarctic Centre for a pre-flight briefing. They were each given three orange bags, containing extreme cold weather gear, such as red parkas and white bunny boots, which they changed into. One man had a mouth for all of the team. His name was Al.

Terry watched his expression when the demonstration moved to the Emergency Passenger Oxygen System. "Goddamn, we're going to hell and we didn't know it," he repeated. The instructor moved on to explain the fact that a C-130 aircraft didn't have a lot of time to stay flying. "If things go wrong, it's over."

Terry smiled and looked around the group.

At seven o'clock the Hercules roared its engines, and the flat plains of Christchurch were left behind. Terry sat across from a southern man who didn't say much. There were four rows facing each other, on webbing seats. The loudmouth Al was busy trying to shout above the roar of the four Hercules engines, laughing about the oxygen mask and the lifejacket. Everything was a joke, and Terry buried his head in his book. The nine hour flight was a tangle of boots, parkas, feet, legs and heads.

The runway was still icy, and the LC's arrived on skis, onto Willy field at McMurdo Sound.

"For Christ's sake. Christchurch...? What a name! That place's not much warmer than down here," Al yelled out to everyone, as they jumped out onto the icy runway.

It was a beautiful clear day, a temperature of zero degrees, with no wind and bright sunshine.

The snow bus was waiting for them and they took off to McMurdo for another briefing on arrival.

Terry's roommate was already working on the field. He set his bags down, and crashed on his bed, slept for a few hours, and went for chow.

Meals were the highlight of a day. Terry's job was to keep the equipment running. The huge air-conditioning units inside had to be thoroughly checked. It gave him time to check out the staff, the officer's quarters, and the sleeping quarters. He planned things carefully, keeping to himself. He liked his writing, and pinned up Allison's photo on the wall by his bed.

Outside chores and engine maintenance continued, and the team had come down to resurrect a plane that had trouble back in the last season. Terry smiled at who it was that almost met his fate. He knew all about Chuck. He knew about everything else as he scoped out his plan in the ice. The area where no one went. He was good in the deep snow. His time in Siberia taught him patience with the thickness of the ice. He had a long steel pole and he jabbed at it. At a clearing over by the wreck he made his mark. He concealed an empty canister and left for the Base. It wasn't time to move.

Chapter 37

It was October and the bitter months of winter were over. The plant was humming. Jack and Josh were excited about their sugar beets. It was a time in economics where fuel was at a crisis, and no one would be interfering with their attempts to create an alternative fuel.

"Kind of like farming, eh Jack?" said Josh as he paraded through the lines of beets. They had begun to sprout and their purplish green leaves were young and tender as they unfolded.

"Well, it's a good cause." Jack had his hands in his pockets, rattling his change, thinking of the money he was going to make - not the leaves of the sugar beet. He walked towards the shed. The ground was still cold, and they both shivered and made a dash for the shed. Inside the air conditioner hummed. A bench ran across the full length of the windowless shed. Jack had set up Bunsen burners, and was staring at the contents, shaking the glass beaker. Josh had the job of crushing the formula. Everything had to be sterile. Some of it they kept hidden back at Bellamy labs, concealed in the vault and locked away.

• • • • •

News of the crash had been in the papers, but Allison hadn't heard anything. She knew she would never hear from Chuck, and Bill had not written.

Classes had ended and the directors invited two of the best plastic surgeons to lecture the students on their procedures. A rhinoplasty operation was Allison's dream... to be rid of Rat Face. She sat listening to the exact procedure, and looking at photos outlining the details. Each surgeon described the techniques in his own style. The first surgeon was a very tight lipped Englishman. To her, he seemed so false, and she thought of his patients. The second man was much older, and his hands looked more like workman's hands, as he pointed towards the procedures up on the board.

"That's who I'm having for my liposuction," whispered Gwen, sitting next to Allison.

When the two surgeons ended their lectures, Matt made an announcement.

"So ladies, I am sure listening to these two surgeons has helped you see into the world of cosmetic surgery. They have very kindly offered a reduction to you for their services before the end of this year. In your profession, it's not required that you undergo any procedures, but it's always a great advantage to be a believer and live your dream. What better way to show your clients?" He turned to the two surgeons, "Many thanks for your generous time." The students clapped.

"You can see how I turned out. Go on... book in," said Gwen.

The students left the lecture room, but some of them were discussing their options with the surgeons.

"I've always wanted to do something with my nose, ever since I can remember, but never had the courage," Allison whispered to Gwen.

"Oh, you don't need courage... only money," replied Gwen with a smile.

"I know. I have some funds left from my mother. I need a boost."

"Well there you are. Wouldn't she love to see you spend it on something that will make you happy and even more beautiful?"

"Make me happy?" Allison thought of Chuck, and how everything had gone wrong. "Yes it's just what I need." She got up, and went over to the older surgeon and booked in a time for a consultation.

She smiled to herself as she rode home, thinking about how she'd look.

Allison's practical exam required a model for the day. Sarah was delighted to be having a special day of pampering, and she promptly arrived at Allison's station at the School. Allison came out looking the picture of perfection in her freshly-laundered white uniform, with her hair done in a French roll.

The day ended and Sarah drove them back towards Allison's.

"Well I don't care what anyone says about beauty therapy... I think you'll make a huge go of it," said Sarah.

"Thanks. That's what I say. I don't care what some of my friends have said. I'm going with my gut feeling. Today made me feel as if I were already working."

"Well, you will be soon," said Sarah, turning into Allison's driveway. "What are you wearing for the do?"

"I got a dress sent out to me from a girl I met back when I was going out with Chuck. I think she felt sorry for me when I lost my mother. I didn't know her all that well, but she sent it to me. It's gorgeous. It fits like a glove."

"Can't wait to see it," said Sarah, as Allison stepped out of her car, and waved goodbye.

The evening of Allison's graduation was beautiful. The sun was low in the sky and the surrounding trees hung still, an orange and green backdrop for Allison and her party, grouped together for photos. Allison had gone inside to get her camera when the phone went. She picked it up and heard a slurred voice...

"Allison, dear Allison, you've done it." There was a hiccup.

She stood there trembling, "Who's this?"

"It's your old protector. Your old wishful cowboy, baby, home from wherever."

"Tom!" Allison recognized his voice.

"You didn't invite me, so I'm having a drink... I salute... congrats baby." The phone clicked off.

Allison couldn't think why he would call her in this way. She tried to forget, and went on opening the camera. She wore the powder blue satin dress with embossed flowers, strapless, and nipped in at the waist. It ballooned out in folds, knee length to give a nice flow. On her feet, she wore her favorite white satin high heels. She moved with elegance. She didn't have time to worry about Tom as she raced back outside.

"Mum, this is Tracy. She plays cricket on the young women's team," said Chris.

"Nice to meet you. I've heard Chris talk about you. Glad you could join us."

"Congratulations," said Tracy. Here… Chris, grab your bat and stand with your mum." Tracy stepped back, a pretty blonde girl with a face full of freckles, and took a photo.

Chris stood next to his Mother posing with his cricket bat and jersey. Allison squinted into Tracy's camera to escape from the piercing last rays of sunlight, and hugged the back of Chris's jersey.

"We made it, Chris," Allison whispered in his ear.

"Well yerrrrr," he smiled back into the camera, and over at Tracy.

Allison put her arm around Tracy.

"Mummy, is it our turn for a photo?" Isabel asked, tapping her Mother. She was dressed in a striped black and white skirt, and Lucy had on a similar outfit that Allison had made. They had their hair braided, and their faces beamed up at Allison.

"Yes, this is Tracy, Chris's friend. She's going to take a photo of us all, under the trees." Allison took Isabel and Lucy and set them in the front.

"Here make sure you get us all." Gary's voice echoed out across the park. He stood behind Sarah with the girls.

Tracy bent forward, and the group smiled into the camera.

"Yes, this young lady's going to be a raging success. Come on, everyone smile," Gary called out.

"Thanks, Gary." Allison turned around and gave him a warm smile. She felt sad for Tom. He'd helped her too. *She'd give him a call*, she thought. *Poor guy, he's probably lonely.*

The phone rang again. Allison grabbed it, thinking it was Tom again, but it was Julie to say she couldn't make it. Allison's new friend, Betsy, had walked up the road to join them. The graduation was held at the big theatre at Canterbury University, only around the corner. When Allison and her party entered the building, there was a scramble to find seats. The rows of seating went down towards the stage, and they grabbed some seats further back. It was a good view down to the two directors, Matt and Ivan, who came onto the stage, and everyone clapped.

"Good evening, Ladies and Gentlemen. I'm one of the directors, Matt," and he took a bow, and walked across the stage. Allison knew he liked his own presence. "Of course, we all know this is a very special occasion for our students," Matt smiled out to the audience. "But first, we must have some light entertainment." The audience cackled. "I'm going to let Ivan introduce the events."

"Good evening, I'm Ivan." He made a slight bow. "I'm the practical part of the team," he looked over at Matt, "so Matt would have me doing this part of the show." There was a slight giggle in the audience.

Allison smiled through misty tears. She loved his quiet manner, and enjoyed his presence. After a happy display of fun and laughter, the audience leapt to their feet when the lights came on, to stretch their legs.

The intermission bell rang and the audience returned to their seats. The lights dimmed and Matt appeared again, and everyone hushed.

"Ladies and Gentlemen. These students have worked hard this year and we have a list of achievers tonight." He cleared his throat.

"I don't think this will be me," Allison whispered to Betsy.

"The first award is to a very special student." He paused and looked out into the audience. "She didn't have it easy, riding that bike every day. All you could see was a huge pink padded coat, a long red scarf, and a nose poking out." Everyone laughed. "You'd think the wind would blow her over." And more laughter filled the theatre.

Allison froze. Surely he's not talking about me? She started to feel hot with excitement. *It can't be me they're talking about, but it has to be?* she thought.

"The person we have chosen," said Matt taking a pause. "Has gone from a moderate achiever, to the most impressive achiever. Through all her hardship, she biked on, dealing with all that came her way. She continued to shine, and we feel confident she is the winner... and the award goes to Allison.... Brownley..."

The crowd roared and she was up on her feet. Hands reached out for her as she walked down the stairs to the stage. There they were… her mentors whom she so much admired, smiling at her and handing her the trophy – a golden angel reaching up to the sky. On the placard the words read, "Southern School of Aesthetics, Most Improved 1989." Allison was overwhelmed with excitement. She held the trophy high in her hands, and went back to sit amongst her family and friends. She never forgot that moment.

Chapter 38

Gwen endured a liposuction operation on her thighs. Allison had only made an appointment, and the two women were eager to exchange ideas on their surgeries, when Gwen arrived around to see Allison at her home.

"Gwen. Wow, look at you," said Allison, opening the door.

"I told you I wouldn't die."

"You're funny. Come on in, and tell me all about it."

"Oh, I'm a bit stiff still," said Gwen, screwing her face up, as she walked into the conservatory.

"Look at my corset." She lifted up her skirt. "It's a bloody harness. I feel like one of those women back in the old days. I have to have this thing on for weeks. But it's what I wanted."

"Yes, and you look so trim already."

"Good, isn't it?" she laughed. "It's a miracle. Now, what about you?"

"Well I'm booked in for tomorrow actually. I can't wait, after seeing you."

"Hey, that was a surprise at the Event the other night. Good on you. Wish I had one of those awards. I might go and buy one at a trophy shop... *Best Legs*."

"Oh Gwen, you can't do that."

"Why not? I earned it too." She gave a wink.

Allison thought she was a funny character. She had liked her company right through, but sometimes her remarks were a little odd.

"Heard anymore from that character in the jungle?"

"Yes I have." Allison went into her room and brought out the photo, and the book she kept by the bed.

"Look at this for something different."

"Well, you can say that again." Gwen stared at the photo, and then at the book.

Allison sat back down in the opposite chair. There was silence in the sunlit room.

Gwen took her time, opening the book and looking at the photo. She put it down, and looked over at Allison.

"You know what I think? I think you better be careful. How do you know it's him in this book? Look at the nose, it's smaller than the guy on the front cover." She handed the photo back to Allison.

"He might have had a nose job. Hey... that's a thought. Now we know noses can be made smaller," Allison replied.

"Hey, you're right girl. You're into deep waters. You better watch your toes."

They sat back and talked about their new careers. Gwen had an interview with a therapist in town, and Allison took Gwen out to her new clinic therapy room.

"It's going to be hard, starting from nothing, Allison. You've got no clients," Gwen said as they walked back out of the little room, and she opened her car door. "Let me know how your appointment went." She waved and drove away.

Allison sat in Mr Simm's surgery. She was comforted about Gwen's success, and was surprised at Mr Simm's manner when she walked into his room. He had been more relaxed at the lecture. His expression was stern, blending beautifully with his antique furniture and ancient desk, where he roosted for his next victim.

Mr Simm looked up at her. "So how can I help you?" he asked, studying her over his thick rimmed glasses.

"I've always wanted to have my nose altered."

"You mean a Rhinoplasty?'

"Yes."

"Turn on the side for me," he looked and began to write some notes. He sketched a nose as Allison watched him draw a nose that was straight, and not bent with a bump in the middle.

"I enjoyed your lecture at the school." commented Allison.

He didn't look up, but went on drawing.

Allison continued, "My colleague, Gwen Thomas, just had liposuction with you, and she is so happy."

"I hope she's wearing her corset." He looked up and his face seemed to lighten. "Your nose will look something like this." He showed her the finished drawing. "I'd like you in at the hospital next Wednesday morning, at ten with nothing to eat or drink from midnight." He handed her the papers for the hospital.

When it came time for Allison to go to the hospital, Betsy had driven her there and dropped her at the entranceway. Allison had insisted she would be fine. After a number of forms to be filled in, Allison was shown to her room and dressed in a gown. It was not long before a hospital warden came for her. She put on the disposable green booties and hat, climbed onto the trolley bed, and was wheeled into the bright lights of the theatre to Mr Simms waiting for her. He put his hand on her shoulder, reassured her, and the bright lights faded as the anesthesia worked its wonders.

The pain hit. No it must be a bus that hit. Allison imagined she could see familiar faces around her. She heard Betsy as she passed in the hallway, but the pain was unbearable. What had she done? She could barely see anything. Her nose was on fire.

"We are going to give you something for the pain, Allison... can you swallow?" asked a nurse and helped her up.

Allison felt nauseous and began to vomit. The pain got worse; an injection was the next step, and most of the night she vomited, until sleep finally came with sheer exhaustion in the small hours of the morning. Betsy came back the next day to pick her up, and it was a slight relief to find herself back at home in her own bed.

Ten days later, taking off the bandages for the first time was a surreal experience... looking at her reflection in the mirror. No large bump anymore - the look that so haunted her all her adult life... Rat Face was gone.

CHAPTER 39

A position as a chef's assistant had been convenient for Terry as he made his move. It was time for the team to leave. The parts of the missing plane had been successfully salvaged and had gone ahead quicker than the team had predicted.

Terry slipped into the role, his apron folded over a large belly. He'd been to the barber's and had an obligatory military buzz haircut. A hairnet hid his new look and thick glasses hid his eyes. He never looked at anyone, just peeled potatoes, scrubbed the pans, and kept the huge dishwashers going. Everything ran on generators. The officers ate at a special time, and Terry had been observing his prey. The man was tall and rotund. He wore glasses, sported a moustache, and had a sort of English accent. He was a New Zealander, and bragged about his fiancé, and how he was looking forward to taking her back to America for Christmas. Terry sliced up the potatoes with his sharp butcher knife and dug it hard into the soft wood of the chopping block – a bit too hard as he licked his finger from the taste of blood.

Bill and the crew had retrieved the Black Box of the missing plane, and were laughing and drinking. It was their last night, when Terry finished his chores. Some of the cooking hands were being exchanged. There was another flight due down in the morning. Timing was crucial. Terry snuck into the Lieutenant's quarters and stuck Reefton in the neck with a syringe. His body flopped into a waiting trash bin, and Terry walked out to dispose of the kitchen waste as usual. Out of the bright lights, he had his concealed area already dug and his plan was easy. He hopped onto the Snowcat, and made his run towards Mt Discovery. Kind of an ironic name, he thought.

There was no sun. He returned the Snowcat and slipped back inside, into Lieutenant Reefton's room and washed up.

He looked at himself in the mirror. He put on his moustache, ran his hand over his cropped hair, puffing out his well-built round body, ready for the flight to Christchurch.

CHAPTER 40

Gary had spent his weekends completing Allison's small addition to the back room alongside her garage. He had become a good friend.

"Cup of tea?" Allison called out to Gary.

"You bet," yelled Gary, turning off his saw and brushing his shorts. "What do you think so far?"

"I can see it already. The waiting room is going to be right here where we stand," said Allison, opening her arms up and twirling around in the space under the clearly lit conservatory roof, that Gary had added on. And I'm going to have a white cane couch just here. They can sit and wait. See...," and she pointed to the back wall.

"You're a goer, Miss Brownley. Come on, where's that tea?"

They sat down on the front step back at the house, and shared some sandwiches Allison had made.

"And who's the addition to the family?" asked Gary gently touching Monty's nose.

"Yes... this is Monty, the phantom shitter," and she giggled.

Gary laughed. "What's Chippy going to say to you when I shift over the fence?" Gary smiled back at Allison.

"Yes, I take possession of the house before Christmas. The family were glad I bought it."

"That worked out well. I'll love having you as a neighbor... we can have lots of cups of tea."

"That's for sure," replied Allison.

Gary got up, "By the way, your nose looks good."

"Thanks."

"I thought it looked good before," Gary looked around with a slight smile, and went back to finish the walls of the small entrance. He sold Allison an old door, and big windows from his other house. It had worked to a perfect fit.

•   •   •   •   •

It was morning and Jack picked up the girls. He had managed to persuade them to leave Monty behind, and they called out to Monty, trying to catch him to say goodbye.

"Do you like my clinic?" said Allison, going over to stand by Jack's car.

"What, the size of a wheelchair toilet?" Jack smiled, and looked directly at her. "What's with the nose? Maybe you should have added your nose onto your room," he sat, laughing sarcastically while starting the engine.

Allison didn't react, but turned and went inside.

"Fuck him." Jack's words clouded her mind, and she picked up the measuring tape to measure the curtains for the clinic.

Gary was busy finishing and skimming the inside wall lining.

"I'm angry as a hornet. Jack's always saying nasty things." She walked over to the back window. "Even my nose… he can't say it looks good."

"Why are you asking for his approval, Allison?" said Gary stopping his work. "If you need his approval, you should be still married to him."

"No, but you'd think he'd give me some credit."

"I can't understand you women. My wife was like your husband, always putting me down. But do you see me complain? Now… get a grip, woman!"

"Yes, you're right. It's times like this I need to hear good words."

"Words are cheap. It's *deeds* that count! Get some action behind those words."

"Yes, boss," Allison saluted, and they laughed. She went on with her measuring.

In the post the next day, the long awaited results arrived. She tore at the envelope, and squealed and jumped for joy, and ran into Chris, who was sitting in the sun in the conservatory. "I've passed. All three exams."

"That's good Mum. Told ya."

Allison took out the certificates and stared at them with their red seals. She had passed and was now certified by the London Confederation of Cosmetology. That was the first for the school as they were doubtful anyone could pass it. In the world of beauty therapy, it was the top achievement. "Jack Brownley... Kiss My Sweet Ass!!!"

There were celebrations ahead. When the girls got home, Allison was in a whirl of excitement.

"Mummy's passed. Look girls, here's my certificates. We're going to celebrate! We're having a party!"

"Mummy, a party. Can we stay up?" Lucy and Isabel both jumped up and down.

"Just for a little while. Then you have to go to bed."

"We promise," Isabel said.

Allison dialed Sarah's number, but nobody was home. Julie was at work, so she went on dialing the numbers of friends. Eventually she dialed Gwen's number.

"Thought it might be you. Yes I passed too. Great isn't it?" responded Gwen.

"Would you like to celebrate over here?" asked Allison.

"Sounds good."

Allison called another couple of her colleagues, and both had passed; but some of the class had missed out on passing.

Gary had said he'd come later, and Chris was coming home after a sports meeting. Allison liked to include the girls in everything she did. They had loved the graduation, and the atmosphere was a family affair. They helped her make some sandwiches, and Isabelle liked stirring the onion soup mix into the sour crème, and getting it ready for the dip, with a big bowl of potato chips.

The party brought a sea of faces, voices echoing into the open spaces of the Park. Betsy had sounded delighted when Allison told her. Allison could hear laughter coming from her sports car. American accents were getting clearer as the group came into vision.

"Allison," said Betsy, clutching a bottle of wine. "Surprise, and congratulations," and gave her a huge hug.

"Bill! What are you doing here?" said Allison, hugging Betsy and looking over her shoulder.

"How did...?" Allison stammered.

"We met again, up at Bourbon Street," interrupted Betsy, looking at Bill. "Thought you'd like a surprise."

"Well, you certainly did that. I'll get some more glasses. Come in and meet everyone," said Allison, going inside to grab some glasses. Bill followed her.

"I didn't write because...," he put his head down.

Allison lifted her hand to her mouth in sudden emotion. She instantly knew by the look on Bill's face that he had some bad news.

"Nobody prepared us for what happened this winter. It was played down in the papers, but I'm afraid... two airplane crashes... but at least we have one of the Black Boxes...," he broke off again with a catch in his voice.

Allison put her arms around his tall frame and they stood in silence without mentioning Chuck's name. It was a moment's silence - another moment Allison would remember as she stood in the same room. The thought of two coffee cups slowly cooling, the waiting, the silence. Allison stepped back and wiped her tear-stained face, and Bill followed her into the lounge. Everyone was laughing and talking. They squeezed through the crowd.

One of Bill's friends was coming out of her room.

"Sorry Ma'am, I was looking for the bathroom. Are you okay?" Allison nodded without replying.

"By the way, this is Gimpy," said Bill.

"That's a funny name," said Allison, clearing her voice.

"Yes, I got my nickname from an accident I had once. Nicknames stick with you."

"Yes I've learned that. I've met a lot of Americans with nicknames," replied Allison. Everything reminded her of Chuck.

"Hey, sorry, I went into your bedroom by mistake. I was looking for the restroom." He moved away, but looked across at Bill.

Betsy walked over and interrupted. "Why don't we take a walk in the moonlight?" she said smiling at Bill.

"The moon's not out yet," Bill said, and sat down on one of the seats with his wine.

"Did you guys complete your work down on the ice?" asked Betsy, sitting next to Bill.

"Yes ma'am. We were ahead of schedule, so we've got some time off for good behavior."

Gimpy came back to join them.

"You must meet the rest of the party," said Allison, introducing everyone. "You'll have to excuse Gwen over in the corner there, she's had a fall."

Gwen raised her drink and smiled. "Hear, hear," said Gwen.

Gimpy walked with a slight limp, and sat down next to Gwen.

As the twilight waned, the spacious lawns outside the conservatory set the scene for a moonlight walk. A small group left Allison's house, and strolled towards the bridge. Walking together as a group and chatting, made Allison realize just how special the Park was.

"Look at these enormous trees," said Bill, almost touching a branch that hung above his tall frame. "The leaves, they're oak, am I right?"

"Yes," said Allison. "And you see these acorns?" She bent down, and picked one up and handed it to him. "They were brought over in a ship called the *Charlotte Jane* back in 1850 from Gloucestershire, England."

"Wow, certainly looks to be in good shape after 185 years. Maybe I'll just sit under this tree and then I can live to be 185."

"Good idea. I remember things in funny ways, and Isabelle had a doll the size of a baby and she called it Jane." She looked up at the new spring foliage, and pulled a leaf off the tree to brush it up against her face.

Allison looked over at the old house across the Park, and saw a car in Jack's driveway. It looked familiar. It looked like Sarah's car. It was blue.

Allison broke from the group, and walked towards the swings, but the car was too hard to identity. She turned and walked back towards the group.

"I didn't realize how much your country is so like England," said Bill, when he caught sight of Allison coming towards them.

"Yes, Christchurch is the new England Downunder," said Allison, catching up to them. "I went on ahead. Sorry, I didn't know you guys weren't following."

"Did you find what you were looking for?" asked Bill

"No, not really," said Allison.

"It certainly is a beautiful part of the world down here. And beautiful women to boot," Bill smiled at Betsy and Allison.

"Well, aren't you a true gentleman for that Bill, my boy? You deserve a nice big hug." Betsy came up behind him, and squeezed his arm. "Who's for a nightcap?"

"Let's go back up to the hotel," said Bill, picking up speed with huge strides.

Bill appeared to Allison like an overgrown schoolboy. He had a note of innocence about him. His dark hair, pale skin, and beautifully shaped face was the first thing that fascinated Allison when she first saw him. She put her slender arm through his big arm and smiled up at him, "I'm so glad it was you who told me the news. Thanks for coming."

Bill nodded his head in agreement.

They all left the Park, and walked towards the brightly lit conservatory. Allison could hear Gary's voice booming out, and Chris was outside the conservatory, sitting on the steps, with his usual can of beer. The music was playing.

Allison called out to Chris, and he looked up, "Have you met all my friends, Chris?"

"Yerrrr, Yerrr. I'm playing them my favorite track, from Billy Idol."

"Hello, who's this?" said Chris, looking up at Bill with Allison.

"Hello, I'm Beeaall."

"Jesus... who?" Chris pulled a face.

"Bill," said Allison.

"Sorry, I didn't understand you, mate," said Chris. "We talk different too. We're Kiwis. Yerrrr, I'll drink to that", Chris raised his beer.

"We're going up the road for a drink," said Betsy. "Anyone want to come?"

"No, what's wrong with here?" said Gary, swinging his glass around, and yelling across to the others. "We're not, are we?" he looked over at the group.

"It's been nice meeting y'all, but my ride's leaving," said Gimpy, getting up to join Betsy.

"And I'm off too. My legs are sore," said Gwen, pulling herself up to a standing position, and rubbing her back.

"I know what that's like," said Gimpy.

"I have to see to the girls… I'll follow," said Allison

"Oh, then the ladies can stay," said Gary, looking over at the two classmates who were sitting together, talking on the couch.

Allison peered into the girl's bedroom. They had tossed their blankets off. She covered them up, and went back out with her keys in her hand, knowing that Chis would be here to watch the girls as usual.

"Here's to Miss Brownley," said Gary, tipping his glass. "Oh, and don't forget to tell all those Yanks up there, you passed your exams with honors," he roared, and waved her goodbye.

Allison parked the car not far from the corner of Jack's house, and crept up to the bay window of the huge lounge. She stood on a pile of timber and weeds under the window, straining her neck. She could see Jack, and a woman standing over by Jack's piano. The woman looked like Julie, but it wasn't her. They were drinking wine and laughing. Allison clung onto the edge of the window to see who the woman was. Then she heard an American accent. The woman was as tall as Jack. Allison gasped… it was Molly!

Chapter 41

Allison's head spun, and entering the White Heron entranceway made her feel even more nervous than ever, after the final blow of viewing Molly.

Julie interrupted her thoughts, "Congratulations! Sorry I couldn't come to your party."

"Oh that's okay. We've had a great time, and I got a real surprise," she turned to Betsy. "This is Betsy. She met Bill up at Bourbon Street."

"Hello Julie. Nice to meet you," said Betsy politely, shaking Julie's free hand.

"You've been busy, Bill, you sly old dog. It doesn't take you long to meet the ladies. Told you he was a catch," Julie patted him on the back.

"Oh come on. Stop that. What are you ladies having... liqueurs?" asked Bill.

"Yes, thanks," said Allison and Betsy together.

"The night's young. I'm still unwinding. I'll have a wine, thanks," said Julie.

Allison could hear his slow American accent ordering the drinks. She was miles away in thought, when Julie said, "You've got a message. Someone has been trying to contact you. They called down from reception. I told them you weren't working up here anymore."

"Who could that be?" said Allison.

"Don't put that one on me. You keep your secrets hidden, don't forget." Julie blew cigarette smoke out next to Allison, and turned away. Allison got up before Bill returned with the drinks, and went across to reception.

The clerk recognized her. "Sorry, we didn't know you'd left." He handed her an envelope. Allison slipped it into her jacket, and went back to join the others.

Allison found it hard to concentrate.

"What'd you find over at Jack's?' asked Betsy.

"I'm not sure, but I'll find out. I got a shock, but it's none of my business anymore what he does."

"No, it's not."

"You look tired, Allison," said Bill.

"I feel it," she sighed, "I haven't told you all the rest of the things that go on. You're not married, so it might be hard for you to understand."

"I suppose so. You ladies down here are so friendly. Why would a guy want to change that? I don't get it," he shook his head, and tipped his liqueur back. "Us boys are going to turn in now. We've had a long, hard week and all." He put his arm around her, "Allison, I'm sorry."

"That's okay."

"We'll give you and Betsy a call tomorrow." Bill stood up to leave.

"That's fine. You get some rest. Betsy and I are going soon too. Goodnight," replied Allison.

"Goodnight," said Betsy. "What happened?"

"That plane crash...," Allison began to speak, and saw Julie watching her.

"I'm sorry too," said Julie moving over to sit with them. "Chuck was killed instantly in the mid-winter drop," Julie said to Betsy, putting her cigarette down as if to salute him in spirit. "He was a true pilot. He didn't deserve that fate," her eyes still fixed on Allison.

"Oh! I am so sorry," Betsy said, and they sat in silence until Julie got up to leave. Betsy looked at her watch. "Bill's such a nice guy. I'm sure it was the right time for him to give you that news, Allison." She put a hand on her lap. "Are you going out to your car?"

"No, I'm not. I need to go to the bathroom. Will you be okay?" asked Allison.

"Oh yes, I'm a big girl. I can see myself home," Betsy walked away, towards the tiled entranceway.

"Take care, Allison," Julie said waving at her. Allison walked in the direction of the bathroom, opening the envelope. It read, *"Meet me in room 245"*

Allison climbed the stairs, and knocked on the door of room 245. There was no answer, but she heard voices that sounded like the news playing. She couldn't tell. She knocked louder.

A waiter was delivering a tray next door when Allison caught his attention. "Excuse me, but have you seen the person from this room?"

"No, sorry ma'am. You'll have to ask at the desk."

Allison hurried back down to the desk.

"Hello. Did you get your message okay?" asked the clerk behind the counter.

"Hi, sorry I didn't recognize you before. Do you know who's in room 245?"

"Let me see… a Lieutenant Reefton."

"What does he look like?"

"I'm sorry, I can't help you. All I know is he works for the National Science Foundation. He's a pilot."

"If he checks in, can you tell him I got the message?"

"Sure, and I'll take a good look at him. See if I can find out anything further. Us staff have to stick together," he winked.

"Thanks heaps," and she turned around to the bar. She was sure she had seen a man drinking there. She must be dreaming. She drove home.

Chapter 42

Terry Ross was good at anything he liked to become. He sat there at the bar, and smiled to himself with his crooked smile. *The lady's beautiful.* But then he already knew. He had met her in the car in Chicago. She looked frightened, poor thing. But then, he liked his women beautiful, and frightened was even better. Allison had gained his trust and display of courage in a clever twist to his novel. *How many men does she need*, he asked himself. He drew in his last puff, and blew the smoke into the air, stubbed his Camel out in the ash tray, and left the bar.

    •   •   •   •   •

When Allison arrived home, the rest of her friends had left. Chris was asleep, and the night was still. Allison turned the lights out in the conservatory. She jumped when the phone rang.

"Thought I'd never catch you."

"What? Terry? What's been happening?" she asked.

Terry's voice was slow and seductive…, "Ever had phone sex, baby?" There was silence, only breathing. "I want you to play a game. Are you lying down?"

Allison lay there, her heart racing, listening.

Terry continued, "Now close your eyes and do exactly what I tell you."

She could feel herself becoming aroused. Placing her fingers in areas she had no control over, she felt mesmerized by his voice, and now her juices were flowing.

He broke off. "This is just a taste of what's to come. I'm arriving soon but I have orders. I'll be delayed. I won't be able to write or call."

"How do you know the time here?" asked Allison.

"Just guessing. Listen, got to go. I'm onto something big. I just wanted to say goodnight."

"Goodnight? That's a good guess."

Terry hung up the receiver in the phone box, and walked around the corner. *She's not dumb*, he thought to himself as he moved across the Park towards Jack's house. It was late, and the trees overshadowed his broad figure.

As he neared Jack's house, a woman was just leaving through the front door, but the woman was not Allison. He made a note of her car's license plate. He was dressed in an officer's uniform. He flipped his cigarette out onto the pavement. He was glad that the lights were still on, and that the woman had left.

He knocked, and Jack opened the door, "Who are you?"

"I'm from the United States Air Force, and I believe you had dealings with a Chuck Bronski?"

"At this hour, what's this about?"

"Late orders, sir. I have a warrant to search your house." Terry stepped up to the front porch and looked straight at Jack. "Yes, orders to search for missing files."

"I want to see those orders. Show me your identification, Mr. Whoever you are. Barging in on local citizens is not the way it works. Now fuck off!" he tried to slam the door.

Terry stopped him, "Don't tell me to fuck off, Mr Dealer Chemist. Yes, I know what you're up to, and we know up at headquarters that you murdered Lieutenant Bronski, in mid-air. Now let me in."

Jack took a step back.

Terry moved in, pushing him down the dark passageway. "I think you've got a lot of explaining to do. It's not polite to keep visitors standing in the cold outside." Terry pulled Jack into the huge lounge, and sat him down on the bench seat. Terry sat opposite him, his uniform creases standing out like railway tracks.

Jack's eyes fixed on Terry. "Wait a minute, you look familiar. You're that son-of-a-bitch from Chicago that my stupid wife's writing to? How the hell did you get down here?" said Jack, springing to his feet.

Terry leaped up, "I'm here for the formula and the cylinder, that's what I'm here for. She's just my ticket out of here. Now do as I say, and do it fast. First, I want the formula... *Now*! The papers, then we'll take a ride." He grabbed Jack, pushing him against the lounge wall, and grizzled into Jack's face, "I had your phone tapped. I know all about Josh boy and how he fooled you. Yes," he threw Jack across the seat. "You're a regular little bully aren't you, Mr Downunder? Can't keep your hands to yourself can you? You fool. It was Josh's new bitch. He didn't like your coming back on the scene, poking around Josh's apartment. Think, boy, think. While you're busy being the hero, your formula's getting duped. Everyone's in on it but you. Even old Mark, whatever his name was... the old gay boy played along. He's the detective, you stupid cunt face." Terry laughed out loud, "I love this... payback time all round."

"Absolute bullshit, what drugs are you on?" stammered Jack.

"Don't try and bluff me," Terry pulled Jack up to his feet, and pushed him towards the door. "We're going for a ride. We'll see who has the drugs. Then you'll take a nice long nap. Yes, you'll see the inside of that bedroom of yours, not for what you think it is." Terry pressed a pistol into Jack's ribs, and Jack backed down the hallway, towards the bedroom.

"Take it, and get the fuck out of my house," Jack threw the briefcase across to Terry.

Terry opened it and threw the papers on the floor.

"How do I know all this shit's what I want?"

"You should know."

"No, I don't know. That's why I have you alive isn't it? Remember, your pretty lady read just how good I am at killing."

Jack bent down, and threw him the papers. Terry looked again at the mismatch of papers. These aren't any formulas you dumb ass. Explain these to me." Terry wadded and threw the papers back at Jack.

Jack looked at the papers. They were a mass of numbers, nothing matched or made sense. He stared at them. "They've been switched. Someone's come in and stole them."

Terry laughed. "Oh yeah…? Where are the gas cylinders? I want them now."

Jack went to the garage.

Terry was close behind him. He was calm. He stood there, not entering.

"Go on, move." Terry shoved Jack forward, digging the pistol into his back, and threw him against the bench in the garage.

Terry held Jack's arm up against his back until Jack called out, "Fuck you, you bastard. Fuck you!"

"All the amounts of fucks are not gonna let you out of this one, bubba Jacko." Terry yanked his arm further up his back, then turned him around like a rag doll, and punched him hard into his stomach.

Jack retched, vomit flying out of his mouth.

"Now that should get rid of your shit." Terry gave him an extra shove.

Jack called out, "I'll take you there." He buckled over and tried to wipe his mouth of the vomit. Trails of saliva, like threads of thick slime, oozed onto his shirt.

Terry shoved Jack towards his vehicle, "Get in and show me, you sick fuck."

They drove off to the plant, with Terry pointing the pistol at Jack's neck, as Jack drove out into the night.

"It's easy when you have what I want."

By now they had returned back to Jack's house. Jack was unconscious, when Terry threw him on his bed. The vomit was perfect.

"Say good night, Mr Casanova." Terry put one of the tanks into the vehicle he was driving, and drove back to the hotel.

Terry entered the White Heron by a side door. He needed to investigate the rooms that Bill and his team occupied. He would go and find a hungry woman. Now was the time to meet her. He liked strong women; they were a challenge to break. He'd bust her wide open before he left town. A woman that liked sex and lots of it. He took in a breath, and walked down the stairs past the restaurant, and glanced in. He could see a tall blonde, and he smiled as he strolled down to reception. He liked the respect people paid him as he approached the desk.

"Good evening Lieutenant, how can I help you?'

"Arrr... Bill Hoffman, Arrr.. Allan..."

"Just a moment, I'll bring up their rooms on my screen." The clerk went away and came back, "Room 255."

"I don't need their room numbers. Please give them a wake-up call at zero four hundred hours; they're shipping out tomorrow." Terry rapped his knuckles on the counter, and the clerk wrote a note next to their names.

He turned and went to the bar, ordered a drink, and sat against the wall where he could see the restaurant; it appeared to be closed. He lit a Camel and sat back. He spotted a woman at the bar, ordering a drink. He stood up, and waved at the waiter, "I'll take that."

She swiveled around on her stool, flicked a cigarette into the ash tray, and smiled at Terry, "That was quick."

"That's me," Terry leaned up against the bar. "Lieutenant Reefton, ma'am."

"Yes, I know. We know everything round here..."

"Been here long?"

"About as long as you have." She was smart and had an answer for everything. She stood up. She was as tall as Terry. "Come on, I want to show you something."

She walked outside with Terry following. "I want you to show me the Southern Cross. Then, I'll believe all this bullshit about your being Lieutenant Reefton. He was not due in today."

Terry laughed, and tilted his head back, turning away from the airport and pointing.

"I don't play games, but for pretty ladies, anything's possible." He leaned towards her, and grabbed her neck and pulled her towards him. She finger-stabbed his throat, and kicked him in the groin.

"Listen Mister whoever you are. I play the shots, not you. You'll find out."

Molly walked away.

CHAPTER 43

Allison woke the next morning. The girls had arranged to go with a friend to the beach. It had worked out well. Allison was preoccupied when she waved good bye.

The phone rang. "Allison, I'm glad you're okay." Gwen said.

"Why, what have I done?" answered Allison.

"You haven't done anything yet. I was talking to that guy. The one with the funny name."

"Gimpy?"

"Yes, that's the one. He told me that photo you have in your room… looks strangely familiar. One of the maintenance guys down on the ice looks just like him. A guy by the name of Terry Riley. He's not even a military guy," replied Gwen.

"But Terry lives with his mother in North Carolina. I have his number."

"I told you I had a funny feeling. You'd better call. Check it out. Don't assume. It might not be him on the book cover. I told you that."

"Yes, he's been a long time writing. You're right, no harm in calling" Allison paused, "Oh and thanks for being so concerned."

"Thanks for last night." Gwen interrupted. "Oh, and I liked the bit about the fall. See, you can cover. Now make that call."

Allison dialed the number in America. There was no answer.

Then she dialed Tom's number. It rang and went to an answer phone. She spoke into the machine when the beep came on, "Hello Tom, it's Allison. I know this sounds crazy, but I think my pen friend's in town."

She let the message click off, drew her hand up to her mouth as she remembered Terry warning her about how his phone was bugged. Allison did not know that Terry was finding it hard to grapple with the authorities, and now she had dobbed him in. Which way was she to turn? Allison dressed, drove back up to the hotel to find Bill and his friends. She ran up the stairs to Room 245. The room door was half open, and she peered in.

"Sorry, room service," said the maid.

"Excuse me, but when was this room vacated?"

"Sorry, I only work here. You'll have to check back at the desk."

Allison's head was spinning. She ran down to see if Julie was on breakfast. Then she thought she'd not involve her, so she went to the reception.

"Is there any message for me? My name is Allison Brownley. I used to work here."

"Yes, I know. No sorry... no messages."

"Did you find out any more about the Lieutenant in Room 245?"

"No, sorry."

Allison remembered asking this clerk before, and thought he wasn't being honest with her. His expression gave him away. "Then can you give me the room number of Bill Hoffman, please? He was with two other men, but I don't have their last names."

"Just a moment please, I'll have to check." The clerk went over to the registrar. "He's up on the second floor, Room 255, but I'm sure they have checked out."

Allison climbed the stairs, walked past Room 245. The door was closed. She walked to Room 255. She knocked at the door, but there was no answer. She went up and down the corridor looking for the maid she'd seen, but there was no one around. A ghostly silence. She paused, and went back and knocked louder on Room 255.

"Is anyone there? It's Allison. Can you hear me?"

She wanted to contact Bill, and she rushed back down the stairs, and over to the clerk. She was out of breath.

"I'm sorry, but Bill Hoffman is not answering his door. Did you say he's still here?"

"Just a minute." The minutes seemed long before the clerk came back. "There must have been a mistake. I'll have to check into this, but now I see a group of them left early this morning. I can ask what happened if you like, Allison." He winked at her.

"I know what you must think, but it's not like that. Oh, never mind."

She turned away and walked into the bathroom. She stood staring into the mirror, trying to come to terms with the assumption she was a whore. Damn it, she'd go find Julie before she'd take another step into the rooms. Women come up here to get laid. Damn it, she'd find Julie. She walked across the entranceway into the breakfast area, and caught sight of Julie.

"What now, or should I say why now?" said Julie, tapping on the register.

"Have you seen Bill?"

"No... why?"

"I'm sorry, Julie. I haven't meant to harass you. Please, I need to find him."

"Honestly, Allison, if I had seen him I'd tell you. But I'll check around."

Allison drove home. She kept thinking about Bill. She opened the front door, and let herself in. It was pleasant and warm, like a greenhouse, as the morning sun streamed into the conservatory through the colored fiberglass roof. She sat down to recapture all that had happened in the last twenty-four hours and called Betsy.

"Hi, wasn't it fun last night? Listen... have you heard from Bill?" asked Allison.

"No, I was hoping to. I'm about to go out."

"I went up to the hotel to find him."

"He must have left... maybe he'll leave a message. I'll call you later, okay?"

"He must have, thanks, talk to you soon." responded Allison.

Whoever was trying to contact her, had to have been mixed up with Bill. They probably got the wrong room, and because it was her, the staff must have thought she would have been fucking him.

Damn them, and their opinions, who needs that? Allison thought. She got up and went to change. It was sunny, and she would mow the lawns. A great way to unwind.

But there was a knock at the door. Allison thought it was Tom. Perhaps he'd come looking for her. She rushed to the door, still pulling on a top for the gardening, when she caught sight of a form standing at the front door, through the lounge window. A tall figure. She opened the door, face to face with her pen friend, Terry Ross.

CHAPTER 44

"Good God... Terry!"

He stood there smiling at her, carrying a small bag.

"Who else do you think it would be, eh? Come here and give me a hug."

He drew her close to him.

Allison stood there. She smelled the tobacco as he breathed down at her, looking at her through the thick lenses of his glasses. The author of the book was finally here.

Terry let her go, and stepped back to look down at her. "You are beautiful." He bent down, and kissed her gently on her nose.

"But it can't be you... you only just called."

"Hey, don't be shy." He put his finger under her chin, and turned her chin up towards him. "Haven't you got anything better to say to your pen friend, who's just travelled thousands of miles to be here? Are you going to invite me in?" He took her arm, and they shut the door.

"Your uniform. You look so....wonderful... an officer. Where did you get the uniform?" Allison walked into the kitchen, a little shaken, and went to put on the kettle for hot water and tea.

"It's mine, dummy. See the initials, L. R." Terry set his bag down on the chair. "Is this what the English do? Make a cup of tea?" he smiled.

"You should know me by now. We always drink tea. How do you take yours?" Allison said, setting out a couple of cups.

"I'll have it just like you, strong and sweet," he laughed.

"There was a message last night for me at the hotel up the road, the hotel by the Base," Allison responded as she poured out the tea.

"Last night? Must be someone else. How many officers can one lady have?" He leaned over the kitchen bench. "I only got in this morning. I called you last night in transit." He reached inside his top pocket to pull out a packet of cigarettes. "My, you sure have a nice place," tapping his cigarette out of the packet. "Pictures don't give you credit. Hey you still got my novel?"

"Yes, it's by my bed."

"I have something I want to show you. Can you get the novel for me?"

Allison set down the cups filled with tea, and left the kitchen. Her curiosity was heightened. She returned, handing it to him. He took it, with his lit cigarette in his mouth, and they walked into the conservatory.

"Mind if I smoke? I did tell you I smoked, or was that some other pen friend?"

Allison walked across and opened the big sliding doors to the garden to let the smoke out, and sat down with her cup of tea.

"You don't have to be so sarcastic."

Terry smirked at her, and went on flicking through the pages, giving it back to Allison, pointing to the antagonist being a New Zealander.

"Yes, it's about your being a New Zealander, isn't it?" queried Allison.

"Yes. That's why it's easy for me to arrange entry. Some things I didn't want to explain. I told you... I'm being watched. I have to be careful what I say. That way... what you don't know, you can't talk about."

"So you came in with the military, this time?"

"Yes."

"You're very edgy."

"What's that supposed to mean?" said Terry, taking a huge draw of his cigarette and turning to look at her.

"Well, first you use sarcasm, and then you have to explain why you're here. You're starting to act like Jack."

For the first time she had the courage to look straight at him. She could tell he was full of confidence, but something was bothering him. His eyes were large open eyes, magnified under his huge glasses. She looked at his nose, and thought of her own reformed delicate nose. Maybe he did have reconstruction. You can never tell. Only the bridge of the nose changes. She could tell he was reading her mind.

"Why didn't you tell me last night? I could have prepared for this moment. It's... it's special."

"Oh baby, you're so pretty in person. I don't know who you think I am, but I sure as hell want you baby." He pulled her towards him, still staring intensely into her eyes.

"Are you going to stay?"

"Listen, Dickless Tracey," he pushed her away. "Only place I'm goin' is with you. I'm being followed... I can explain, but let me get out of these khakis."

"You can change in the bedroom."

He looked at her. "You make it sound so formal." He pushed her hair back from her face, and bent forward and kissed her so gently.

It made her heart race. The instant throb of passion was waiting like Dracula's fangs to take her. She stood up and he followed her into the bedroom.

"I see you have me displayed." He picked up the photo, and smiled at her, "Just like me... I have your photo by my bed. But now we don't have to rely on photos." He looked down at her, put the photo down, pulled her towards him, and bent down to kiss her, pulling at his shirt and throwing it away over on the bed. He began loosening his trousers, still kissing her.

Allison could feel his passion rising, as they fell back over on to the bed.

"I've booked us into a little hideaway place. Can you get away?" he mumbled, still kissing her face, neck and body.

"I'm not sure." Allison pushed him away and tried to sit up. "All this has come as such a surprise... I..."

"Shhhh... I didn't even ask about your kids. Where are they?" Terry sat up and brushed at his hair. He got up, and leaned down to look in her mirror. His hair was a soft, light brown, not much of it, but he was particular in his appearance.

"They're out. They've gone to the beach," Allison stopped. She didn't think she'd say they'd gone for the night and Chris was at cricket. Somehow her instinct told her not to say.

"But they'll be back, right?" he turned, and helped her up off the bed.

"Yes, so I can't go with you."

"Yes you can, for the day you can." Terry stood there next to his photo.

Allison looked at him. His presence was overwhelming, and his confident air began to shine through. "I didn't intend to come and stay, you know. I am a gentleman."

"But you haven't even looked at my clinic, or anything."

"Listen, if we're to have the time together, we need to go... now. I'll see everything when I drop you back. That way I can meet the kids, and they can show me around."

They walked out of the bedroom, Terry carrying his military khakis over his arm. At the door he turned back to face her, "Your children. It's their house too... they'd like to show me around, wouldn't they?"

"Yes, you're absolutely right."

"Do you mind? I'm going to put these out into my car."

"Of course, I'll put the cups away," replied Allison.

Terry opened the door and walked out.

Allison watched him walk down the steps in his well-worn pair of jeans, and his white tee. Was there time to call Tom? She went to the kitchen, but before she rinsed the cups or reached for the phone, Terry was back, his arms around her.

"Isn't this the most exciting thing that's ever happened?" he stood there, turning her around and taking in her every gaze. "I just can't believe how beautiful you are, and you're all mine." He bent down to kiss her, pushing her up against the old kitchen table. He pushed against her. She could feel his hard penis ready to penetrate straight through her, right there on the old kitchen table. Suddenly, he lifted her up onto the table, and started going down her body, ripping at her clothes, his tongue working its way down past her nipples and belly button, when the phone rang right beside him.

"Fuck the God Damn phone." And he threw it out of the socket, and over against the kitchen sink. "Fuckin' phone."

Allison pulled her blouse closed, slid off the table, and charged down the hallway. She felt dizzy.

"Hey! Come on, baby... you're coming with me... where there's no fuckin' phones." He jerked her outside, slammed the door behind him, and shoved her into his car. He locked her door, and looked at her through the window of the car with a cold stare.

Allison hadn't noticed, but the car was right outside her front door. He must have shifted it when he went to take out his bag, while she was in the kitchen. *Had he planned all this*, she thought. She felt nauseous and drugged. They only had a cup of tea. The streets started to look blurry, and she could feel his hands climbing up her legs, and parting her thighs, as he drove. He stopped what he was doing with his hands, lit another cigarette, and smiled across at her. His gaze was starting to become blurred, and she had a feeling of drunkenness, when sexual pleasures become wickedly inviting. Her pubic bones throbbed for penetration, and she relaxed as his hands wandered back after he'd flicked his cigarette out the window.

They drove towards the airport and along the main back road, passing Orana Park.

"Don't y'all have such nice parks? Nearly as beautiful as you," he smiled at her, as they arrived at a small, secluded hotel set in the trees. Terry got out and opened the car door. Before Allison had time to catch sight of anyone in the car park, he had ushered her into a side door, and down the narrow corridor. There was no one around as he turned the key to one of the doors, and it opened into a beautiful room with a wooden veranda.

"There," he threw his small bag across the room to land exactly on the nearby chair, and hung up his uniform in the closet. Terry was still wearing his jeans and white tee shirt. "Isn't this inviting?" He walked over to the sliding doors, opened them, and stood outside, quite different to his attitude back at her house, more relaxed. He turned, and leaned against the wooden railing, pulling out another cigarette. For a quick moment Allison likened it to the railings of the bridge, she so often leaned over, weeping for love. Now it was here, staring at her in the face. How ironic?

"Come," he beckoned her, "come on, what's wrong?"

"Nothing, I'm thinking that's all."

"About what?" he drew a puff, and flicked the butt into the moving stream. A duck gave a startled quack and swam past. "I guess he thought we'd feed him," he laughed and turned around to face Allison and lit another cigarette. "I guess I must have frightened you. Is that what you're thinking?"

"I'm just not used to a man anymore. So much has gone on. The letter writing only gives us words, not touch, and having you here and not on paper is such a shock. I have you in my dreams, but the physical is all too much." Allison could feel waves of sickness, and then with the fresh air, she breathed in fully and leaned up against the railing. Her head cleared a little. "I feel sick, as if I've drunk something strange."

"We only had a cup of tea." Terry dropped another cigarette into the stream, and picked her up, carried her back into the room, slid the door closed, and pulled the curtains.

"The physical is about to begin. You've wasted too much time dreaming, little miss Alice in Wonderland. Isn't that what you like to call yourself?" He threw her onto the bed. "Time you stopped chasing that fuckin' rabbit, and fucked me."

Allison caught the close breath of his spoken words as he lunged forward, and landed on top of her.

"How does it feel now to be a pen friend? Hmmm?" kissing her nose. "So they fixed your nose did they? God, what was wrong with it? You sent me pictures in your classroom photo. There was nothing wrong with your nose."

"Oh... the bump." Allison tried to put her hand up to her face.

"No, put your hand down, I can see." he kissed her nose again and the side of her neck, slowly loosening the buttons of her blouse again, without any more effort. He snapped off her bra straps and pulled her panties down. "It's fun half-dressed." He pulled her one leg out of her panties and parted her legs.

Allison lay there as the room was going round and round. By now she was totally mesmerized and unable to even resist his deep thrusts over and over again. Her hands pulled his buttocks into her as she craved his hard penis banging into the end of her vagina... until blackness became blackness.

She sat up. She had been dreaming. She had been asleep. Terry was still dressed in the uniform and moving towards the door. He opened it and left the room. She tried to see but, her vision failed her. She fell back on the bed. She sat up again, grabbed her panties, stood up… but slumped back until jerking herself forward with all her might. She staggered into the bathroom and retched into the toilet bowl. She could hear Terry coming back down the corridor. She wanted to run, but her legs wouldn't let her. She heaved again, and thick, acrid stomach bile gushed out. Her body shook as the globs of red blood and semen flowed down her legs. She pulled the toilet roll hard, put on her panties and tried to stuff them with paper, when an arm drew her up.

"We're going for a ride, pretty lady." She couldn't see and couldn't move. Something in her lower legs was numb. The blood dripped, and Terry stashed a towel between her legs. He carried her down the hallway to the car. The car door closed, and he backed with no lights. They sped off in the direction of the airport. She groaned to herself.

"It won't work being the victim, Mrs Brownley. You and Jack are no more."

"What do you mean?" Allison's mouth was completely dry, and her tongue stuck like glue to the roof of her mouth. Her head was throbbing with pain.

"Jack's met his fate. I know all about you and Jack. Phone taps, baby. I told you about phone taps back in America, but you're so much in love with love, you're going on a ride." He laughed, "You're finally going to get your dream." Terry sped around the corner heading towards the American Base down the back gravel road. "Yes… little baby's going home to America, as my fiancé. You're my ticket out of here. It's all arranged. I'm Lieutenant Reefton, and you're my fiancé returning to the States after a mission to the ice. Yes it was easy doing my research. I work for the C.I.A. you know."

Allison's mouth dropped but she couldn't keep awake. All she could hear was the word Reefton. It was too late. They approached the Deep Freeze Base, and Terry got out with his clipboard and saluted the guard. Allison lay in the car seat, slumped over, her head jammed between the seat and the window.

"I have a passenger. She's my fiancé. We're headed back to Travis Airbase. I have some precious cargo to deliver." Terry pointed to the car with the engine still running, and Allison visible.

"Certainly, Lieutenant Reefton. Is Madame all right?"

"I've sedated her, she gets travel sickness." He winked and opened the door.

Allison moaned out, "He's an imposter."

"Don't listen, she's delirious." Terry picked her up and hurried past the guard. Allison waved her arms around as he strode towards the runway, and carried her onto the plane. "We're going to have to strap her in. She's not been feeling well," he yelled at one of the crew members.

"Yes sir, Lieutenant."

"Women, and their periods. I've sedated her for the trip." Terry bent down, and placed Allison gently into one of the seats by the side of the plane.

"Sorry sir. We'll get her seated, and made comfortable."

"Make sure you strap her in tight. She's very wobbly and will fall."

"Yes sir."

"Don't... don't... I don't feel well."

"Sorry, Lieutenant's orders ma'am."

"Just give me a few minutes. My back hurts, please." She could feel herself dribbling as she slurred out the words, but not to alarm them, she slowed down her speech. The crew member clicked the belt in place and left her. She looked around. She remembered being inside one of these aircrafts with Chuck, and knew the layout.

Terry went back out to the car. Allison, floating in and out of consciousness, knew she had to move. Her head spun. She unfastened the belt and stood up, keeping her grip on the ropes along the side of the plane. The men were busy packing and getting ready to clear the decks for takeoff, and didn't notice her slip out down the gangway. Allison hid, bending down, keeping to the other side of the cargo, out of view of the men. Terry called out to them to get ready to close up, and their attention was taken away from where Allison hovered. Over by the gates, Allison heard sirens, and when there was a break, she staggered towards the gates. Terry rushed to get the cylinder, which he'd concealed in a suitcase, leaving the car. He turned to look in the direction of the sound. Allison made it over to the car, and crouched beside it. She could see his figure, haloed in the lights from the aircraft. He caught sight of her. He stood for a moment, not moving. Then he leapt up the gangway at the sound of the Police sirens. He turned and waved at the guard and they closed the hatch. The engines roared. Allison's hair and clothes flapped in the air, as she fell against Tom, and collapsed. The huge Hercules lifted above them, like a giant bird, and Terry Ross, whoever he was, was gone.

CHAPTER 45

"We'd better get her to the hospital," yelled Tom to the Police. Allison's small form lay on the stretcher and the door of the ambulance closed. Tom sat next to Allison, holding her unconscious hand.

The ambulance silently backed towards the huge doors of the hospital, and Allison's stretcher was transferred to an operating bed. A drip was already in place, and the bright lights faded as Tom watched the nursing staff close the door.

Allison was wheeled into the Operating Room. Masked faces nodded, gloved hands held upright as the injection raced its way through her body... through to save her. The hysterectomy was successful. The theatre doors opened.

"She's going to be alright," said the surgeon to Tom in the waiting room.

Allison stared up at Tom.

"Where am I?"

"You've just had an operation. Don't say too much. There's been a lot going on."

"What? I don't understand. What happened?" She began to cry.

"Listen, shhhhh. It was your pen friend, Terry. He tricked you. I could see it coming, and if it wasn't for the help of FBI agent, Jean Mullen, we might not be able to prove anything.'

Allison clung to him, "But I can't remember."

"I know. He drugged you with Rohypnol. He gave it to Jack as well."

"Is Jack okay?"

"Don't worry about him," said a voice in the background. "He's going down. Good morning. Special Agent Mullen, call me Molly."

"Then call me Tāne."

"You didn't tell me?" interrupted Allison.

"Listen, you're not meant to be speaking. Anyway, you wouldn't want to know the meaning." He turned to Molly and winked, "In Maori, Tāne is your Adam... I am named after the man who started it all. He pulled out a dollar bill, and pointed to the fantail bird on the back of the note. "Tāne, also means, Lord of the birds, the forest... all us creatures, cool eh?"

"I'll remember that," said Molly, smiling and shoving the brown dollar bill in her pocket. "And yes, you did well on this case. You had to take her call," Molly looked at Allison, "and I had to break off and get Jack to the hospital."

"It's always hard pretending," Tāne looked down at Allison. "I know you saw me at your house, Allison. Sorry, I had a job to do. I couldn't say anything. It's a shame I put you through this. You're a gutsy lady. Now get some rest."

"The fantail is the bushman's friend," said Allison stirring, the pain was coming back.

"I know," said Tāne. "Get some rest."

Allison lay with her eyes closed, listening to Molly and Tom murmuring... "But we have work to do back in the U.S. We've been hunting Riley for years." Molly had an American accent. She looked down at Allison. She was as tall as Tom. She put a hand on Allison's bed. "I'm sorry Allison."

"We all are," said Sarah, walking in with Chris and the girls. Sarah nodded at Molly and Molly moved away saying softly, "Listen, I'll leave you to your family."

"Mummy! What happened? Are you alright?" said Isabelle pushing past Sarah, and running up to kiss her mother with Lucy right behind her.

"Yes, I'm lucky." Allison tried to close her eyes.

"So, who are you?" said Sarah looking over at Tom.

"It's a long story, but my Maori name is Tāne... but call me Tom if you wish."

"Well, we've got time to hear all about it, haven't we?" Sarah replied as she sat down beside Allison, and took her hand. "Listen Allison... I haven't been honest with you. I've been wanting to say about Jack."

"You don't need to, you're here."

"Yerrrrr you can say that again, Mum," Chris looked across at Tom.

"Don't forget... it's the ones that care about you... love you that matter," Allison whispered. "I'm so glad to be alive."

•   •   •   •   •

Jack's eyes opened slowly, his body jerking.

"Steady him! He's had an overdose," said Molly standing next to the doctor. The hospital lights came clear and Jack looked around the room. A policeman stood over to one side of the room, by the door.

Jack tried to move.

"You won't be going very far, my boy." Josh still had his giggle. He looked over at Mark.

"Yes, it's been a difficult case, this one, but we finally nailed it. If it weren't for my assistant Detective Briggs and Agent Mullen, all the way from Chicago, we'd never have done it," said Mark, standing with his hands behind his back.

Molly looked down at Jack and smiled, "Yes! Some of these motherfuckers can't resist a good fuck. We have the papers, formulas, and the tanks."

Jack stirred, and Molly patted his pajamas, "Rap this one up... I've a plane to catch."

She walked out into the corridor and paused. She beckoned the Policeman, standing by the door. She gave him her orders, "Have this box delivered to the Women's Ward, to a Mrs Allison Brownley. I believe it's her daughter's toys she left behind in Chicago... they're just in time for Christmas."

Molly stepped outside and breathed in the warm Southern air. Once again her task was finished for this drug bust. As for Terry Ross... there was always a next time.

The End

About the Authors

Lynette grew up listening to her mother Mattie's stories about her WW2 love for US Navy Diver Charlie. She used Mattie's 30 letters from Charlie, and together with her insightful Co-author, editor/advisor husband Bud, they completed extensive research to give reality to *The Rigel Affair* and its *Sequel*, and now *Broken Wings* to extend *The Rigel Affair Series*. Both Lynette and Bud have completed numerous Creative Writing courses at Auckland University. Lynette is an accomplished expressionist Artist, with works sold internationally and paraded on their website, www.lmhedrick.com